LOVE FORBIDDEN

OTHER BOOKS BY BARBARA CARTLAND

Romantic Novels, approaching 700, the most recently published being:

THE QUEEN SAVES THE KING
LOVE LIFTS THE CURSE
A TANGLED WEB
JUST FATE
THE WINDMILL OF LOVE
HIDING
LOVED FOR HIMSELF
A KISS IN ROME
NO DISGUISE FOR LOVE
HIDDEN BY LOVE
WALKING TO WONDERLAND
THE WICKED WIDOW
THE QUEEN OF HEARTS
LOVE AT THE RITZ
BORN OF LOVE
THIS IS LOVE
LOOK WITH THE HEART
LOVE IN THE RUINS
THE WONDERFUL DREAM
THE DUKE IS TRAPPED
A DOG, A HORSE AND A HEART
LOVE AND A CHEETAH
THE EYES OF LOVE
NEVER LOSE LOVE
SAVED BY A SAINT
THE INCOMPARABLE
BEYOND THE STARS
THE INNOCENT IMPOSTER
THE LOVE PIRATE
THE MASK OF LOVE
A DREAM FROM THE NIGHT
THE DARE-DEVIL DUKE
A ROYAL REBUKE
LOVE RUNS IN
THE LOVE LIGHT OF APOLLO
LOVE, LIES AND MARRIAGE
IN LOVE, IN LUCCA
THE ADVENTURER
ALONE IN PARIS
THE DEVIL IN LOVE
A WITCH'S SPELL
THE GLITTERING LIGHTS
A SECRET PASSAGE TO LOVE
THE INCREDIBLE HONEYMOON
DANCE ON MY HEART
LIGHT OF THE MOON
PURE AND UNTOUCHED
RIDING TO THE MOON

Autobiographical and Biographical:

THE ISTHMUS YEARS 1919–1939
THE YEARS OF OPPORTUNITY 1939–1945
I SEARCH FOR RAINBOWS 1945–1976
WE DANCED ALL NIGHT 1919–1929
RONALD CARTLAND (with a foreword by Sir Winston Churchill)
POLLY—MY WONDERFUL MOTHER
I SEEK THE MIRACULOUS
I REACH FOR THE STARS

Love Forbidden

Barbara Cartland

NEATH PORT TALBOT LIBRARIES

ROBERT HALE · LONDON

© Barbara Cartland 1957
This edition 2001

ISBN 0 7090 6950 2

Robert Hale Limited
Clerkenwell House
Clerkenwell Green
London
EC1R 0HT

The right of Barbara Cartland to be identified as
author of this work has been asserted by her
in accordance with the Copyright, Designs and
Patents Act 1988.

2 4 6 8 10 9 7 5 3 1

NEATH PORT TALBOT LIBRARIES	
2000326058	
	8/01
HR	£17.99
	CS.

Typeset by Derek Doyle & Associates in Liverpool.
Printed in Great Britain by
St Edmundsbury Press Limited, Bury St Edmunds, Suffolk.
Bound by Woolnough Bookbinding Limited.

1

"Sorry to be late, dearie, but the milk didn't arrive from the farm till a few minutes ago. Your tea's waiting for you now."

Aria rose slowly from the table at which she had been sitting and smiled.

"I thought Bill must be late again," she said. "Don't worry, Nanny, and for goodness' sake don't say anything to him. You know what a job Charles has to get cowmen."

"It's a job to get anyone these days," Nanny answered tartly. "Now you run along and get your tea. Did anyone come this afternoon?"

Aria looked down at the box on the table in which reposed six half-crowns.

"As you see, we haven't been overwhelmed by the crowds," she smiled, "There were four Americans and a horrible couple on a motor-cycle. The woman said 'Reely,' in her opinion, she didn't think the house was worth half-a-crown and she wondered how we had the cheek to charge it."

"What impudence!" Nanny ejaculated. "I wish I'd been here. I'd have given her a piece of my mind."

Aria laughed. She had been conversant with the "pieces" of Nanny's mind for as long as she could remember. They always sounded very fierce in anticipation, but in actual fact they were not likely to make anyone over the age of three quake in their shoes.

"We mustn't drive away the few customers we have," she said. "Despite the woman's nasty remarks her husband bought a couple of postcards. You will find the money in the drawer. Charles said we were to keep it separate."

"I haven't forgotten," Nanny said irritably.

She invariably got any money there was in a muddle and disliked the slightest suggestion that she was not a meticulous accountant.

"Six people in an afternoon!" Aria said, stretching her hands over her head. "Fifteen shillings! It's hopeless, isn't it, Nanny? I shall talk to Charles tonight. He was so tired when he came in yesterday evening that I didn't like to worry him."

"Now, think before you do anything rash, dearie," Nanny admonished her. "And I'm not agreeing with your wild ideas—mind you."

"But you know as well as I do, Nanny, that something has got to be done," Aria insisted.

Nanny gave a sigh that seemed to come right from the very depth of her frail little body.

"Yes, dearie, I suppose something has got to be done," she agreed. "But what? That's the question."

"And I know the answer," Aria said. She bent down unexpectedly and kissed her old nurse's withered cheek. "You are not to worry, whatever happens. It will all come right in the long run, you see if it doesn't. Doubtless it's all for the best! Don't you remember how often you used to say that to me when I was little?"

"Indeed I remember," Nanny answered. "It used to cheer me up to say it; but I'm not sure in my bones that it was always right."

"Well, I'm sure this time," Aria smiled.

She walked from the table across to the window. Outside the sun was shining and a light breeze was rustling through the pale green, early summer foliage of the trees. There was a soft murmur of bees in the rose-bushes which stood in front of the house. Otherwise everything was very quiet—the soft, quiet peace of the English countryside.

"Too quiet!" Aria suddenly said aloud, following the trend of her thoughts.

Nanny looked up in surprise from the table where she had seated herself.

"What is?" she enquired.

"This place," Aria replied. "Too quiet; too off the beaten track; too small to command much attention. And we can't afford to advertise. What chance have we got of attracting visitors when within a few miles of us are Hatfield House, Luton Hoo and Woburn Abbey? And with all the attractions the Duke of Bedford is introducing to bring the crowds into Woburn, why should anyone worry about us?"

"Why shouldn't they?" Nanny enquired almost angrily. "Queen's Folly is as old and as beautiful as Hatfield House."

"And about a tenth of the size," Aria retorted, and then laughed. "Don't listen to me, Nanny. I am just feeling envious of those who can collect so many more half-crowns than we can because they have so much more to offer. Not that Charles would admit that any place in the world could be as wonderful as Queen's Folly."

"There isn't a place to touch it!" Nanny said stoutly.

Aria laughed again.

"You're prejudiced, both of you."

"And rightly," Nanny snapped.

"And rightly," Aria echoed softly.

Her eyes were gentle and she looked at the bent figure of her old nurse sitting at the table just inside the open front door waiting to collect money from the visitors to Queen's Folly.

It seemed such a splendid chance of making money when they first decided to open the house to the public. Naturally Charles had at the outset been against the idea of allowing strangers to intrude on his privacy and disturb the peace of the house which he loved to the exclusion of all else.

It was Aria who had convinced him that their only chance of keeping the roof over their heads was by gratifying the curiosity of those who liked to stare at the relics of past glories.

When Charles was finally convinced that to open the door of Queen's Folly was not only necessary but expedient, he, too, became enthusiastic, only to be thrown

7

into a fit of depression and bitterness that the response to their gesture was so half-hearted.

It was not surprising, really, that few people heard of Queen's Folly, let alone found it.

It lay down narrow, twisting lanes, in the wild, rural, green belt of Hertfordshire, which is still untouched and unspoilt even though it lies within twenty-five miles of London.

There were no gay road-houses with swimming pools and coloured lights, along the road which led to Queen's Folly. There were no public houses which had been taken over by smart caterers who were prepared to serve a Ritz luncheon under ancient beams and in front of ancient open fireplaces.

Yet a few people did visit Queen's Folly, the more intelligent of them to exclaim with delight at the mellow beauty of the red bricks which had been erected five centuries earlier; to go into ecstasies over the mullioned windows; to stare incredulously at the pictures which hung in the Banqueting Hall, finding it hard to believe they were authentic.

And that was all! There was nothing more to see!

Queen's Folly was quite tiny. The legends said that it had been built at the command of Queen Elizabeth as a place where she might spend a few informal nights without being surrounded by courtiers, ladies-in-waiting and attendants.

Legends also hinted that there was something romantic in her desire for a small hiding-place; but there was nothing to substantiate any of these stories.

Queen's Folly was undoubtedly Elizabethan and a perfectly preserved gem of the period.

Its name was undoubtedly as old as its foundations and one could only conjecture as to the reason for its existence, for in the records of the County of Hertfordshire there was nothing save the bald information that it had been built at the order of one Sir Charles Milborne.

Had he, perhaps, been yet another gallant who had laid his heart at the feet of the woman who had raised

England to unprecedented greatness and whose adorers had christened her Gloriana?

The Queen's portrait hung over the mantelpiece in the Banqueting Hall. It was not a particularly famous portrait, but it portrayed very successfully the vivid red of her hair.

As a child Aria loved it. "She is red like me," she had said when she was quite tiny, pointing with a small finger up towards the jewel-spattered tresses of the Virgin Queen.

"She was a great woman," Nanny had answered. "And that's more than you will be if you don't learn to control your temper."

Then she had taken Aria by the hand and shown her an old carving on the staircase and made her spell it out loud.

"When a Milborne is red, there's trouble ahead."

Looking at her charge now, with red hair rioting over her tiny head, the sunlight streaming through the open door making each curl dance and sparkle as if, indeed, it was a golden flame rather than ordinary hair, Nanny felt her heart contract suddenly.

The child was lovely! And what was there for her in this empty, crumbling house save the companionship of an old woman and the unceasing grumbling of a man who had been nearly broken and destroyed by the blood and carnage of war!

"She must go away from here," Nanny thought to herself. But even as she moved her lips ready to say the words aloud, Aria had turned on her heel and was no longer listening to her. She was looking out through the open door.

"There's a car coming," she said. "It looks expensive. My goodness, it is, too! It is one of the new Bentleys."

She moved forward into the embrasure of the window so as to see more clearly. Standing between the faded damask curtains which had once been red and were now a soft threadbare pink, she was hidden from anyone entering the hall.

She watched the Bentley pull up outside. A man got out. He walked round to the other side to open the door for a woman who had been sitting beside him. He was wearing a casual grey flannel suit, his head was bare and his skin was very sunburned.

There was something purposeful in the way he walked, in the squareness of his shoulders and the carriage of his head.

Aria decided all that from his back view, and then, as she saw his face, she realised that her first impression of him was not exaggerated.

There was something arresting about him; something which made her stare almost breathlessly through the small panes of the mullioned windows. He had high cheek-bones, deep-set eyes and a full, yet rather cruel mouth.

He was not exactly good-looking, but he was obviously a person one could not ignore or be likely to forget. He smiled, and she decided he was also definitely attractive.

And then there stepped from the car a woman who made Aria forget the man. She was silver blonde and so breathtakingly pretty that Aria knew without being told that she must be a star of film or stage.

Dressed in deep sapphire blue with a long stole of platina mink, she had diamonds twinkling in her ears and at her wrists; and she stepped from the car to stand outside the house with her hands still in her escort's, her face upturned to his.

"Must we really look at yet another boring old museum?" she enquired in a soft, almost caressing tone. "I am so tired."

"This is the last," the man answered, in a low, deep voice with a faint American accent.

"Well, I promise you I'm not climbing any stairs."

"Would you like me to carry you?"

The question was charged with meaning and two blue eyes gleamed at him from beneath long, dark lashes.

"I would love it—but not here."

10

He slipped his arm through hers and drew her up the steps to the front door. There was no mistaking that they were lovers, Aria thought, turning from the window to watch them as they paused at the table in front of Nanny.

"Five shillings! Is that right?" the man asked.

"Yes, that's right, sir," Nanny answered, taking her time in giving him change from a pound note.

"Do we need a guide or can we look round on our own?"

"You just walk round on your own, sir. There's no-one to take you. The Banqueting Hall, where the pictures are, is straight ahead."

"No stairs, mind," said the blonde.

"If there are any, my offer still stands," he replied, speaking in a voice that was intended for her alone.

Still arm-in-arm they walked across the hall and into the Banqueting Hall. Nanny leant back in her chair and looked round to where Aria was watching them.

"That makes eight altogether today," she said. "It's better than yesterday, anyway."

"Yes, it's better than yesterday," Aria answered automatically.

She moved as she spoke and opened a door on the right marked "Private." She did not know why, but she had no desire to go on watching the American and his lovely companion. Usually the visitors' reactions were a matter of indifference to her, but for some reason she could not explain she did not want to hear these two exclaim:

"Is this all? Aren't there any other rooms to see?"

How often had she heard that complaint? And usually she merely despised those who preferred quantity-to-quality. But now the idea of hearing it from these visitors made her feel depressed.

She walked along a short passage and opened the door of the sitting-room where she knew her tea would be waiting. Nanny had left it on a tray and an old-fashioned tea-cosy covered the teapot and kept it hot.

The room was small and shabby. When her father

11

had been alive it had been the housekeeper's room. Now it housed all that was left of their furniture.

Aria sat down at the table and poured herself out a cup of tea. There were cucumber sandwiches and a piece of home-made cake. She ate absent-mindedly, her thoughts far away, until with almost a start she heard the sound of a car being started up.

Then she rose to her feet and went to the window which overlooked the front of the house.

She could see the grey Bentley just beginning to move. She had a fleeting glimpse of a sunburned face with high cheek-bones and dark eyes, and then the car was past and was moving swiftly up the drive, seeming to flash by in the sunshine as if it were something from another world.

"Swiftly come, swiftly go!"

Aria whispered the words aloud and then wondered why she had said them. The car was now out of sight. There was only the same peace and quiet that she had commented on a little earlier.

They were the richer by five shillings, and yet Aria felt as if the man in the grey Bentley with his lovely amoretta had left disruption behind him. Or did that lie merely within her own heart?

The door behind her opened.

"They didn't take long, did they, Nanny?" she said, without turning her head.

"Who didn't?" a man's voice enquired.

She swung round.

"Charles! I wasn't expecting you."

Her brother walked across the room and sat down at the table.

"Have you a cup of tea for me?" he asked.

He was wearing dirty, stained corduroys and an open-necked shirt.

"Of course," she answered. "But what has happened? Why are you here at this time of the day?"

"I have got a blade broken on the silage cutter," he answered. "It's a damned nuisance, too. We would

12

have cleared Greenacres tonight if we hadn't been held up like this. I had to go into Hertford to get another."

"How sickening for you," Aria said.

She fetched another cup from the cupboard in the dresser.

"Eat that sandwich," she said, "and I'll cut you another."

"No, I don't want anything to eat," he answered. "I have got to get back to the fields in a moment, although we can't get on until Joe has fixed the new blade."

"You look tired," Aria said quietly. "Can't you leave it until tomorrow and start fresh in the morning?"

"You know darned well I can't," he said sharply. Then added quickly: "I'm sorry! I didn't mean to snap at you, but it makes me so irritable these blasted things always breaking. It isn't only the delay, it's the fact that I can't afford to pay for new ones."

"Yes, I know, Charles. But you are driving yourself too hard. You are trying to do too much, too quickly."

"Too quickly! Do you know what the overdraft is at the bank? And by the way, I have had a letter from the manager this morning. He has asked me to go in and see him. You know what that means!"

"Oh, Charles! You don't think he is going to be difficult and ask us to repay some of the loan?"

"I wouldn't be surprised if he did. But I can't do it, you know that, Aria. I just can't."

There was a sudden high, almost frightened note in her brother's voice and quickly Aria put out her hand and laid it in his.

"No, I know you can't, Charles. But don't worry. Don't cross the bridge until you come to it. It may be nothing; just a routine talk."

"But if it isn't, what am I to do?"

Again there was that note of panic in the man's voice.

"Charles, something will turn up. We have survived until now, haven't we?"

"By the skin of our teeth."

13

"Nevertheless they are still there."

Aria tried to smile. It was not a very successful effort.

Charles beat both fists on the table.

"I won't give this place up, I won't, I tell you."

"You are not going to," Aria said soothingly. "Who has ever suggested such a thing? It's yours, Charles. We are living here. We have managed so far; we will go on managing. You've not to doubt that."

The passionate sincerity in her voice, the pressure of her hand, seemed in some measure to bring reassurance. For one moment Charles was tense, fighting a rising panic, and the next moment at Aria's words he seemed to relax, the terror faded from his eyes.

"Drink your tea," she said quietly. "And eat that sandwich, if nothing else. I insist on it."

He obeyed her without further argument and once he had started to eat she went into the kitchen and brought back a loaf and a pat of butter.

"Did you have any lunch?" she asked casually.

"Of course . . ." he began, then stopped and looked at her guiltily. "I . . . think I did."

"That means you didn't," Aria said. "Charles, how ridiculous you are! You'll kill yourself if you work like this. No-one can work from dawn till dusk without food. Now don't you dare move. I am going to fry you a couple of eggs and you will eat them and like them."

Her brother looked at his watch.

"I have got to get back."

"You will stay where you are until you have something inside you," Aria said firmly.

She hurried into the kitchen and while she was frying the eggs on a small gas stove which stood beside the great useless range with its spit and huge bread ovens which had been there in her grandfather's time, she thought almost despairingly of Charles' face when he told her that the bank manager had asked to see him.

She knew this meant that he would not sleep until the interview was over; knew, too, that he would drive

14

himself to work-even harder than he was working already—forcing himself to do the work of ten men, to have an almost superhuman strength.

"Poor Charles! Poor, poor Charles!"

The soft hiss of the gas seemed to echo the words which moved Aria's lips. She thought suddenly that it was difficult now to remember the time when she had not had to worry about her brother and be sorry for him.

She had seen so little of him when she was small. He had been at boarding school. She had been with her father, often abroad when the holidays came round, so that Charles had gone to relatives and brother and sister had not even met. During the war Aria had seen Charles only twice.

And then, when the hostilities in Europe were over, Charles had volunteered first for Korea and then for Malaya.

He had been in Malaya only a week when he was captured by the terrorists. They tortured and ill-treated him until, when he was finally rescued, he was little more than a corpse. He had come back to England a nervous and physical wreck—to face disaster in his own family life.

Charles' and Aria's father, Sir Gladstone Milborne, had died in 1953 when Aria was eighteen and Charles was twenty-four. It was only after his death that they discovered how he had managed to live for so many years in luxury and comfort.

Everything had been spent—there was nothing left. Even the money which should have been in trust had somehow been used up by methods which would certainly not have stood a legal investigation had there been any point in having one.

Worse still than the fact that there was no money was the discovery that he had stripped Queen's Folly in his desire to finance his enjoyment of what he termed "a gentleman's way of life."

He had gone abroad immediately after the war, tak-

15

ing Aria with him. They had stayed in Italy, in Paris and had gone to Egypt in the winter.

They always stayed at the best hotels; but while Sir Gladstone amused himself with beautiful women, luxurious food and the night life of the cities they visited, Aria was strictly chaperoned by an elderly governess, who never ceased to express, not in words but by her manner, her disapproval of her employer.

Why her father wished to have a girl still in her teens with him Aria afterwards could never understand. Perhaps it gave him, in his own way, a sense of security, a feeling of homeliness although no-one who knew him could have suspected him of wanting anything so alien to his character.

There was no doubt at all that as he grew older Sir Gladstone became more dissolute. There were ever-recurring scandals, scenes, recriminations and often violence, which meant that they packed their possessions hastily and moved on to another gay city, another part of the globe. Rome, Madrid, New York, Buenos Aires—Aria knew them all, but only through the pane-glass of an hotel window.

The fact that his home had been sacked and the family treasures sold had been a worse torture to Charles than anything he had experienced from the terrorists. Knowing her brother so little, Aria had not at first understood his passionate, almost fanatical devotion to his home.

"It's mine! Mine! Do you understand?" he had shouted at her once. "Queen's Folly has belonged to a Milborne since Queen Elizabeth's day—father to son, father to son—and now it's mine and I'll never give it up. I will die first; die on the threshold and be buried in the soil which belonged to my ancestors and now belongs to me."

His voice had risen shrilly to what was almost a scream. He was shaking, his hands were icy cold and yet the beads of perspiration were running down his forehead.

"Only time can heal his nerves," the doctor had told

16

Aria. "Try not to let him upset himself; try to make him take up his ordinary everyday life as easily and smoothly as possible. It is not going to be easy, I know that. Those devils have jerked him out of gear, so to speak. We have got to get him back into the rhythm of living. Do you understand?"

Aria had not understood at the time, but as the years went by she began to understand a little of what Charles was suffering, to learn how to handle him. Sometimes she must be soft and tender and sympathetic; but at other times she must be firm, hard and cold, and must even bully him a little.

Sometimes she must cling to him, at others she must be a rock of strength itself.

There were nights when she wept into her pillow and felt she was being a failure; days when she thought Charles was mad and that nothing could save him from the asylum.

These were the occasions when she hated Queen's Folly because it must mean so much to the man who loved it as though it were his mother, wife and mistress.

She hurried from the kitchen now, back into the sitting-room. To her relief Charles was still sitting at the table.

"Here are your eggs," she said. "And if you go without your lunch again, I shall instruct Joe to force it down your throat, however much you abuse him for doing so."

"I won't forget it another time," Charles said with a sudden good humour. "It's been a hell of a day today. Everything has gone wrong. The fox got six of our pullets last night."

"Oh, not again!" Aria exclaimed. "How did he manage it?"

"Bit a hole in the hen-house. You know we want some new ones. The wood is rotten; as soon as I repair one hole, two or three others appear."

Aria sighed. The hen-houses were like everything else, falling to pieces for want of money. And what could they do about it? She pondered for a moment,

17

her eyes on her brother's face as he ate his eggs, and then she said quietly:

"I've been wanting to talk to you for some time Charles. I've come to a decision—a rather important one."

"What about?" he asked, not looking up, and she knew he was not really attending to her but thinking of his problems on the farm.

"Listen to me, Charles," she said urgently. "This is important. I have decided to go away; to see if I can get a job."

"A job! Whatever for?" Charles had raised his eyes to her now and she saw for once she was really holding his attention.

"To make money, of course. I've been talking it over with Nanny. There are so few visitors that she can manage them and the house. We thought at first that we should have crowds here, but hardly anyone comes until the afternoon, and if they do we can always put a notice on the door for them to ring the bell. Nanny can sit in the hall in the afternoon, and if things really get busy it only means that your supper may be a bit later than usual."

"But you can't go away. You can't leave me, Aria."

Aria's face softened and there was a sudden light in her eyes as she held out her hands to her brother.

"Oh, Charles! That's the nicest thing you've ever said to me. Would you really miss me a little? But, dearest, I am really wasted here. I am hale and hearty and I have got a few brains, I think, tucked away somewhere. If I could earn a decent wage, think what it would mean to all of us. Even two or three pounds coming in regularly would pay half Joe's wages. We might even be able to afford another man."

She saw by the look on Charles' face that he was taken with the idea. Then abruptly he dismissed it.

"It's nonsense!" he said. "You have never tried to earn your own living. God knows the old man never brought you up to do anything sensible."

"Yes, I know," Aria answered. "But Nanny heard

18

from her niece yesterday—you remember, the girl who came here last Christmas. You thought she was rather half-witted, but she has got a job in an aircraft factory and she is earning ten pounds a week with overtime. Just think of it, ten pounds a week, Charles! Why, it would make all the difference in the world to us."

"What on earth is the use of your trying to go to an aircraft factory?" Charles asked. "You would crack up within a week. You're not strong enough."

He looked at his sister as he spoke as if he saw her for the first time. He noted the little, pointed, heart-shaped face, the dark eyes that looked too big for it, and the red mouth which dropped a little wistfully at the corners.

Dark eyes and red hair; it was a strange combination, even though the red Milbornes had cropped up all through the centuries.

Aria was five feet six in height with a tiny waist and long, thin legs which carried her with a grace which owed much to a lissom slenderness and much more to the discipline of deportment lessons which she had endured all through her childhood.

She certainly did not look capable of any great feats of endurance, and yet Charles knew that she was stronger than she looked, having a resilience and determination which at times had even equalled his own.

"What can you do?" he asked.

"I don't know yet," Aria answered. "And I am not going to suggest things so that you can laugh at them. I am going to find out. I have made up my mind. I am going to London tomorrow for the day. I shall go to all the registry offices; I will get a job. I shall then find a room somewhere. I can't go up and down from here, as you well know."

They both smiled at that. It was a family joke that the buses, which passed the end of the drive only twice a week, took them from nowhere to nowhere and in the slowest possible time.

"Well, there's no harm in trying, I suppose," Charles said uncertainly. "But I think you will find that you won't get a job at anything more than five or six pounds a week, and if you have got to live in London you are more likely to be out of pocket at the end of it than to have anything to spare."

"In which case I shall come home," Aria told him. "I am not a fool. I want to make money for Queen's Folly. If I can't do that, I will stay here and go on scrubbing the floors and taking the half-crowns."

Charles had turned towards the door. Now he swung round and walking across to Aria unexpectedly put his arm round her shoulders.

"Do you hate it so much?" he asked.

She sprang to her feet as if he had insulted her.

"Hate it! You know I don't hate it," she answered. "I love it as much as you do. No, that's not true—no-one could love Queen's Folly as much as you. But it is my home; it is the place I dreamed about when I was wandering with Father round those boring hotels.

"I used to think of my own little room and wish I were back in it. I used to remember the oak tree where I could climb up and no-one could find me; the shrubbery where you and I played Indians when we were very small. Queen's Folly was the lodestar, the goal, the ultimate end of everything I wanted most—to go home!"

"And when you did come back it was to find it empty and ruined," Charles said with a sudden bitterness.

It was a dangerous subject and Aria replied quickly:

"Nonsense! It is still home for you and me. It is still here, that's what matters."

Her words seemed to touch him.

"Yes, it is still here," he said quietly. "I suppose that really is what matters."

"Of course it is," Aria smiled. She kissed him lightly on the cheek. "Go along and don't be too late. I want to talk to you and if you are too tired to listen you will fall asleep immediately after dinner."

"You make me sound like a rather boring, middle-aged husband," Charles retorted.

"You often behave like one," Aria told him.

He laughed at that and she heard him whistling as he went through the back door and across the yard towards the farm.

Aria stacked the tea-things and then, just as she was about to carry them into the kitchen, she fetched another cup and filled it for Nanny. There was never a time of day or night when Nanny was not pleased to drink a cup of tea. Aria put in the milk and sugar and carried it along the passage and into the hall.

Nanny was sitting at the table, knitting one of the interminable brown pullovers which Charles wore on the farm and which seemed to get worn out with irritating regularity.

"I've brought you a cup of tea, Nanny," Aria told her. "And, what do you think? Charles came in. Something had broken down on one of his machines and so he had to go to Hertford for a new part. Of course, he had forgotten his lunch."

"There now, and I made him his favourite bacon sandwiches," Nanny sighed.

"I fried him a couple of eggs for tea," Aria went on. "But he's worried, Nanny. The bank manager has written asking to see him."

"I guessed that was it," Nanny answered. "I saw the mark on the back of the envelope. It's always bad news when one of those comes."

"I hope the bank doesn't start harrying poor Charles just at this moment. I thought he was a bit better lately, didn't you?"

"Much better," Nanny nodded. "He'll get all right, you'll see if he doesn't. Give him another year or two and he'll be just like he used to be, my bonny boy."

"He gets so worked up," Aria sighed. "The slightest thing and up he goes."

"Yes, I know," Nanny answered. "But you can't expect anything else when his nerves are all of a jangle. He'll get well, dearie, don't you fret yourself."

"I told him I was going to London tomorrow to see if I could find a job."

21

"What did he say?"

"He was really very sweet about it. I think he realised for the first time that he might miss me. At the same time, when I said it was for Queen's Folly he was all for it."

"If you get something good, it will be worth while. If not, you come home, dearie. I don't like to think of you living in London on your own; you're too young."

"I shall be twenty-one next month," Aria said. "Old enough to look after myself, Nanny."

"I hope that's true," Nanny answered, her eyes on Aria's face.

Aria was looking at the money in the box.

"Those people didn't stay long," she said at length. "The man in the Bentley. Did they say anything when they left?"

"He thanked me most politely," Nanny replied. "I thought he was a nice gentleman. 'Your pictures are well worth a visit,' he said. He couldn't say fairer than that, could he?"

"I'm glad he was pleased."

Aria didn't know why, but she really was glad. She felt a sudden warmth in her heart. Rich, important and attractive he might be, and yet he had liked the pictures of Queen's Folly. Idly she wondered if she would ever see him again, and then she laughed at herself.

Tomorrow she would begin a new adventure. Perhaps it was the opening of a new phase in her life. She was going to London; she was going to find a job. What did it really matter if a man in a grey Bentley liked the pictures or not?

2

Aria paused at the foot of the stairs leading up to Mrs. Benstead's Secretarial and Domestic Agency.

It was the fifth Agency she had visited that morning, she thought a little wearily, and a dusty mirror on the side of the wall reflected her face, showing her, even in its damaged and untruthful surface, looking pale and a little drawn.

She had set off from Queen's Folly with high hopes. She had imagined, foolishly, that jobs were waiting for the asking—only to find herself speedily disillusioned.

There were jobs, of course—a large number of them. But they were not what she was looking for, for the simple reason that the salaries were not large enough for her to be able to send more than a pittance back to Charles.

That, after all, was the main reason for her coming to London. To be able to contribute something in support of the home they both loved, to be able to relieve just some of the lines of anxiety round Charles' eyes, to release the tension which seemed to keep his lips pressed together as if in an almost superhuman effort of self-control.

"You mustn't let your brother worry." How often Aria had listened to those words from their family doctor and known that he might just as well have asked her to stem the tide or change the weather by some magical formula!

Charles' nerves were on edge. The slightest thing could set them jangling until at the end of it he was in little better shape than he had been when he was rescued from the terrorists. And what always upset him worst was the thought of money!

23

Aria knew that always at the back of his mind was the fear that he would not be able to hold on to Queen's Folly; that the house would have to be sold.

The land was mortgaged up to the hilt. It was hard enough to manage to pay the premium year after year and only by the superhuman efforts of Charles on the farm could they contrive to live at all.

Money! Money! Money! It seemed to Aria that the sound of it was ever drumming in her ears, haunting her in the daytime and being a familiar part of her dreams every night.

On the way to London she had calculated how much it would cost her to live. Even the cheapest type of hostel would not be less than three guineas a week, and then there was her food.

With a little sigh she felt ashamed of her appetite. She often felt hungry, and yet any other girl of her age would have envied her because, however much she ate, she never seemed to put on any weight.

She glanced at herself in the mirror. The black coat and skirt she had bought in Paris the last winter she had stayed there with her father still looked smart and up-to-date. It was fortunate that she had been able to have a black one. So many of her clothes were definitely schoolgirlish.

When the news had reached them that her grandmother had died, Sir Gladstone at first had poohpoohed the idea of Aria going into mourning but he had finally consented to her buying enough black in which to meet a cousin who was passing through Paris after the funeral.

The cousin had later gone out to live in South Africa and she was the only relative Aria could remember with the exception of her brother. Their mother and their father had both been only children, and if there were any other relatives living, Charles and his sister had lost touch with them.

"There are only two of us against the world," Aria said aloud, and then, seeing her lips move in the mirror, she gave herself a little smile as if at her own absurdity.

24

It was hard for her to be depressed for long. Her spirits were rising again.

She gave the little black hat she wore over her red curls a twist towards her right eyebrow; then took out her vanity case and powdered her nose. It was wisest to look her best before she went up the narrow stairs to the Agency.

Who knew what might be waiting there?

She was indulging in what Nanny called one of her day dreams when she heard people coming down the stairs. She looked up to see a man and woman descending.

"The best thing we can do," the man was saying, "is to give the servants our income and ask them to return us a few shillings pocket money."

"Oh, don't be so ridiculous, John!" the woman exclaimed irritably. "You know we have got to have someone in the house. We can't go on as we are."

She pushed past Aria with a disagreeable expression on her face, followed by her rather bored-looking husband, and the street door slammed behind them.

Aria took one last look at herself in the mirror and climbed the stairs. Mrs. Benstead's Agency was exactly like all the others she had visited that morning.

There was the same smell of a gas fire and stale tobacco, the same dingy brown walls and peeling paint, the same general air of depression about the whole office.

Aria spoke to an indifferent, rather sulky-looking girl at a desk who, after hearing that she was seeking to be employed rather than an employer in need of staff, appeared a little more interested.

"Mrs. Benstead'll see you in half a mo'," she said. "Better take a seat."

Aria sat down on an uncomfortable chair with one leg shorter than the others, which had its back to the wall just inside the door. The girl turned again to her typewriter and rattled away at the keys with an almost derisive sound as if she mocked at anyone for coming

25

to such a place in the hope of finding anything unusual and interesting.

A door at the other side of the room opened and a large, flamboyant-looking woman with green feathers in her hat and a particularly virulent shade of lipstick flounced out. She came jauntily across the room, winked at the girl at the desk and said,

"Cheeri-bye, dearie. I'll be seeing you."

Then she slammed down the stairs with a noise which seemed to make the whole office vibrate.

A moment later Mrs. Benstead appeared through the door of the inner office. She was a middle-aged woman wearing horn-rimmed spectacles and having a cigarette hanging out of the corner of her mouth.

That this was habitual to her was shown by the bright yellow nicotine stains on her fingers and the fact that the smell of cheap cigarettes in the inner room was almost overpowering.

"I'll see you now," she said abruptly to Aria, adding over her shoulder to the girl at the desk: "I've sent Lucy Jarvis to see Lady Grimblethorpe. You had better telephone and say that she's on her way."

"Lady Grimblethorpe wanted a married couple," the girl answered.

"She'll take what we can send her and like it," Mrs. Benstead replied.

The last sentence was shouted from her desk as she sat down and motioned Aria to a chair in front of it.

"Now, let me see; have you been here before?" she asked.

"No," Aria replied.

"In that case, I'll have to take your particulars," Mrs. Benstead said grudgingly, as if Aria was putting her to an incredible amount of trouble.

She searched amongst the general debris on her desk until among half a dozen ledgers exactly alike she found the one she required.

"Name?" she enquired.

"Milbank," Aria replied.

She had decided the night before not to use her own

26

name. Of course, it was absurd snobbery, as she said to Nanny, to think that anyone was likely to have heard of her. But still, Charles was a baronet and their father had known a vast number of people.

She didn't know why, but she had an absurd reluctance to explain to anyone why she was having to work or to talk of her father's death.

She would never forget the horror of those headlines and the sensational, sordid reports which had filled every paper together with photographs of her father, of the woman with whom he had died and even of Queen's Folly.

"WELL-KNOWN BARONET KILLED IN CAR RACE AFTER CHAMPAGNE PARTY."

She could see the words now spread across the newspaper and many others:

"SENSATIONAL NOBLEMAN PLUNGES TO HIS DEATH."
"THE LAST OF THE REGENCY BUCKS."

She had hardly been able to believe what she read.

It didn't seem credible that her father, whom she had seen only the night before, was dead. But as the reporters had swarmed into the hotel, the telephone had never stopped ringing; and she had been interviewed by the police, the Press, the management—by anybody and everyone wanting to know more and yet more of what had happened—until she had felt it must be some terrible, ghastly nightmare from which she could not awake.

No-one would ever know what a relief it had been to arrive back at Victoria Station on a wet, misty morning in March to see Charles standing on the platform.

She had thought of him at that moment as someone who would rescue her from her own misery, someone to whom she could cling for succour and strength. She did not realise that she was to be the one who must be strong, she must be the rock to which he would cling.

27

Together they had slipped away to the obscurity of Queen's Folly.

They had left behind the sensational stories of Sir Gladstone's extravagances; the details of how he won a fortune at Monte Carlo one night only to squander it the next; of his fancy dress parties where fabulous entertainers were brought from all over the world to amuse and delight the guests; of his wagers in which vast sums of money changed hands; and of his own extraordinary, bizarre personality which made him copy for the Press in whatever he did or whatever he said.

"Forget it," Charles said to her in the train as they journeyed towards Queen's Folly, and she sobbed out her misery and horror of what had happened since the moment that their father's death had hit the headlines.

"Forget it and . . . him!" he added later in a low voice as if he was half ashamed to say the words.

Holding tightly on to her brother's hand, Aria had believed it was possible. That was until they arrived at Queen's Folly. She would never forget the expression on Charles' face as they walked into the house to find it bare.

"He must have stored the furniture somewhere," Charles said in a bewildered manner.

But Aria had known the truth even before Nanny, who had remained in the house as caretaker all the years that they had been away, had come trundling down the back stairs to tell them what had happened.

"It went bit by bit, dearies," she said. "A van would arrive from London and the men would give me a letter from your father to say I was to hand over the Sheraton chairs or the Elizabethan silver mirror."

"Has that gone?" Charles asked sharply.

Nanny nodded.

"It was sold at Christies two years ago. It fetched three thousand pounds."

"I will buy it back!" Charles had shouted. "I will buy it all back. The things were mine, mine—do you hear?"

His voice had echoed round the empty rooms. But

Aria had known in her heart it was but bravado even before the lawyer came down to show them in hard figures how little was left.

"He has made our name stink," Charles had said furiously, but there were tears in his eyes.

Now with an almost defiant air, Aria spelt out the new name she had taken.

"M.i.l.b.a.n.k."

"Christian name?"

"Aria."

"That's unusual," Mrs. Benstead said, and for the first time sounded almost human. "Then we do get some fancy names here. It's the fashion not to be called anything ordinary and easy. Well, I was christened Gladys, and I haven't bothered my head to think of another."

Aria said nothing and after she had finished writing down the name Mrs. Benstead looked up.

"Secretarial, I suppose?"

"I wanted something a little different from that," Aria said hesitantly.

"In what way?" Mrs. Benstead enquired.

"I don't know exactly," Aria replied. "You see, I want something which . . . will bring me in a . . . good salary. Perhaps I should say an . . . exceptional one. As I can't do shorthand, I'm afraid being a secretary is not exactly a job I should do well."

"You can't do shorthand!" said Mrs. Benstead, her voice almost disdainful. "That makes it much more difficult. Even though there's a shortage, people do ask for shorthand these days. You can't blame them; it's speed that counts."

"Yes, I am sure it is," Aria said. "I just wondered if there was anything else."

"What were you thinking of?" Mrs. Benstead enquired. "I have got a woman who wants a social secretary to live in. That means she doesn't pay much and expects you to help in the house when the other servants are out." She flicked the book open as she spoke. "Nice address—house in Upper Grosvenor Street. Like to give it a try?"

"No, thank you," Aria said. "It wasn't the sort of thing I meant."

"Let's see what else we've got," Mrs. Benstead said. "Housekeeper to one gentleman. You have to be a good cook if you go to him. He's ever so particular."

"I can't cook," Aria said. "Not well enough for that, anyway."

"That's no use then. Now, there's a place here . . ." Mrs. Benstead paused.

The girl from the outer office had appeared suddenly. She came in shutting the door behind her.

"She's back!" she said in a low voice to Mrs. Benstead. "He's sacked her!"

"Not Mrs. Cunningham?" Mrs. Benstead said in incredulous tones.

"Yes! And she's brought a message from him to say you are to ring him at Claridges at twelve o'clock."

Mrs. Benstead looked at her watch.

"It's after that now."

"Yes. She said as how her train was late getting up to town."

"What did he sack her for?"

"Need you ask?" the girl enquired, her lip curling. "The usual reason!"

"I never thought Mrs. Cunningham would be such a fool," Mrs. Benstead said. "Oh dear, I had better ring him up and promise him someone else. Find the book for me."

"You needn't bother," the girl replied. "There's nobody on it."

"Well, we've got to do something for him."

In her agitation Mrs. Benstead was pulling at her cigarette until the smoke from it seemed to envelop her like a cloud. She picked up the telephone receiver and dialled a number, and after a moment said:

"Put me through to Mr. Dart Huron."

There was a pause; and then, as she said "hello," her voice changed to one of ingratiating subservience.

30

"Oh, good morning, Sir! This is Mrs. Benstead speaking. Mrs. Cunningham has just called at the office. I'm ever so sorry she was not satisfactory."

The voice at the other end seemed to have plenty to say on this point. Mrs. Benstead appeared to be listening attentively.

"Yes, yes, of course, Sir. I understand. I'm only so sorry. She was so well recommended—I can't understand it. . . . Yes, I will do my best. . . . No, no, we are certain to find someone. There is no reason for you to enquire elsewhere. We'll meet your requirements, as we have always done . . . Yes, yes, that's definite. Three o'clock. . . . Yes, certainly, Sir. I will try and have someone round by then. Good morning!"

She put the receiver down and slumped back exhausted in her chair.

"That's torn it!" she said to the girl, who had been bending over the desk concentrating on every word that was being said. "He wants someone else tomorrow. Expects to interview someone, too, by three o'clock this afternoon. What about Mrs. Jones?"

"She's in Scotland."

"So she is, I had forgotten. Mrs. Harris?"

"Goodness knows what has happened to her. The last letter we sent her was returned, address unknown."

Aria felt as if she had become suddenly invisible. The two women not only seemed to have entirely forgotten her presence but did not even realise that she was still there. Pushing her nicotine-stained fingers through her grey hair, Mrs. Benstead was looking almost wildly through the ledger she had in front of her.

Finally Aria spoke.

"Would you like me to go?" she enquired.

Mrs. Benstead started and stared at her for a moment as if she had never seen her before.

"Yes, yes, of course, Miss Milbank! We'll let you know if we hear anything," she said, oblivious of the fact that she had not yet taken Aria's address.

As Aria rose to her feet, the girl leaning over the desk looked up at her.

31

"I suppose you can't speak three languages by any chance?" she enquired.

"I speak French, German and Spanish," Aria answered.

The words seemed utterly to astonish the two women facing her. It seemed to her that their eyes widened and their mouths literally fell open.

"You do?" Mrs. Benstead said. "How well?"

"Fluently," Aria replied. "I have visited those three countries for quite considerable periods."

"Can you write in those languages as well as speak?" Mrs. Benstead asked suspiciously.

"Yes," Aria answered simply.

The two women looked at each other.

"Well, I don't know," Mrs. Benstead said.

"It does seem a coincidence!" the girl remarked.

"Is that what the gentleman on the telephone requires?" Aria asked.

"Do you know who that was?" Mrs. Benstead asked.

Aria shook her head.

"Why should I?"

"It was Mr. Dart Huron," Mrs. Benstead said. She paused as if waiting for Aria to give an exclamation or show some recognition of the name. When she remained looking blankly polite, she repeated: "Dart Huron. You've heard of him, of course."

"No, I am afraid I haven't."

"Well, really, Miss Milfield—I mean Milbank—I can't think where you've been these past years. Why, he's as famous in America, as well as over here, as . . ."

She hesitated for a name.

"As Billy Wallace or Douglas Fairbanks," the girl put in glibly.

"I think I have heard of them," Aria smiled.

"I should think you have. What do you read?" the girl asked. "The *Church Times?*"

"Well, don't let's waste time," Mrs. Benstead remarked sharply. "The position is this. Mr. Dart Huron, who is a very distinguished American gentleman and very wealthy, has arrived in England and taken a house

32

in Surrey. He has come over to play polo and what he calls 'do the Season.'

"He left it to us to staff his house for him and also to find him a housekeeper who at the same time would be a kind of social secretary.

"He would have brought his own secretary with him but she was ill and so he had to leave her behind in New York. The one essential thing is that she should speak German, French and Spanish—Spanish particularly because Mr. Huron has very big interests in South America."

"What does being a social secretary imply?" Aria asked hesitantly.

"Well, I can't rightly tell you that," Mrs. Benstead replied. "I think she sees to his guests, arranges the rooms and the table, and that sort of thing. Mr. Huron's unmarried, you see."

She glanced at the girl meaningly and then looked back at Aria.

"You must have seen about him in the papers lately."

"I am afraid I haven't," Aria answered. "Has anything particular happened?"

"Oh, really, I don't know where you have been living, Miss Milbank. There have been pages about him— literally pages. You see, he was engaged to Beatrice Watton. You know, the richest girl in America—the Oil Queen they call her. But it was broken off on account of Lulu Carlo—the famous film star. You must have seen her in *Penny Plain*."

"I have heard of her," Aria admitted cautiously.

"That's something, at any rate," Mrs. Benstead said sarcastically. "Well, his engagement to Beatrice only lasted a week or so and then Lulu swooped down on him and off they came to Europe, leaving Beatrice to make the best she could of a bad job."

"Is Lulu Carlo with Mr. Huron now?" Aria asked.

"I imagine so because she is making a film over here. You must have read about that. *Love on a Windmill* it's called. It's being made at Elstree."

"I don't know that I should be very suitable for Mr. Huron's job," Aria said quietly.

She had a sudden horror of being involved with film stars and the type of people who were continually in the columns of the newspapers. Once again she could see the headlines that had heralded her father's death.

Once again she could remember the feeling of being besmirched and dirty after she had read of the way he lived, the people with whom he had associated.

"You don't know what you are saying," Mrs. Benstead snapped angrily. "This is the finest job any woman is likely to get this side of the Atlantic, I can tell you that. Do you know what Mr. Huron pays?"

"I really don't think I should be interested," Aria said.

"Do you know what he pays?" Mrs. Benstead repeated.

"No, why should I?" Aria answered, merely because an answer seemed to be expected of her.

"Twenty pounds a week," Mrs. Benstead said.

"Twenty pounds a week!" Aria ejaculated.

There was no doubt that she was impressed.

"That's the exact sum," Mrs. Benstead said. "And you don't have to pay me any commission either—he pays that. It's the same salary that he gives in New York and he told me that he wanted somebody good and he wasn't going to stint the price he paid for her either."

She looked at the girl beside her and went on:

"Goodness, that Mrs. Cunningham! There's a fool if ever there was one! And she wants the money; I know that, because she's got a child to keep."

"She told me that she just couldn't help it," the girl interposed. "There's something about him," she said. "And you know, I can believe it. You can see it even in his photographs."

"What happened to Mrs. Cunningham?" Aria asked.

Again Mrs. Benstead and the girl looked at each other.

"You had better know the truth," Mrs. Benstead

said. "She fell in love with him; followed him about; made a nuisance of herself. Those were his very words on the telephone. Now, what do you think of that?"

"Are you quite sure that he wasn't being objectionable to her?" Aria asked.

"Who? Mr. Huron? Objectionable to Mrs. Cunningham when he's got Lulu Carlo there!" Mrs. Benstead laughed so much that she had to take her cigarette out of her mouth. "That's a joke if ever there was one. You should see Mrs. Cunningham!"

She laughed until she had to wipe her eyes with the knuckle of her first finger.

"Love! It's the one thing he won't stand. He's got a complex about it. When he was over here before—last autumn wasn't it, Vera?—I got him fixed up in a flat in Grosvernor Square. He had trouble with one of the maids. She mooned about, looked at him with sheep's eyes and went into hysterics when he told her she had better get her work done or go.

"He told me then that he was fed to the teeth with that sort of thing, and now Mrs. Cunningham does the same thing. I could slap her, that I could; letting me down like that after all the trouble I took to get her the job."

"I can assure you that I am not likely to be . . . er . . . interested in Mr. Huron," Aria said stiffly.

She felt a great reluctance to have anything to do with the job or with this man to whom she had already taken an almost intense dislike.

At the same time the thought of twenty pounds a week was too much for her. If she lived in, she need spend hardly anything. It meant that there would be almost twenty pounds to go back to Queen's Folly—twenty pounds a week!

It would mean another man on the farm; repairs to the roof. They could begin to pay some of the bills which were always standing in an ever increasing pile on Charles' desk. However distasteful, however irksome the job might be, she must take it for the sake of Queen's Folly.

"Do you think Mr. Huron is likely to engage me?" she asked.

It seemed as if Mrs. Benstead looked at her for the first time.

"You're a bit young," she said. "Isn't she, Vera? He asked me for someone middle-aged. That's why I sent Mrs. Cunningham—she isn't far off it."

"I am older than I look," Aria said quickly.

Mrs. Benstead shrugged her shoulders.

"Well, we can but try," she said. "I've got no-one else to send him and I don't like to let him down. If he went to any other Agency, it would be disastrous for us. You pop along to Claridges at three o'clock and have a tidy.

"For goodness' sake don't look so sloppy or let him think that you might fall in love with him. That's what he dislikes. It must be uncomfortable, in a sort of way, if you think about it—being a sort of Frank Sinatra. Bother that Mrs. Cunningham; I'm furious with her!"

"Will you give me a card of introduction?" Aria asked.

"Yes, here you are," Mrs. Benstead said, scribbling her name on the top of one of the printed cards. "Send this up at three o'clock. If you get the job, telephone me at once. I'll ring through now and say you're coming. I'll have to say I've known you for some time. I'm taking a chance mind, but somehow you look trustworthy, and if you know three languages you must have had a good education."

"A passable one," Aria said with a smile. She took the card and thrust it into her pocket. "Good-bye!" she said, holding out her hand.

"Good-bye, Miss Milbank, and good luck!" Mrs. Benstead replied.

Aria passed into the outer office. Sitting disconsolately in the chair against the wall was a woman wearing rather fussy, over-elaborate clothes. She was a faded blonde and must once have been very pretty. Now she was middle-aged, her chin-line was sagging and her figure thickening.

"This must be Mrs. Cunningham," Aria thought with a pang of pity. And then, because she felt embarrassed at taking a job from an older woman, she passed down the stairs and out into the street.

She had a cheap and solitary luncheon at a small tea shop off Oxford Street. She found her mood alternating between excitement and optimism at the thought of the salary and depression at what might be expected of her should she actually get the job.

At ten minutes to three she walked into Claridges and asked the hall porter if Mr. Huron would see her. The hall porter telephoned upstairs and then said:

"Mr. Huron is not yet in his suite, Madam. If you like to wait, I will inform you when he comes in."

"I have an appointment for three o'clock," Aria said.

"Mr. Huron should be back by then. He is very seldom late if he makes an appointment," the porter informed her.

The seats in the hall were all filled so Aria walked into the lounge where quite a number of people were still lingering over their coffee.

She seated herself in a chair which had its back to a pillar; beyond was another lounge arranged with low sofas and comfortable armchairs which were intended for the residents in the hotel. Aria had hardly sat down before she heard a voice behind her say:

"I shall kill myself! I shall, really."

It was a woman who spoke with such a passionate intensity that it was with the greatest difficulty that Aria restrained herself from turning round to see who had spoken.

"Now, honey, you are being ridiculous," a man's voice with a soft American accent said soothingly. "You know as well as I do that people who threaten suicide never do it."

"Then I shall be the exception."

"Nonsense! You are too pretty and life holds far too much for you."

"It holds nothing, nothing, without you."

"Now, listen. We have been through all this before.

37

We agreed, you and I, that there was nothing serious between us but a desire for fun. And we've had fun, haven't we?"

"Must you put it in the past tense?"

"No, of course not. It is you who started this conversation."

There was silence and then what sounded suspiciously like a woman's sob.

"Come, honey, cheer up," the man said. "Can I buy you a drink?"

"No of course not. Is that your cure for every ill?"

"I've known diamonds pretty near as effective."

There was no mistaking the slight humour underlying the words. In response there was a sudden chuckle and then two people were laughing in what seemed to Aria a warm accord with each other.

"When do we go and get them?" the woman asked after a moment. "Now?"

"No, I've got an appointment," the man replied. "What about tomorrow morning? Shall we visit Cartier or Boucheron?"

"Why not both? You know I can never have enough of a good thing!"

They were laughing again as if at some familiar joke. Then suddenly Aria glanced down at her wristwatch and saw that it was five minutes past three. She jumped to her feet, anxious lest because she had been listening to a quite irrelevant conversation between two strangers the porter had overlooked her and that she had missed her appointment with Mr. Huron.

She hurried to the desk. She had to wait a moment or two while a large fat woman gave an order about her Pekinese which apparently had to be walked at regular intervals in the park.

At last she gained the head porter's attention. He glanced at the clock before he spoke to her.

"Ten past three," he said. "Mr. Huron ought to be back by now. I'll try him again, Madam."

He picked up the receiver and held on for what

seemed to Aria an unconscionable time. Then at length someone answered.

"There is a lady here who says she has an appointment with Mr. Huron at three o'clock . . . Yes, very good."

He replaced the receiver.

"Mr. Huron's valet is upstairs, Madam," he said to Aria. "He suggests you go up and wait. He doesn't think his master will be long. The page-boy will show you the way."

A diminutive page in silver buttons led Aria to the lift. There were two long mirrors on either side and as they travelled swiftly towards the sixth floor, Aria, glancing at herself, thought how terribly young and inexperienced she looked.

Nervously she pushed back the hair curling over her ears. Perhaps a more severe hair style would make her look older.

She felt suddenly very nervous, her heart dropping at the thought of the interview which lay ahead. Suppose, after all, she didn't get this job? Twenty pounds a week would mean so much to Queen's Folly.

She could imagine the sudden light in Charles' eyes when she told him, the excitement in his voice as he repeated after her, "Twenty pounds a week!"

It was then that she remembered a pair of sun glasses she carried in her handbag. They were not very dark ones, but plain and rather severe in shape, which she had bought many years ago when she was in Rome.

She seldom used them nowadays, but they had been in her black bag when she picked it up to wear it with the black coat and skirt and she had not bothered to take them out.

As she followed the page along the passage, she drew the glasses out of their case. She slipped them on her nose, as she did so pushing her hair still further back behind her ears. The page knocked at a door. It was opened almost immediately by an elderly man dressed in the conventional rounded coat and striped trousers of a man servant.

"You have an appointment to see Mr. Huron, Madam?" he said. "My master should not be long. Will you wait for him in the sitting-room?"

He led the way into a comfortable room and indicated a sofa on which Aria should sit.

"I do not know whether you have seen the *Telegraph* this morning," he said, laying it beside her. "Or if you prefer it here are the *Mail* and the *Express*."

"Thank you," Aria said with a faint smile.

"It's a pleasure," the valet said with what was almost an old world courtesy.

He went from the room, but Aria did not look at the papers. Instead she inspected herself in the small hand mirror she carried in her bag. The glasses certainly made her look older. She looked, too, with her swept-back hair, rather businesslike and efficient. She hoped Mr. Huron would think so, at any rate.

She heard an outer door open and a voice speak, and only just had time to slip the mirror back into her handbag before someone came into the room.

"I'm sorry to keep you waiting, Miss Milbank," he said apologetically, his voice low and deep and with only the faint trace of a transatlantic burr.

Almost instinctively Aria's hand went out to grasp his. It was then, as she felt his fingers touch hers, that she looked up into his face and recognized him.

It was the man who had come to Queen's Folly. The man with the high cheek-bones who had driven the grey Bentley and whom she had thought so attractive that she had found herself thinking of him, not once but continually.

3

"I am sorry to have kept you waiting. Will you sit down?"

Dart Huron indicated a hard chair set beside the writing-desk. Aria crossed the room to it uncomfortably. She had the feeling, absurd though it was, that she should not have been seated on the sofa.

Dart Huron lit a cigarette, then sat down at the desk. He took some sheets of writing-paper out of a drawer and picked up a fountain-pen.

"Mrs. Benstead told me your name but gave me no other particulars," he said. "I think it would be best if I put them down."

He spoke in what seemed to Aria to be an abrupt, rather harsh voice, and now that her first surprise at meeting him was over she was able to look at him calmly and without feeling that curious leap of her heart which had occurred when he came into the room.

His was a strange face, she thought. Not exactly handsome but arresting and, as she herself well knew, unforgettable. He had high cheek-bones and his eyes very deep set, dark and strangely penetrating.

It was easy to understand that some people must find it difficult to look him straight in his eyes. His mouth was full-lipped but firm, and in repose his face had a rather hard expression as if he were a man with little tenderness and not much sympathy for weakness.

"Well, Miss Milbank!"

It almost made Aria jump as he looked up at her suddenly, his pen poised over the paper.

"What do you . . . want to know?" she stammered.

"A few particulars about yourself," he said. "You look extremely young for a job involving responsibility."

41

The cold impersonality of his tone somehow robbed the words of their rudeness. But nevertheless Aria felt herself stiffen.

"I am older than I look," she said. "But if, in fact, you are looking for someone middle-aged, then perhaps it would be better not to waste any more time."

She was surprised to hear her own voice saying the words, and even as she spoke them she wondered how she could throw away this one chance she had of helping Queen's Folly.

Yet there was something in the stranger's attitude which was bringing to the surface a pride she did not even know she possessed.

"I am looking for an efficient housekeeper and social secretary," Dart Huron replied. "I have not any particular prejudice about age. I only want somebody who is capable of filling the position."

"If the particulars Mrs. Benstead has given me are correct," Aria said quietly, "I think I could fulfil your requirements."

"You speak Spanish?"

"Yes."

He gabbed a sentence to her in Spanish, asking her whether she lived in London or whether she had merely come up for the day. She answered him quickly and without any hesitation, replying that she had come from Hertfordshire and that it usually took about an hour-and-a-half to get to London from her home.

"Good!" he said in English. "And you are as fluent in French and German?"

"I have lived in both countries," Aria replied.

"Good!" he said again, and then throwing down his pen as if he had no further use for it added: "Mrs. Benstead will have taken up your references so we need not bother with them. You can start at once, I presume?"

"Do you mean today?" Aria enquired.

"Today or tomorrow. I have a house party coming to Summerhill for the week-end and I want someone to look after them."

"I shall have to go home and get my clothes," Aria said. "I could start tomorrow if that is convenient to you."

"You had better make it as early as possible," Dart Huron replied. "The telephone number is Guildford 8877. If you will telephone the butler and tell him what time you are arriving, he will arrange for there to be a car to meet you at the station. I shall be down at luncheon time. We can discuss then what arrangements are to be made."

"Thank you," Aria said and added, because she was suddenly afraid of all she was undertaking: "I will do my best."

"Thank you, Miss Milbank."

He rose to his feet as if the interview was at an end. And then, as Aria rose too, he hesitated and his lips tightened as if he was making a sudden decision.

"There is one thing more I want to say," he began.

Aria waited, and after a pause he continued:

"I think it best to be quite frank with you, Miss Milbank. I have had trouble in the past with my English housekeepers becoming—how shall I put it?—too attached to me personally. In America I am fortunate in having an exceptional secretary for whom I have the utmost respect.

"She manages my affairs admirably and she never intrudes her own personality on mine. She is, unluckily, ill at the moment, and as she has to undergo an operation is likely to be in hospital for some months."

Dart Huron flicked the ash from his cigarette and continued:

"I miss her not only because her work is first class, but because of her very detached attitude towards me. I think you will understand what I am trying to say."

He looked at Aria in what seemed to her a very disdainful manner. Instinctively her chin went up.

"I assure you, Mr. Huron," she said stiffly after a moment, "that you need not worry that I shall inconvenience you with any unwanted attention or affection. My position in your household will, of course, be exactly as you have defined it, and my attitude towards you will be strictly that of an employee towards an employer."

"I am glad of your reassurance, Miss Milbank," Dart Huron answered. "As I have said, in the past I have been perhaps singularly unfortunate."

Aria thought of Mrs. Cunningham sitting disconsolately in the dusty Agency in Baker Street and felt slightly sick.

"I can give you my assurance that I shall be interested only in my job," she said, and heard the slight edge on her voice which betrayed her inner resentment and rising irritation.

If Dart Huron heard it, he made no sign.

"I shall trust then, Miss Milbank, to your good sense."

"Thank you."

She turned away from him and walked towards the door. Deliberately she did not offer him her hand, knowing at that moment that she would like nothing better than to tell him she had changed her mind and she had no desire to take the position he offered her.

She longed almost intensely to see the surprise in his face, to realise it was not only he who could pick and choose, but other people as well.

Only the thought of Charles' worried face kept her from speaking the words that were trembling on her lips, and when she had reached the door she looked back with what she hoped was dignity and said quietly:

"Good-bye, Mr. Huron."

"Good day, Miss Milbank."

He had not moved from beside the desk and in the light coming in through the soft curtains which veiled the window she got the impression that his eyes were hard and the expression on his face harsh.

Then she closed the door behind her. The valet was waiting in the outer lobby.

"Here's the full address of our house in the country, Miss," he said. "I thought you would like to have it and the telephone number. I have also written down the butler's name—Mr. McDougall it is."

"How kind of you!" Aria exclaimed.

The valet smiled.

"It makes things easier if we all work together, Miss. That's what I always say. You'll find Mr. McDougall a very reliable man."

"Thank you!"

Aria took the piece of paper and slipped it into her handbag.

"I'd like to wish you the best of luck now that you're coming to us," the valet said.

Aria thanked him and shook his hand.

She would have liked to stop and ask the man innumerable questions, but she thought Mr. Huron might hear her, so she walked away down the empty corridor, feeling suddenly very apprehensive now that the die was cast.

"Twenty pounds a week!"

She had to say it over to herself to give her confidence and attempt to restore that sense of excitement which had been hers when she left Mrs. Benstead's Agency. But she knew that Dart Huron's manner had dispersed her first excitement so that it would not return.

It was only as she got into the lift and saw herself in the mirror that she realised she had a bright patch of colour in either cheek. It was anger, she thought, that had brought them there. Anger at his manner towards her, at all that he had insinuated and suggested.

As she stepped out of Claridges into the busy street, she had an insane desire to go back and say that, after all, she had changed her mind. She had a feeling that the whole thing was a mistake, that nothing good would come out of it, and that even the money was not worth what she might have to endure.

It wasn't often that Aria was depressed, but she felt now as if a wave of depression and anticipation hung

45

over her like a cloud. Metaphorically speaking she shook herself.

"I am being ridiculous," she thought.

And yet that uncomfortable feeling of having been subtly insulted made her seethe with anger and resentment all the way to the station.

Her train for Hertford was leaving in a quarter-of-an-hour. Aria seated herself in the corner of a third-class carriage and attempted to read an evening paper. The words danced before her eyes. She kept seeing, instead, the face of a man whom she had at first thought attractive but who now, she had decided, repulsed her.

His words kept echoing in her ear—words spoken coldly and with a personal detachment which was somehow even much ruder than if he had accused her openly of falling in love with him.

"How could Mrs. Cunningham have been such a fool?" she asked herself. "And all those other women who had worked for him and grown to love him?"

If he had been equally unpleasant to them, they must have been demented to have dared to show him the truth of their emotions. And yet perhaps, unaware of what might happen, he had shown them the charm which had been so very obvious when he spoke to the blonde beauty whom he had escorted round Queen's Folly.

It was fortunate that he not enquired what was her address, Aria thought. But if he had, she supposed she would have been quick-witted enough to give the name of the farm or even of one of the cottages in the village. He was very trusting in taking her with so few enquiries, but apparently he had implicit faith in Mrs. Benstead, and Aria could understand the latter's desire not to lose so lucrative a client.

She pulled the piece of paper which the valet had given her out of her handbag. It was thick, white, expensive writing-paper and was engraved *Summerhill House, Puddlefield Green, near Guildford, Surrey.*

Aria wrinkled her brow. Somehow she felt that she had heard of Summerhill before. She could not re-

46

member where, and after a moment resolutely she opened her paper again, striving to think of something else.

But the headlines were not particularly interesting and after a moment she turned to the gossip page. Then, as her eyes glanced at it casually, she felt herself start, for there was a picture of Dart Huron in the centre of the page.

It was not a good portrait—an informal snapshot taken of him on the polo field—but there was no mistaking his high cheek-bones and deep-set eyes, the way his dark hair grew back from his square forehead and the almost aggressive prominence of his chin.

The paragraph beneath the picture told Aria at least one thing she wanted to know.

Mr. Dart Huron's polo team scored a resounding victory at Hurlingham yesterday against Lord Cowdray's team. Mr. Huron is the American millionaire whose feat in flying under Brooklyn Bridge in his private aeroplane was recorded in this paper last year. Mr. Huron, who inherited vast estates in South America, is interested in many things. He has explored unknown parts of Brazil and Peru and has written a book on the Indian tribes which has had an enormous sale in the United States. Mr. Huron, if legend is to be believed, has Indian blood in him, for one of his ancestors, it is said, was a chieftain of the Iroquois tribe from whence he gets his name.

That would account for his high cheek-bones, Aria thought. Perhaps, too, for the unusual look about him. He had not seemed like the ordinary American. This was something else, something which had, in fact, attracted her and now repelled her.

There were a few more words at the bottom of the paragraph.

While Mr. Huron is in this country he has rented Summerhill House near Guildford. It is expected that he will entertain there extensively as he did on a previous visit.

Aria remembered now where she had heard of Summerhill House. There had been pictures of it in an old copy of *Country Life* that she had found in the library at Queen's Folly. She couldn't remember much about it except that in the pictures it had looked like an Italian villa—white and supported by pillars with a wide terrace in front of the windows.

So there was Indian blood in him—Red Indian! She wondered if that would, indeed, make him different from other men. Was that why so many women loved him?

Her thoughts were interrupted by the carriage door being opened and somebody stumbling into the carriage just as the guard blew his whistle and the train started to move. A girl sank down on the seat opposite Aria, the porter threw her suitcase on the floor and slammed the door.

"That was a narrow squeak!"

The girl smiled in a friendly fashion at Aria, who smiled back. She was rather pretty in a heavy, somewhat buxom way. She had fair hair, frank blue eyes, and now she took a handkerchief out of her bag to wipe her face. It was a large, sensible handkerchief and she wiped her face vigorously before she put it back in her bag.

"I thought I had missed the train," she said. "The traffic was awful. I ran like a stag down the platform; I didn't think the porter would keep up with me."

She bent to move her suitcase out of the way of Aria's feet.

"I'm always frightened of missing trains," Aria said, feeling it would be unfriendly not to be conversational.

"My train from the north was late, that was the trouble," the girl said. "It didn't get into Euston until nearly four o'clock. I thought at first it was just hopeless to try to catch the connexion, but I've done it."

48

The girl settled herself more comfortably in the corner seat.

"Have you any idea what time we get to Hertford?" she asked.

"About a quarter-past-five," Aria replied.

"Are you getting out there?"

Aria nodded.

"Yes, I don't live very far from Hertford."

"Oh, really, how interesting—well, interesting to me! You see, I'm going to visit a farm near there. Plover's End is the name of it and Mr. Fuller's the farmer. Do you know him?"

"I have heard of him." Aria said cautiously.

She was anxious not to say more. She did, as a matter of fact, know quite a lot about Fred Fuller, who was a byword in the neighbourhood for the way he drank and what was locally called his "goings on with the girls."

Mrs. Fuller was a rather pathetic, crushed little woman whom Aria had met on various occasions. But her husband was an unpleasant man and although some of their property marched with Queen's Folly both she and Charles contrived to see as little of the Fullers as was possible.

"Oh, do tell me about them," the girl opposite said. "You see, I'm thinking of going there as a pupil."

"As a what?" Aria enquired.

"A pupil. I want to learn farming. You look surprised. Most people do when they hear me say that. Father wanted me to go into business, but my mother didn't want me to do anything. There's no reason for me to work, but somehow I can't sit about doing nothing day after day."

"What made you think of farming?" Aria enquired.

"I've always wanted to be out of doors; to have something to do with animals," the girl answered. "You see, living near Liverpool I've never had the chance to have anything but a dog of my own. I've always wanted to milk cows, look after chickens, to learn to plough. Instead of which I've had to go to tea parties with

49

Mother and listen to Father talking about the variations in trade. He owns a whole chain of stores all over the north. My name is Tetley," she added. "Betty Tetley."

"And mine is Aria Milborne," Aria said. "As a matter of fact my brother's farm is quite near Plover's End."

"Oh, is it?" Betty Tetley said eagerly. "Well, perhaps we shall see something of each other—that is, if I go there."

"Tell me what being a pupil on a farm involves," Aria said.

"Well, I don't know much about it myself," the other girl answered. "We just saw the advertisement in the *Farmer and Stockbreeder*. We answered it and Mr. Fuller wrote a nice letter saying I could live in the house with his wife, that he would teach me everything about farming and we would only have to pay one hundred pounds for my year's board and keep."

Aria's eyes widened.

"You mean you have to pay?" she asked.

"Oh, but of course!" Betty Tetley answered. "And that's cheap really. I should have to pay more if I was apprenticed to any other trade. Why, the Secretarial Colleges charge an awful lot. I forget what it was my cousin paid where she went, but it was a great deal more than that."

"Yes, I see," Aria said. "But I never thought of there being farm pupils."

"Well, you've got to learn somewhere," the girl answered. "And after I have done this for a year I might go on to a college—in fact I intend to do so. My father has bet me I shall get tired of it before that. He doesn't know. It's what I've always wanted to do!"

There was so much enthusiasm in her voice and an expression almost of ecstasy on her good-humoured, frank little face, that Aria found it hard to find words in which to tell her that the last place she ought to go was to Plover's End with Fred Fuller.

This was obviously some new idea of his. He was

50

always complaining that staff were hard to get, and that was not surprising because a lot of decent men wouldn't stay with him.

Aria could well imagine what would happen to this girl once she got to Plover's End. Fred would be charming to her, of course, and he wasn't bad-looking in a coarse, rather flashy way.

There was always the chance that she would be foolish enough to fall in love with him. Then she would find herself in a terrible mess. There were half-a-dozen local girls who had lived to rue the day when they had met Fred Fuller. And as far as he was concerned he was safe enough.

There was always his wife drudging along in the background looking after the children and apparently indifferent to what he did or how he behaved as long as he gave her enough money to keep the house going.

On impulse Aria bent forward.

"Listen!" she said. "I don't know whether your father and mother have made enquiries about Plover's End, but I don't think you would be very happy with Mr. and Mrs. Fuller. It's not a very happy house. If you want to be a pupil on a farm why not come to my home?

"My brother is very anxious to get help and he has got a mixed farm where you could learn everything you want to learn. He is very nice, except that he was a prisoner in Malaya and was badly treated by the terrorists so that at times he becomes utterly exhausted and his nerves get the better of him.

"But nobody works harder than he does and you could live at Queen's Folly and my old Nanny would look after you. She is a very sweet person who has looked after both my brother and myself since we were children."

"It sounds wonderful," Betty Tetley said. "And Queen's Folly is such an unusual name. Is it a very old house?"

"Elizabethan," Aria said. "I think you would like it. Most people think it very beautiful."

"I would love to come and see it," the girl said. "But what ought I to do about Mr. and Mrs. Fuller? Shouldn't I see them first?"

"Yes, of course," Aria said. "I expect they will be meeting you at the station. But you might suggest that you have other people in the neighbourhood to visit and come over to us before you make a decision. I dare say Mr. Fuller would bring you in a car. If not, and you ring up, I will come and fetch you myself."

"I say, it's awfully kind of you," Betty Tetley said a little shyly.

"I think really I am being selfish because I know that my brother would like to have you to help on the farm," Aria said.

Then suddenly her face clouded.

"There is only one thing. I suppose your parents would think that Nanny was sufficient chaperon? We treat her as if she were one of the family. I suppose really she's more of a companion now than a Nanny. She has meals with us—or rather we have meals with her, because she usually cooks them."

"I am sure that would be all right," Betty Tetley said quickly. "Father and Mother aren't a bit stuffy about that sort of thing. They know I can look after myself."

How blind some parents were, Aria thought. They always imagined their children could look after themselves in the most impossible circumstances. And yet she wouldn't have given sixpence for Betty Tetley's chances of looking after herself where Fred Fuller was concerned.

"Of course, I don't want to press you," she said. "But it just seemed that as you have come all this way you might as well see two farms as one. My brother is Sir Charles Milborne, by the way."

She saw Betty's eyes widen slightly and realised that the child was impressed. That, at any rate, might swing the decision in Charles' favour and save her from Fred Fuller. But still, one never knew. Girls were funny creatures; she might take a fancy to Plover's End and that would be that.

Aria felt she could do no more. At the same time, it would be nice for Charles to have a pupil, for Nanny to have someone to look after, and a hundred pounds would always come in useful though they had to spend most of it in feeding Betty.

The train ran into Hertford exactly on time. As they came out of the station Aria saw Fred Fuller in a rather loud sports jacket and a cap pulled over one eye, waiting beside his new Land Rover which had only been delivered a few weeks earlier.

There was one thing she had to admit—that rotten though he was as a man, Fred was a good farmer. He made Plover's End pay, which was more than she could say of poor Charles.

After waiting for ten minutes Aria caught a bus which set her down about a mile-and-a-half from Queen's Folly and she started to walk home across the fields. In the winter this short cut was impossible and it meant going round by the roads, a distance of well over three miles. This evening the fields were dry underfoot and the warmth of the day was dispersing to the soft mist rising from the distant river.

Aria suddenly felt a warm affection for the countryside that she knew so well and which was somehow so much a part of herself that its every aspect seemed as dear and familiar as a person whom she loved.

The hedges, budding green; the chestnuts just ready to break their sticky buds; the glimpses of the bluebells vividly blue in the woods and the primroses on the banks made her feel, with a sudden aching nostalgia, that she could not leave them.

This was her home, this was where she belonged. However much money she earned, however much she was offered, how could she leave it all?

And Charles needed her, too. She knew how to talk to him when he was tired, how to inspire him when he was low and miserable. Nanny fussed over him too much. To her he was always the little boy who must be cosseted and put to bed because he had eaten too many green apples.

53

"I must be mad to think I can go away," Aria said, and then she remembered that pile of bills on Charles' table—bills that would be whittled down very considerably by the sum of twenty pounds a week.

She stood for a moment as she reached the stile leading to another field. Ahead of her in the distance she could see Queen's Folly.

It stood a little higher than the ground surrounding it, its red bricks warm in the glory of the setting sun. It was so lovely that she felt as if she wanted to cry at the sight of it—so old and yet so impervious to the passing of the years, that one felt as if it must stand for ever, a monument of the past and yet still with a vision of the future.

Was any sacrifice too great when it came to the point of saving Queen's Folly?

Aria was smiling as she came through the front door to find Nanny still sitting at the table in the hall, although it was after six o'clock and the door should have been closed to visitors.

"Oh, there you are, dearie!" Nanny said, rolling up her knitting and getting to her feet. "I've got the kettle on the boil and you'll be wanting a cup of tea, I'm sure of that. Did you have a long day? It must have been hot in London."

"Did you have any visitors?" Aria asked, looking into the box where the money was kept.

"Eight," Nanny replied. "And all American. Two car loads of them. They were doing a round of all the houses, they told me. They thought this was 'real quaint' because it was so tiny."

Nanny trying to imitate an American accent made Aria laugh.

"Close the door," she said. "It's after hours and I've got lots to tell you."

"You've got a job," Nanny said. "I can tell it by the look in your eyes."

"Can you guess what it is, as you're so clever?" Aria enquired.

54

"I'm not going to waste my time guessing," Nanny said. "Come along and tell me all about it."

She led the way towards the sitting-room. Aria threw herself in a chair and pulled off her hat. It was only as she did so that she realised her hair was still brushed back from her ears as she had arranged it for the interview with Dart Huron.

She had taken off her glasses in the bus which had carried her to the station, but she had forgotten about her hair, and she wondered now why Nanny had not remarked on it.

Perhaps it hadn't made such a difference as she thought. Perhaps she would have looked just the same to Dart Huron if her curls had been rioting against her cheeks.

Nanny came back from the kitchen with the tea-things.

"I've cut you a nice lettuce sandwich," she said, "I'm sure you didn't have a proper lunch, seeing that you had to pay for it."

"I had a salad, some cheese and a cup of coffee," Aria answered. "And you'll hardly believe it but it came to four-and-sixpence. I was furious afterwards that I hadn't gone somewhere cheaper."

"These London places are all the same," Nanny snorted. "It's a wonder that the wretched people who have to work in the town don't die of starvation. They never give you enough in those eating places to put a bit of flesh on your bones."

She poured out Aria's tea and sat down at the table.

"Now, tell me what you have been up to," she said.

Aria told her from the very beginning. How she had gone from agency to agency until finally, at Mrs. Benstead's, she had been offered the fantastic job of housekeeper and secretary to Dart Huron. She described her interview with him at Claridges, only omitting what he had said to her about becoming too affectionate to him, even as she had omitted all reference to Mrs. Cunningham in her description of the Agency.

"And so I've got the job, Nanny," she said at last.

55

"It doesn't seem possible!" Nanny ejaculated. "All that money! He must be rolling in it if he can throw it away as easily as that."

"I think he is rolling in it," Aria said.

"And what's he like, dearie?" Nanny asked. "Is he a decent man? I wouldn't like you to be going to a house where you would not be mixing with people like yourself. No money in the world is worth some things which you might encounter."

"You need not worry about that," Aria replied. "And if you want to know what Mr. Dart Huron's like, I can tell you. You've seem him."

"I've seen him!" Nanny ejaculated. "When?"

"Do you remember the man in the grey Bentley with that very pretty blonde American who came here yesterday?"

"Of course I remember him," Nanny said. "Do you mean to say that's Mr. Huron?"

"Yes, that's him."

"Well, fancy that now!" Nanny exclaimed. "Oh, well, I'm glad that he has seen your home and knows the sort of place that you come from. It's better that he should have an idea of who you are and the respect to which you are entitled."

Aria did not disillusion Nanny by telling her that she had given a different name from her own. Nanny had very exaggerated ideas as to what Charles' title and Queen's Folly meant to the average person.

She would never have understood even, if Aria had tried to explain to her, how ashamed she was by the notoriety of her father's death or the gossip that Sir Gladstone Milborne had always caused in his lifetime. To Nanny, the gentry, good or bad, were still people to be looked up to.

She had no idea that times had changed or that Aria, as well as Charles, were not proud of their position or their history.

"Twenty pounds a week!" Nanny said. "Well, it seems a lot of money. Do you think he will want you to stay a long time?"

"I have no idea," Aria answered. "The summer, I suppose. But now I've got something else to tell you, Nanny."

She related how she had talked with Betty Tetley in the train and what she had suggested about her coming to Queen's Folly as a pupil if she was not entirely satisfied with the Fullers.

"No decent girl ought to go into Plover's End, and that's a fact," Nanny said. "That Fred Fuller's a bad man. Why, Mrs. Hurcombe was telling me only last week that he's been after the Deaken girl at the Post Office. Goes down to meet her in the evening—and him the father of four children."

"I suppose Mrs. Fuller knows it's no use protesting," Aria said. "Anyway, we can only see if she turns up here. I couldn't say more, could I?"

"No, dearie, of course, you couldn't. Though I'm sorry for the poor creature if she goes into a house like that."

"That's what I felt," Aria said. "You don't think Charles would mind?"

"Well, I was thinking that it would be company for him when you're away. He'll feel a bit lonely in the evenings when there is no-one to talk to, and you know what I am for dozing off when supper is over. I've tried everything but I can't keep awake."

Aria laughed.

"And there's no reason why you should, Nanny. You have your forty winks; and if our pupil comes, Charles can instruct her in the rotation of crops or something equally thrilling."

"If she's a decent sort of a girl it will do him all the good in the world to have someone fresh to talk to," Nanny said. "If you ask me, the way he keeps himself all buttoned up is bad for him. He ought to try and be young again. Do you know, I haven't heard him laugh, not once, this past year.

"I was thinking the other day how he used to laugh when he was a little boy. 'It's funny, Nanny! Don't you see how funny it is?' he used to say to me, and

57

laugh till I thought his sides would burst. Now he's as solemn as a judge. It isn't natural."

"No, Nanny, it isn't natural," Aria said, thinking of the tortures that Charles had endured as a prisoner, some of which he had once revealed to her in a wild moment of misery and depression.

She picked up her hat and bag and got to her feet.

"I'm going upstairs to change," she said. "I hope Charles will be in soon. I can't wait to tell him all the things that have happened today."

"I'm just praying that young girl will come here," Nanny said, and Aria realised with a little sigh that, as usual, Nanny was thinking more of Charles than of anyone else.

He had always been Nanny's favourite; and as she walked slowly up the uncarpeted stairs, Aria felt as if already she had gone from the house and out of Nanny's and Charles' lives. It was almost like being in no-man's-land. Today was finished; tomorrow had not yet begun!

And what would tomorrow bring her? She heard again that harsh, cold note in Dart Huron's voice and felt herself shiver. It had made her angry at the time and yet now, in retrospect, there was something slightly sinister about it.

Was he cruel? she wondered. As cruel as his Indian forbears had been? She felt suddenly afraid.

4

Aria arrived at Guildford Station to find a large limousine awaiting her.

The chauffeur put her luggage into the back of the car and they drove through the town and out into the Surrey hills; and although Aria was prepared for something rather impressive as they turned in at the drive gates with huge stone newels and a rather ornate lodge, Summerhill House, when it came into view, took her breath away.

Originally built by an Italian in the reign of George the Third, it had been added to by subsequent owners until it sprawled, large, a little unwieldy, and yet contriving to be strangely beautiful, over several acres of ground.

It was situated on the very summit of the hill; the ground sloped sharply on the other side of it into the valley below and on clear days one had an uninterrupted view towards the distant sea.

Not only was this house unique, but the gardens also were unique. Everything that money could do to make a garden beautiful had been done at Summerhill. There were flowers and statues, fountains and arbours, rockeries and rippling streams until the eye was bewildered with it all.

For a moment Aria sat open-mouthed in admiration, and then a feeling of nervous anticipation supplanted everything else. This was so much bigger and more impressive than she had expected, and suddenly she remembered why she was there—to run this awe-inspiring house, to manage it for the man who was prepared to pay her twenty pounds a week for her services.

She wondered what the respectful and rather uncommunicative chauffeur would say if she commanded him to turn round and take her back to the station.

Yet that was what she wanted to do more than anything else—to run away, to evade this responsibility which she was quite certain was more than she could shoulder.

But it was too late. The car had drawn up under the portico of the front door, a footman in livery was hurrying down the steps, and a moment later Aria found herself being greeted by McDougall who looked, she thought with a sudden flash of humour, like a rather dissolute archbishop.

"Mr. Huron said we were to expect you, Miss Milbank," he said politely but with just that hint of familiarity as of one servant to another.

"Perhaps you will be kind enough to show me round," Aria said. "But I should like first to see my own room."

"You will, I presume, be using the same apartments as Mrs. Cunningham," McDougall said, and once again Aria fancied that there was something lurking underneath the words as if secretly he was poking fun at her.

"I imagine that will be most convenient," she said stiffly.

He took her upstairs and she found at the end of an enormously long corridor two extremely pleasant rooms.

The bedroom was small but exquisitely furnished, while the sitting-room had large windows overlooking the garden and besides a serviceable-looking writing-desk, which appeared to Aria to be piled with papers, there was a comfortable sofa, armchairs and a television set, all, she gathered, for her own exclusive use.

"What charming rooms," she said, forgetting for a moment to be formal in front of McDougall.

"So Mrs. Cunningham thought," he said. "She was sorry to say good-bye to them."

There was no mistaking the sidelong glance of his eyes or the expression on his face. Aria felt her heart sinking. If all the staff knew why Mrs. Cunningham had left, she could see very clearly that her new position was not going to be an easy one.

"I think now it would be best if you introduced me to the staff," she said. "Mrs. Benstead informed me that they all came through her Agency."

"That's right, Miss," McDougall smiled. "We're all from the Benstead stable, so to speak. Some of us have been with Mr. Huron when he has been over here before, and some, if I may be permitted to say so, are not up to our usual standard. But there you are, one has to take what one can get these days."

Aria agreed with him as they went down the back stairs to the kitchens. There she met the chef, to whom she took an instant liking, and shook hands with an enormous miscellaneous collection of men and women without for a moment having any conception what their duties were or how any of them fitted in to the household management.

"Here's my dining-room, if you would care to see it," McDougall said.

He flung open the door of a very large, beautifully proportioned room as he spoke, but Aria knew there was a warning for her in the possessive "my." McDougall did not intend her to interfere in his department.

"And now perhaps you would like to see the front rooms," he suggested.

Aria shook her head.

"There is no hurry for that," she said. "Perhaps later you could inform Mr. Huron that I have arrived and let me know if there is anything which needs doing in the meantime."

"There's the seating for dinner," McDougall said a little grudgingly. "Mrs. Cunningham used to do that, but Mr. Huron would be quite prepared to leave it to me."

"I think until Mr. Huron gives definite orders I had better see to it," Aria said firmly.

She saw only too clearly that she and McDougall were going to have a silent battle as to who was the real authority in the house.

It means, she thought a little wearily, ceaseless manœuvering, and although the butler was doubtless very good at his job she felt somehow he was not the type of man she could either like or trust very far.

"I think I had better go back to my own sitting-room," she said, and realised that already she was completely lost.

They had passed down so many passages, gone into so many rooms of one sort and another that now she had to wait until McDougall led her back to where she had come down from the first floor.

She climbed the stairs and passing through a swing door which divided the staff quarters from the other part of the house, found herself once again in what already she had begun to think of as her own sanctum.

She put her hat and coat down in her bedroom and glanced at herself in the mirror, only to feel, with a sense of dismay, that she was looking absurdly young. The excitement of her arrival had brought the colour to her cheeks, and her eyes, though wide and a little apprehensive, were also sparkling.

Try as she would she could not control the red curls rioting around her white forehead or the roguishness of those which lay against her cheeks and at the nape of her long neck.

"I had better put on my glasses," she told her reflection in the glass with a little grimace.

She put them on her nose and they certainly did give a new severity to her appearance. She thought, too, that her white blouse, severely tailored, and her black skirt gave her a workmanlike look which was well in keeping with her new position.

Curbing an impulse to hurry, she walked slowly from her bedroom into her sitting-room.

It was even more attractive on second impressions than it had been at first. Pale-green walls and deep rose-coloured chintz were a fitting background for a few really nice pieces of furniture and a lovely picture which Aria recognised as being by one of the early nineteenth-century landscape artists.

The picture made her mind fly back to Queen's Folly. She wondered how Nanny was managing alone this afternoon with no-one to relieve her from her post at the hall door. She felt a sudden pang of unhappiness at the thought of being away from home.

How would Charles get on without her? she wondered, and then remembered, with something akin to jealousy, that he might have Betty Tetley to talk to in the evenings.

It was only now, she thought, that she realised how happy she had been these past years, despite the fact that she had been worried about Charles and troubled about money. Yet how infinitely preferable that was to worrying about her father.

Looking back, she knew that even when she was a

child she had been aware that he was dissolute and un-
reliable.

He had had charm, no-one would deny that, and yet
Aria could not remember a time when she had not
realised that he was uncertain and not to be trusted. He
would break promises as readily as he had made
them—a new interest, a new attraction, a new face,
and old friendships, however valuable they might have
been in the past, were cast aside without a moment's
hesitation.

Little wonder that Sir Gladstone Milborne had had
many acquaintances and no friends.

With a little sigh Aria turned away from the picture.
The past was something she had got to forget, and yet
she knew that neither she nor Charles could ever forget
that their home had been emptied to pay the bills of
some luxury hotel and to buy jewels for a pretty blonde.

Only the pictures had remained; and they could have
gone, too, if the solicitors had not, in a moment of unexpected shrewdness, persuaded Sir Gladstone to make
them heirlooms under the National Trust so that they
should not be liable for death duties.

How often he had regretted what he termed his "one
quixotic action." But he could not cancel or repudiate
it, so although Charles had nothing else and could not
sell them even if he wanted to, the best pictures of the
Milborne collection were still in his possession.

The door behind Aria opened suddenly and she
started rather guiltily, her thoughts so far away that she
had forgotten for a moment her new duties.

"Can I come in?"

It was a man's voice which asked the question, but
there was no trace of an American accent in it and it
was not Dart Huron who stood there. It was, indeed,
someone very different.

A slim, smiling young Englishman with fair hair and
twinkling blue eyes and a mouth which, even in repose,
turned upwards a little at the corners.

"Good afternoon!" he said, advancing across the

63

room. "McDougall told me you had arrived. My name is Buckleigh."

"I'm Aria Milbank," Aria replied, shaking hands with him.

"Yes, McDougall told me your name, but he didn't prepare me for what you were going to look like."

"What . . . what do you mean?" Aria asked.

"But you're a beauty! Dart told me he had engaged a new lady housekeeper and that she was extremely accomplished. He didn't add that she was also a raving beauty."

The newcomer had a whimsical way of speaking which made Aria want to laugh. But remembering that she was supposed to be older and more staid than she looked, she quickly put the glasses that she had been holding in her hand back on her nose and began sternly:

"Mr. Buckleigh——"

"Actually I'm a Lord, if you must be formal," he interrupted.

"Lord Buckleigh, then. I think it is a mistake for us to talk at cross purposes. Would you please tell me what position you hold in the house? Are you a guest?"

"Yes and no," he answered, smiling. "Shall we say I'm a long-term visitor? If you want to know what I do, well, I'm general factotum, adviser, smoother-out of troubles—in fact the perfect A.D.C."

"Mr. Huron employs you?" Aria asked. Then added quickly, "Please don't think it rude of me to ask these questions, but I must understand a little of what goes on in the household, mustn't I?"

"Of course you must," he said soothingly. "That's exactly what I have come here for, to explain to you about everything. I was expecting . . . well . . . shall we say a 'lady of uncertain age'—another Mrs. Cunningham!"

His eyes were twinkling so much that it was hard for Aria not to twinkle back at him. With an effort, however, she turned away and picked up a block from the writing-desk.

"I was just going to jot down the approximate number of servants in this house when you came in," she said. "I wonder if you could help me with it?"

"Good lord, no!" Lord Buckleigh answered. "It's no use asking me things like that. You'll have to get McDougall to work it out for you, though I doubt if he really knows who everyone is. Haven't you realised by now that Dart Huron does himself *en prince?* And why shouldn't he? If one's got American dollars these days, one may as well enjoy them."

"And let your friends enjoy them too?" Aria suggested.

Lord Buckleigh threw back his head and laughed.

"Touché," he said. "I see I was mistaken. You're not the simple girl I thought you were when I came into the room. Yes, there are quite a number of people living on Dart one way or another and if he likes us to do so, who are we to complain?"

Aria began to write his name down in block capitals on the pad in front of her.

"Do you spell Buckleigh with a y or a gh?" she asked.

"gh," he replied. "Tell me about yourself. Where do you come from?"

"Hertfordshire," she replied.

"It's quite a big county if I remember right," he said. "Whereabouts?"

"Not far from Hertford."

"Not very communicative, are you?" he said. "Do you have to earn your own living?"

"Naturally, or I wouldn't be here," Aria answered.

"I think it's a mistake, you know. You're too pretty for this sort of thing."

Aria put down her pencil.

"What exactly do you mean, Lord Buckleigh, by 'this sort of thing'?"

It was a challenge, but he did not take it up.

"You'll find out for yourself," he said. "I warn you, this isn't an easy household."

"You needn't try and make me any more frightened than I am already," Aria said.

For the first time since he had come into the room she dropped her rather formal manner and spoke naturally. In response he seated himself on the side of the desk and put out his hand.

"I like you," he said. "And I think you're lovely. Shall we be friends?"

She hesitated a moment and then laid her hand in his.

"I should be grateful for your friendship," she said.

"Well, don't put too much accent on the word *friend*," he said. "It was only in the manner of speaking."

The admiration in his voice made her drop her eyes and turn her head away from him. She would have taken her hand away, too, but he held on to it. She could feel the warmth of his fingers and then at that moment, as they sat there linked together, the door was burst open and Dart Huron came striding into the room.

"Good afternoon, Miss Milbank," he said. "McDougall told me you had arrived. I've got three cables I want sent off to South America. Will you see to them?"

It was as if a tornado had entered the room. There was something virile and alive about Dart Huron which seemed to galvanise the whole atmosphere.

As he entered, both Aria and Lord Buckleigh had almost instinctively risen to their feet. And now, as they faced each other across the desk, Aria felt the blood rising in her cheeks at the thought that as he had entered the room Mr. Huron must save seen Lord Buckleigh holding her hand.

What must he have thought? she wondered, and knew there was no explanation she could possibly offer even while the embarrassment of it seemed to restrict her very voice within her throat.

"Good afternoon, Mr. Huron," she managed to murmur at length in a low voice.

"I'm glad you arrived safely," he said indifferently,

66

as if it was of no consequence. "Will you take down the cables."

He rattled the cables off in Spanish so quickly that Aria, who could not do shorthand, found it almost impossible to keep up with him.

"I . . . I'm sorry," she said at length, "but I'm afraid I must ask you to repeat those addresses again."

"I thought I said them quite clearly," Dart Huron answered, with an impatient note in his voice. "However—Señor di Palando."

He dictated them again and Aria scribbled away only praying that her spelling would not be at fault. When he had finished speaking Dart Huron looked at his wristwatch.

"It's time for tea," he said. "Will you come down and pour out, Miss Milbank? I'm not much of a tea drinker myself but my guests seem to expect it."

"Oh, but . . ." Aria began to expostulate.

"Lord Buckleigh will doubtless show you the way." Dart Huron walked quickly from the room before Aria could say any more.

She turned to Lord Buckleigh with a look of consternation on her face.

"I didn't think he would want me to do anything like that," she said. "To mix with his guests, to——"

"To play hostess," he finished for her. "If you ask me, Dart has got a good motive behind that request."

"What sort of motive?" Aria enquired.

"You'll find out," he said enigmatically. "And hurry up, for Dart is unlike the usual American, he's never late. This is the only house where with American dollars paying for the meal I get my food served on the dot."

"I think perhaps I had better tidy myself," Aria said a little agitatedly.

"You're all right. Don't worry," he said, smiling down at her as she stood there looking very small and young, the sunlight making a halo of her red curls.

"Will I have to come down to every meal?" Aria asked.

She did not know why the idea should agitate her so tremendously except that she had planned in her own mind that she would be expected to eat in her own room and alone.

"Only when you're invited," Lord Buckleigh replied. "But I've an idea at the back of my mind you're going to find yourself invited pretty consistently."

"But why?" Aria enquired. "Mr. Huron can't possibly want me there! He doesn't know me. I don't know any of his friends. You must see how terrifying it is for me."

"I'll look after you," he promised.

There was something consoling in the thought even while Aria told herself she should not smile back at him in such a friendly manner.

"Come along," he said. "I'll lead you into the lions' den, and what's more give you a personal introduction to each of the lions!"

Aria found there was nothing she could say, and so, with a new shyness that she had not known for many years, she walked beside him along the passage which led to the main staircase. Despite her apprehension of what lay before her Aria could not help but admire the panelled hall and the pictures which hung in it.

"They are nice, aren't they?" Lord Buckleigh said, following the direction of her eyes. "You know whom this house belongs to, don't you?"

"No," Aria replied. "Although I realised that Mr. Huron had only rented it."

"Well, it was originally built for the first Duke of Melchester," Lord Buckleigh said. "It remained in the family until the last war, and by then it was in a very bad state of repair. In fact, the story was that if you weren't careful you would put your foot through a rat-hole every time you got out of bed. So the present Duke sold it to Nognossos, the Greek millionaire.

He spent a small fortune in doing it up and uses it himself for perhaps three months of the year. The rest of the time it is let to people like Dart, or to any of my friends who are prepared to pay me commission for arranging it for them."

"Pay you commission?" Aria questioned.

"Yes Haven't you realised by this time that I'm a commission boy? I get a cut here and a cut there. How else would I live?"

There was something so disarming in his frankness that Aria found herself almost convinced that there was nothing else for him to do. And then, before she could say anything, they had entered the drawing-room and she saw the tea-table with the silver tea-things, arranged at the far end by the fireplace.

It was a long, low room and the curtains and covers were of oyster satin set against eggshell blue walls. But Aria had eyes only for the people assembled round the tea-table.

One face she recognised instantly—the beautiful platinum blonde who had been with Dart Huron when he visited Queen's Folly. She was looking lovelier than ever as she lay back in a big armchair, wearing a dress of emerald green jersey, her small wrists festooned with chunky gold bracelets of every size and shape.

"Oh, there you are, Tom," she said to Lord Buckleigh. "We were wondering where you had vanished to. You knew we wanted to finish our game of Canasta."

"I'm sorry, Lulu," he answered. "We'll finish it after tea. May I introduce Miss Milbank?"

Lulu Carlo turned to look at Aria and there was no mistaking the way the smile faded from her red lips or the antagonism in her expression.

"The new secretary?" she asked, raising her eyebrows but without extending her hand in a manner which Aria privately thought was extremely rude.

"Miss Lulu Carlo, of course, needs no introduction," Lord Buckleigh said to Aria. "You must have seen her in so many films."

Aria managed to repress a start, Lulu Carlo's name was as well known to her as Rita Hayworth's or Jane Russell's, but she was not prepared to say so.

"I am afraid I never have time to go to the cinema,"

she said demurely and felt, with a little feminine glow of satisfaction, that she had paid the film star back for her rudeness.

Aria found herself being introduced to half-a-dozen other people in quick succession. Several of them had titles, two others had names which she thought vaguely had some connection with the film world.

Then, while she was still shaking hands with a tall young man whom she recognized as one of England's foremost polo players, Dart Huron and another man came into the room through an open window from the garden.

"Carl says he's certain it's going to rain tomorrow," he announced. "But he's only saying that because he knows my ponies dislike the heavy going."

"It's not going to rain, I feel it in my bones," someone replied, but Dart Huron was already addressing Aria.

"Oh, there you are, Miss Milbank. Will you pour out the tea?"

Aria was seating herself by the table when Lulu's voice, low and decidedly petulant, came from the other side of the hearth.

"I thought you would like me to do that, Dart darling."

"Why trouble? You know you don't drink anything at this hour."

"It's no trouble for me to pour out for . . . you."

There was a caress on the last word, but it seemed as if Dart Huron did not hear it. He was offering a plate of sandwiches to his other guests while Lord Buckleigh took the cups from Aria as quickly as she filled them.

Lulu rose suddenly from her chair and walked across to the table.

"Why can't one of the footmen pour out?" she enquired in a voice that was deliberately aggressive. "After all, the butler shakes the cocktails."

There was a sudden uncomfortable silence, as always happens when people become aware that an emotional scene is brewing. But with deliberation Dart Huron chose a sandwich for himself from the plate which he was still holding, and replied:

"On the contrary, I usually shake the cocktails myself. It is only because McDougall keeps assuring me that he learned to mix cocktails from Old Harry himself that I am weak enough to let him do it occasionally. But I assure you I have not yet discovered who Old Harry might be."

There was laughter at this but Lulu, standing beside him, did not smile. She was not so beautiful when she was being petulant, Aria thought. Her whole attraction lay in the fact that she had an air of irresistible gaiety about her, a lissom joyfulness which even came over in her films.

Aria had seen one film a long time ago in which Lulu had played the part of a girl who suddenly inherits ten thousand dollars and goes to Paris to spend the whole of it in one mad spree. Lulu's wide-eyed excitement was something she could still remember.

"Dart, you're being unkind to me!"

Lulu's voice had changed completely. She was no longer sulky and petulant but a little girl who was too young and frail to face the unkind buffets of a cruel world. One even had the illusion that there was a suspicion of tears in her big blue eyes as she threw back her head.

"You're hungry, honey," Dart Huron said lightly. "I always find women who are miserable before meals need sustenance. Have a sandwich, they're delicious."

"You know I never eat anything at tea."

The petulance was back in Lulu's voice again.

"Shucks, forget your figure for once," Dart smiled. "A sandwich a day keeps the blues away. Try it."

"I don't want anything, I've told you."

Lulu gave the plate he was holding out to her a sudden push. She knocked it from his hand and it fell to the ground, smashing into a hundred pieces, the sandwiches falling on to the carpet.

"That's entirely your fault," Lulu said, her voice

71

sharpening. "But doubtless Miss Milbank can pick them up for you. That's what she's employed for, isn't it?"

As she spoke Lulu Carlo walked across the room with a sudden sweep of her skirts and jingle of her bracelets. Then, before anyone could move or speak, she had swept through the drawing-room door and slammed it ominously behind her.

There was a moment's uncomfortable silence and then Lord Buckleigh laughed.

"That's another item on the dilapidations, Dart," he said. "But not such an expensive one this time. I forgot to tell you, I broke one of the billiard cues last night."

"How could you manage to do that, Tom?" Dart Huron asked.

His voice was quite natural and if it had not been for the broken plate at his feet and the sandwiches spread over the carpet it would have been impossible to believe that a rather ugly and embarrassing scene had just taken place.

With an effort Aria pulled herself together. She rose and pressed the bell by the side of the fireplace. A dog which appeared from under one of the chairs began to eat the sandwiches.

"Be careful that he doesn't get a piece of china in his paw," somebody said.

They were all concentrating on protecting the dog when one of the footmen came into the room.

"Will you get a pan and brush, please?" Aria said in a voice of authority which surprised even herself. "One of the plates has been broken by mistake."

"Very good, Miss."

The footman hurried away. Dart Huron looked at Aria directly for the first time since he had entered the room.

"Can I have a cup of tea, Miss Milbank?" he enquired.

"I'm sorry. I thought you said upstairs that you weren't a tea drinker," Aria replied. "Otherwise I would have poured you out one."

"Highballs are more in his line!" a pretty girl laughed.

72

"Not tonight they aren't," Dart Huron answered. "We've got to win that match tomorrow. And if we don't win the cup, it will be soft drinks at dinner for everyone as a punishment."

There was much laughter and jesting about this and while everyone was talking the footman came back with a pan and brush and swept away the debris.

"Shall I bring some more sandwiches, Miss?" he asked Aria.

"No, thank you. I think everybody has finished," Aria replied.

The man disappeared. Aria sipped her own tea and felt the colour which had risen in her cheeks at Lulu Carlo's insult beginning to die down and the beating of her heart return to normal.

The polo player, whose name she discovered was Jim, asked her if she had seen the garden yet and what she thought of the view. It was banal, very common-place conversation, but it gave her time to pull herself together and realise that it was possible for her to speak quietly and naturally and as if nothing had happened.

"What about a game of tennis," someone suggested, and as they rose to their feet Aria realised thankfully that this was where she could escape.

Lord Buckleigh was involved in a conversation as to who should partner whom, and she thought no-one would notice that she had left. She had, indeed, almost reached the door when Dart Huron's voice arrested her.

"Miss Milbank!"

She swung round. He had detached himself from his guests and was walking towards her. He walked like no other man she had ever seen. There was something almost feline in the grace of his body and she wondered if this was due to his Indian ancestors.

She waited while he approached her, feeling a little nervous. Feeling, too, absurdly young and somewhat out of place in her white blouse and plain black skirt.

"You have got everything you want?"

She realised the question was merely a formality and yet perhaps in its way an effort on his part.

73

"Yes, thank you, Mr. Huron!"

"I may have another cable to send later this evening. You got the other ones off?"

"No. I was going to send them after six o'clock at the cheaper rate."

The severity of his face relaxed a little and for the first time since she had known him he smiled at her.

"I don't usually worry myself about cheap rates."

"I'm sorry! I didn't understand that you wanted them sent at once."

"My usual instructions to anyone who works for me are to do it immediately!"

"I will send them as soon as I get upstairs," Aria promised.

There was a pause as if Dart Huron did not know what to say and she did not quite know how to go, and then he remarked a little abruptly:

"That will be all then. I shall see you at dinner."

"Oh! You don't want me to come down to dinner, do you?" Aria asked.

"Why not?"

"I . . . I would rather not."

His lips tightened as if he was incensed at being argued with.

"Are you stating your usual preference in such matters or are you upset at what has just occurred?"

"My usual preference," Aria answered. "I did not expect to have meals with you and your guests."

"Most women I have employed in your position have sought such invitations," he said.

She felt a sudden surge of anger because she was certain that inwardly he was sneering at her.

"I am afraid I have no knowledge of what has gone on here in the past," she said, holding her head very high. "But I should like to make it clear to you Mr. Huron, that whatever did happen, I am not particularly interested. If you wish me to dine downstairs I will, of course, obey your orders; but I would prefer, especially when I have more work to do, to have my meals in my own sitting-room."

The anger and dislike that she had for him permeated her voice despite her efforts to speak entirely impartially. He looked down at her and for a moment their eyes met.

Both were conscious of the sparks passing between them; and then, as Aria waited, holding herself very erect, her chin up and with a sudden fire behind her dark eyes, Dart Huron turned on his heel.

"I shall expect you to dine with us tonight," he said, and walked away.

5

"I see that you have put down two dishes with white sauce," Aria said, as she glanced up from the menu at the chef standing on the other side of her writing table.

"*Ma foil mais c'est impossible,*" the chef exclaimed dramatically, and then as Aria held out the menu towards him he added: "*Oui, c'est vrai. Je vous demande pardon, M'selle.* It was—how you say—a slip of the pen."

He made the alteration in pencil and then, as Aria approved his suggestions, gave her a very Latin bow and went from the room.

She gave a sigh of relief when she was alone. At the same time she could not help feeling almost childishly elated that she had held her own and been quick enough to spot the mistake in the menu.

Years of eating in hotels were likely to stand her in good stead now, but she could not help a little tremor of apprehension whenever she had to deal with the upper servants.

She was well aware that they looked on her curiously, thinking her far too young for the post and being ready to resent any suggestion she might make to them.

Fortunately Aria had a very good idea of how a big house should be run. One summer her father had rented an enormous villa in the south of Italy, and another winter had been spent in Switzerland, where, because he had a row at the hotel, he had hired a large castle and they had lived in almost feudal state for the few months that it had amused him to ski.

But experience had not prevented Aria from feeling very lonely and very frightened when she went down to dinner the night before, to encounter the hostility of Lulu Carlo and the rather supercilious curiosity of the rest of the guests.

It seemed to her that for some extraordinary reason Dart Huron was singling her out for attention; asking her opinion on various matters; giving her instructions for the staff which he could quite well have given himself.

She hated every moment of the evening and her host most of all, and it was with a sigh of relief that she managed to creep upstairs to her own room as soon as the party had settled down to games of cards.

She had not gone to sleep as she had hoped but had lain awake hour after hour, staring wide-eyed into the darkness, puzzling over so many things and finding no satisfactory answer to any of her questions.

She had thought that she would wake up depressed, but instead, with the sunshine coming in through her bedroom window, she had felt excited and light-hearted when she had arose at eight o'clock.

Her breakfast was brought to her room and with it the morning papers. She glanced through them to find a large picture of Dart Huron in the *Daily Mail* and several references to him in the gossip columns of other papers.

His photograph did not do him justice, she thought. They seemed to accentuate his high cheek-bones and to give his face almost a savage look as if he were much

76

more uncivilised and uncultured than he really was in reality.

She found herself wondering about him as she dressed. There was a harshness in his voice when he spoke to her that was not there when he addressed other people. And yet if he disliked her there was no explanation for his continually singling her out and his insistence on her being present at dinner the previous night.

As soon as she was dressed, Aria went to her sitting-room, where she found the morning's post waiting her. She opened Dart Huron's mail with the exception of the letters marked "Private" or "Personal."

There were over a dozen fan letters from idiotic women writing to tell him how much they admired his pictures in the Press and invariably suggesting on some pretext or another that he might care to see them.

Aria set these on one side and made another pile of those which concerned business matters.

There were at least a dozen invitations, all from important and distinguished people inviting him to dinner, to luncheon or to stay the week-end; and not unexpectedly there were dozens of appeals from charities, all begging a donation towards some particular worthy cause.

Aria arranged them all carefully and wondered whether she should take them down to Dart Huron's own study or whether he came to her. She had decided that she must consult McDougall on the matter when the door opened and the Head Housemaid arrived to enquire what guests were expected that day.

When she left, the telephone rang and Aria had just finished taking down a message about the boxing of a polo pony when the door opened and Lord Buckleigh came in.

He was wearing riding-breeches and a well-cut tweed coat.

"Good morning!" he said. "Would you like to come riding with me?"

77

"I should love it!" Aria answered. "But you know I can't."

"Why not?"

"Because I have got work to do. Do you know whether I take these letters down to Mr. Huron's study or do I wait until he sends for me?"

"I think you wait until he sends for you," he answered. "If he does! He has a habit of leaving his correspondence to his secretary."

"But I don't know how to answer these," Aria said helplessly.

Lord Buckleigh came over to the desk and stood beside her.

"Let me help you," he suggested.

"Oh, would you really? Thank you so much," Aria replied.

She looked up at him as she spoke and then something in his face made her turn her eyes away quickly.

"You're very pretty," he said in a very different tone. "I'm prophetically aware that I'm about to fall in love with you."

"Oh, don't be so silly," Aria pleaded.

"I am not being silly, as a matter of fact," he answered. "The very first moment I saw you yesterday something very strange happened to my heart. Are you engaged to anyone else, by the way?"

"No, of course not," Aria replied. "And you're not to say such things to me."

"It wouldn't have made much difference if you had been," Lord Buckleigh went on. "But an infuriated he-man ramping about the place wanting to punch me on the nose has never seemed to me a particularly desirable asset to a love affair."

"Well, there isn't such a person and there won't be any love affair," Aria said firmly "I am here to work for Mr. Huron."

"You're not thinking of falling in love with him?" Lord Buckleigh enquired.

"No, I am not," Aria said almost angrily.

To her surprise Lord Buckleigh put his hands on her shoulders and turned her round to face him.

"You said that almost too vehemently," he said. "What's Dart been doing to you?"

"Nothing!" Aria answered, trying to free herself. "Please, Lord Buckleigh, go out riding and leave me alone. I have got a lot of work to do and I am not in the mood for being teased."

"I'm not teasing you, you ridiculous child. Yes, you are a child, despite the fact that you try to look grown up. Tell me about yourself. Where you have come from and who are you?"

With an effort Aria wrenched herself free from him.

"Please go away," she said. "I haven't got time to relate my family history at this time in the morning. Mr. Huron may be wanting me."

"You look adorable when you try to be cross," Lord Buckleigh smiled. "I've always fallen in love with girls with red hair. But yours is different from most; it looks as if it has specks of gold in it. There is gold, too, in the green of your eyes."

"It's likely to be the only gold I shall ever have then," Aria said sharply.

Lord Buckleigh sat down on the edge of the writing-desk. Although Aria felt embarrassed by his behaviour and by what he was saying, she could not help feeling that his charm and his air of boyish irresponsibility made it difficult for anyone to be really angry with him.

"Do go away!" she begged. "It's hopeless to try and talk sense to you and I really haven't got the time to talk at all."

"You will need me as a friend, you know," Lord Buckleigh said.

"Yes, I know that," Aria answered soberly. "I think I am going to need friends here."

Lord Buckleigh grinned.

"Are you thinking of Lulu?"

Aria nodded.

"Dart's inviting trouble, if you ask me. But actually he's got no right to drag you into it."

79

"But I don't understand," Aria said. "Why should she hate me?"

"You are being rather obtuse, aren't you, sweetie?" Lord Buckleigh asked. "She wants to marry Dart. She hasn't hooked him yet and he's being pretty wily. She's not the first or the last woman who will fight like a tiger to get him into the matrimonial net."

"What has that got to do with me?" Aria enquired.

"Surely it's obvious!" Lord Buckleigh replied. "Lulu wants to marry Dart and he is determined not to commit himself, especially in public. Hence a housekeeper who is a hostess, who makes the arrangements of the household, who looks after the guests and pours out the tea."

He laughed as he spoke, but Aria's face was serious. Much that had seemed unaccountable was now becoming clear.

"Dart has got rather a unique position over here," Lord Buckleigh went on. "He knows everyone—Royalty, Society, the Stage, Diplomatic big-wigs and, of course, all those who are interested in sport. He doesn't want to do anything so stupid as setting up house with Lulu Carlo, which is just what she intends he shall do.

She never stays here unless there is a married woman in the party. But Dart also has to prevent her from assuming a position inside the house where his other guests are concerned. And you, my dear, are the answer to that!"

"Why didn't he explain it to me?" Aria asked.

"Dart explain anything!" Lord Buckleigh threw back his head and laughed. "He is a law unto himself; a man who really believes he can do as he likes without being accountable to anyone, not even to his fellow men. That's why I like him, I suppose—and envy him. One has to have a lot of money to get away with that sort of thing."

Aria sat down in the writing-chair.

"I don't know whether you have made things better or more complicated! Now at least I understand what is happening, but it is not the sort of situation that I am likely to enjoy."

"I expect Lulu is thinking the same thing," Lord Buckleigh said with a wicked grin.

"She is very beautiful," Aria sighed. "I can't think why Mr. Huron doesn't want to marry her."

"Can't you?" Lord Buckleigh questioned. "Well, I can! And now, enough about Dart and his women. Let's talk about us."

"I have told you, I haven't got the time," Aria replied.

"I don't believe you have got anything to do at all," Lord Buckleigh retorted. "You're just making excuses. But I don't mind. I'm a simple sort of fellow. I'm content just to sit here and look at you. There's something about the way your mouth turns up at the corners which fascinates me."

Aria put her hands to her cheeks.

"Please!" she cried. "You are making me so embarrassed. I don't know what to say to you."

In answer Lord Buckleigh held out his hands towards her. "Say that you like me a little bit," he said pleadingly.

"I don't . . ." Aria answered. "I don't know anything about you. I only met you yesterday for the first time."

"I met you yesterday, but I know exactly what I think about you. You are lovely, you are sweet, and at this moment I would like more than anything else in the whole world to kiss you."

Aria got to her feet. "Go away," she said. "You are not to talk to me like this. If you don't go I will . . ." She hesitated.

"Well, what will you do?" Lord Buckleigh enquired

"I . . . Don't know," Aria said helplessly. "You're being hateful!"

"Darling, I am a beast to tease you," he laughed. "But you're so adorable when you are annoyed, and so utterly fascinating when you are not. Please tell me you like me a little bit."

He took her hand in his and raised it to his lips.

They were standing in the sunshine from the window, her hand close against his mouth, when the door opened.

Aria started guiltily, but to her relief it was a woman who stood there, not, as she had been half afraid, Dart Huron himself.

"Miss Carlo would like to see you, please, Miss," the woman said, and Aria recognised her as Lulu Carlo's personal maid.

"Yes, of course," Aria answered, disengaging her hand from Lord Buckleigh's. "Where is Miss Carlo?"

"In her bedroom. I'll take you there, Miss, if you like."

"Thank you! I will come back at once," Aria said.

She picked up a notebook and pencil from her desk and without even looking back at Lord Buckleigh followed the maid from the room. She hoped that she appeared composed, for her cheeks were burning and she felt both embarrassed and irritated that she should have been so weak with him and that the maid should have seen him kissing her hand.

Lulu Carlo's bedroom opened off the wide landing at the top of the stairs. The maid knocked on the door and as a petulant voice answered she opened it and Aria passed into the room.

It was a large, high-ceilinged room with long windows opening onto a balcony, facing which was a huge bed upholstered in peach velvet and ornamented with carved angels.

Lulu Carlo was lying back against a pyramid of large pillows, a dressing-jacket of pink chiffon trimmed with swansdown covered her nightgown, and her lips were a slash of red against the pale purity of her face.

"Good morning!" Aria said tentatively from the end of the bed.

"Where's Mr. Huron?" Lulu demanded in a hard, rather aggressive voice.

"I have not the slightest idea, Miss Carlo. I have not seen him this morning."

"That's a lie!" Lulu Carlo ejaculated.

Aria felt herself stiffen.

"I am afraid I don't understand," she said quietly.

Lulu Carlo gave a rude laugh.

"You understand me well enough," she said. "I sent down a message to Mr. Huron some time ago and was told he couldn't come to see me as he was attending to his correspondence. You're his secretary, so I imagine he was with you."

"I am afraid you have been misinformed," Aria said.

"Well, then, go and find him for me," Lulu Carlo commanded. "I want to see him—and at once."

Aria wanted to tell her to get out of bed and go and find him herself, but she decided that if there was any argument Lulu was much more likely to be ruder than she could ever possibly contrive to be. So without saying another word she went from the bedroom and down the stairs which led into the hall.

There was no-one about and after hesitating for a moment Aria opened the door which led into the Study. She had learned the night before that it was a room which was considered Dart Huron's sanctum and into which the guests did not percolate unless specially invited.

It was a pleasant room lined with books and having an essentially masculine smell about it, which in itself was a relief, Aria thought, after the heavy, exotic fragrance of Lulu Carlo's bedroom.

The room was, however, empty, and Aria would have left at once if her attention had not been attracted by a picture over the mantelpiece. It was a framed portrait of a man by Lawrence. It was not unlike one which hung at Queen's Folly. There was the same wonderful green tone to the coat; the same exquisite drawing of the turn of the head.

The picture at Queen's Folly had been damaged and was not in particularly good preservation. This one was perfect and Aria stood staring at it, taking in every detail of the beautiful painting and the charm which always seemed evident in anything portrayed by that nineteenth-century master.

"Delightful, isn't it?" a voice said behind her.

She turned with a start to see Dart Huron standing just inside the doorway.

"I . . . I am sorry . . ." she began.

But he interrupted her as he crossed the room, saying:

"I think if I could own anything that is in this house I would choose that picture. There is so much life in that face, and a light in the eyes which seems to tell me the gentleman has just achieved something he most desired!"

"You are like my brother," Aria said impulsively. "He always makes up stories as to what people were thinking about when they were painted."

"Your brother is interested in pictures?" Dart Huron said.

Aria remembered that this was on dangerous ground.

"Yes," she said briefly. "But I came to tell you——"

"That can wait for the moment," Dart Huron said. "Come and look at this picture."

He led the way across the room to where another picture hung between two windows. It was the portrait of a girl by an unknown artist and had obviously been painted some time in the eighteenth century. It was not such a finished picture as the one over the mantelpiece, but it had a charm of its own.

"I like that, too," Dart Huron said.

"So do I," Aria agreed. "But she looks frightened."

"Perhaps that is why I like it," Dart Huron said.

Aria looked at him in surprise.

"Does that sound brutal?" he enquired. "If people are frightened of one, they are not likely to become too possessive or familiar."

Aria did not know what to say to this, so she was silent. Then, in an entirely different tone, as if his mood had changed in an instant, Dart Huron said:

"You were looking for me?"

"Yes. Miss Carlo wants to speak to you."

"Where is she?"

"In her bedroom," Aria answered.

"I am busy right now," Dart Huron said. "Tell Miss Carlo I shall see her at luncheon, or before if she comes down."

"I . . . I think it is urgent," Aria answered.

She knew by the sudden tightening of his lips, the squareness of his jaw, that her remark did not please him. He did not answer it, but after a moment said:

"Are you comfortable, Miss Milbank? Have you found everything you want? I have instructed the servants to take all their orders from you."

"I hope I shall be able to manage the household to your satisfaction," Aria replied formally.

"I hope so, too," he answered gravely. "You are younger than I thought. Younger than you appeared when we met at Claridges. Do you think it will be too much for you?"

"No, I don't think so," Aria answered. "It is a little difficult to get into things right away."

"Good!" He picked up a letter from his writing-desk. "Will you translate this for me?"

It was a business letter written in Spanish and with only two very short hesitations Aria read it through. Only as she finished did she realise that it was a test to see if she was capable of understanding it.

"Where did you learn to speak so well?" he asked as she handed him back the letter.

"I have been in Spain and South America," Aria replied. "I was not very old when I visited Buenos Aires, but I had a Spanish nurse that winter and that, of course, helped my language a great deal."

"Yes, of course it would," Dart Huron said. "But most girls do not have such advantages—at least that's what I have always understood, although I don't know much about English girls. Tell me about your family."

That was the last thing that Aria wanted to do and her voice was as cold as it could be as she replied:

"I have a lot to do, Mr. Huron. There are several piles of letters upstairs for you to see when you have the time."

"So you think I am being curious or impertinent," he

85

said. "Well, perhaps you are right. It's your own business."

Aria inclined her head.

"Shall I fetch the letters, Mr. Huron?"

"Yes, yes! Fetch them if you must. I hope when you have been here a short time, Miss Milbank, you will be able to answer them yourself."

Aria turned towards the door. She had the feeling that he was watching her go. Because she wished to appear dignified she walked a little slower than she would have done had she followed her own inclination.

Outside in the hall she lightly ran across the marble floor and up the wide staircase. At the top of the landing she hesitated, remembering that she must first give a message to Lulu Carlo before she went to her own room to fetch Dart Huron's correspondence.

She knocked at the door. A voice that was all honey and sweetness answered:

"Come in."

Aria did as she was told. Lulu Carlo was lying back against her pillows, her fair hair freshly combed and floating over her shoulders. She was looking very lovely.

"I found Mr. Huron . . ." Aria began, only to be interrupted by a voice that was sharp and angry.

"Well, why hasn't he come? Did you tell him I want to see him?"

"I gave him your message. He replied that he would see you at luncheon, or before if you were down."

"He is showing off in front of all these damned snobs he has got staying here!" Lulu Carlo exclaimed. "Afraid of what they will think if they see him coming into my bedroom. Well, I could tell them a thing or two if I wished to."

Aria looked at her and wondered if Dart Huron had ever seen or heard her talking like this. If he had, surely the vulgarity and commonness must have disgusted him, despite the loveliness of her face which remained unchanged despite the harsh stridency of her voice.

"Will that be all, Miss Carlo?" she asked.

"Oh, I suppose so," Lulu Carlo answered petulantly,

and then as Aria turned to go she added: "You know that I am going to marry Mr. Huron, don't you, Miss Milbank?"

"No, I did not know it," Aria replied. "May I offer my congratulations to you both?"

"It is a secret, of course," Lulu Carlo said lightly. "We are not telling anyone yet. It naturally doesn't matter you knowing. A confidential secretary should always know everything, shouldn't she?"

"I don't know about that," Aria replied. "But it is nice of you to tell me."

She spoke with deliberate politeness, determined that this unpleasant woman should not be able to accuse her of bad manners.

"Mr. Huron's a difficult man," Lulu Carlo went on. "Very difficult! As his friends will tell you, and as you will soon find out. But I love him. I love him very much indeed, and we are going to be very happy together."

There was a ring in her voice when she spoke of her love which told Aria that she was, indeed, speaking the truth. And there was a look on her face which confirmed this.

Quite suddenly Aria was sorry for her. This spoiled and pampered film star, who was the envy of half the cinema-going world, was in love; and unless she was mistaken, Aria thought, Dart Huron was not very much in love with her.

"Did you see my last film?" Lulu Carlo asked suddenly.

Aria shook her head.

"I have seen only one of your pictures. I haven't been able to get up to London very often—or even to the cinema in Hertford, which is near my home."

"I wish you had seen it," Lulu said. "I wore a really lovely wedding dress in it—all tulle and diamanté. I thought of having something very much the same for my own wedding."

She was longing to talk, Aria could see that. She was wanting to confide in someone her dreams and her

87

fantasies about her wedding which might never come off.

"I wish I had seen it," Aria agreed. "But I have got to go now. Mr. Huron is waiting for me. I have got a lot of letters to ask him about."

"So he has time for you, has he?" Lulu said, her voice sharpening again. "Oh, well, I had better get up. Tell him if Mohammed won't come to the mountain, the mountain must come to him."

She threw back the bedclothes as Aria went from the room, hurrying along the passage to her sitting-room to collect the piles of letters she had left on her desk.

There was no time to think about Lulu-Carlo now, with her curious mixture of intense rudeness and almost pathetic confidences. At the same time, Aria realised that she did not dislike her as much as she had done the night before.

Dart Huron was waiting in the study, seated at a big, leather-topped desk, when Aria re-entered the room.

"Two replies have just come to the cables you sent last night," he said. "They are both unsatisfactory: you will have to cable them again."

"Very well," Aria said. "What shall I say?"

He dictated the cables rapidly and then turned over the pile of letters she had set down beside him. He told her to accept one or two of the invitations and to refuse the others. Then he looked at the pile of requests from charities, whose Chairmen, mostly distinguished people with titles, wrote asking for a donation.

"You can refuse all those," he said.

"You are not going to send any of them anything?" Aria asked. "Some of the requests are from personal friends."

"I have got my own charities in America," he answered. "Do you suppose these people would worry about me if I wasn't rich? All they want of me is money, and in my opinion the money I spend on those less fortunate than myself should be spent in the country from which it comes."

"I . . . I think you are right there," Aria said. "I will answer them as kindly as I can."

He pushed the pile on one side.

"No! Don't do that," he said. "Send them each twenty pounds."

"All of them?" Aria enquired.

"Yes! All of them," he answered. "It won't hurt me and it will please them."

"That is very generous of you," Aria said.

"Generous!"

He gave a bitter laugh.

"Well, I suppose I get something out of it. The adulation of people who are always trying to get something out of me and a niche in the social life of England. Money can buy all those things, you know. It can even buy friendship—and love."

"It depends what sort of love," Aria said quietly.

"Any sort of love," he said firmly. "Shall I tell you something it cannot buy?"

He got to his feet as he spoke and walked across to the mantelpiece to stand looking up at the Lawrence picture.

"That's what it cannot buy!" he said.

"But . . . I don't understand," Aria said, wrinkling her brow. "Do you mean that particular picture is not for sale?"

Dart Huron shook his head.

"No! I mean ancestors; family portraits handed down from generation to generation. This picture is of a former Duke of Melchester, and until Nognossos came here, spreading his money all over the place and ruining the atmosphere of centuries, the Duke's great-great-grandson sat in this room and looked at the portrait, even as I am doing.

That is something that money cannot buy. Treasures handed down the centuries; treasures which belong to you, personally, and not just to any collector who's got the money."

There was so much intensity in his voice that Aria

89

listened surprised. Then suddenly, as if he thought he had said too much, Dart Huron said sharply:

"That will be all, Miss Milbank! Please get those cables off immediately."

Aria picked up her notebook and the pile of letters. She wanted to say something and yet she could not think what. And so in silence, conscious that Dart Huron's eyes were watching her, she went from the room.

She had so much to think about that she wanted to be alone, but when she reached her own sitting-room it was to find McDougall was waiting for her with a list of household requirements, and no sooner was he gone than the telephone started to ring.

Nearly half an hour later Aria turned with a sigh to the pile of letters, and then, before she could even begin them, Lord Buckleigh was once more in the room.

He came in, threw his riding-crop and gloves down on the sofa, and said accusingly:

"You have spoiled my ride for me. I kept seeing your green eyes looking at me. Have you missed me?"

"Not in the least," Aria said severely. "You must go away at once. I have got too much to do to talk to you."

"You are being unkind, you know. I thought about you all the time I was riding—and I am in love with you! There's no mistaking the symptoms."

"Then you will just have to get over it," Aria said.

"You are heartless and unkind. I shouldn't have thought it of you."

Despite her resolution to be severe Aria could not help smiling.

"You are being ridiculous," she asserted. "Do go and find someone else to talk to—Miss Carlo for instance."

"You know I can't help feeling that it was fate that brought you here," Lord Buckleigh said, paying no attention to Aria's suggestion. "I was only thinking two days ago how most people bore me and I was rather dreading the house party this week-end, and then suddenly you appeared."

"Like a new cabaret turn," Aria suggested. "You will soon be bored with me, too, and I am certainly going to be bored with you if you don't let me get on with my work."

"I love you!" Lord Buckleigh said. "Remind me to tell you about it some time."

"I'll make a note of it," Aria answered. "But one thing is quite certain, I shall get the sack very shortly if you don't let me do any work."

Lord Buckleigh moved to her side and before she could realise what he was about had put his hand under her chin, tipped back her head and kissed her gently.

"You are adorable!" he whispered against her lips.

"How . . . dare you?" Aria managed to stammer.

She wanted to say more, to berate him for daring to touch her, for insulting her by that easy, lightly given kiss. It was too late. He had gone from the room as swiftly as he came into it, leaving behind an impression of ephemeral charm, of a gray, elusive personality that it was almost impossible to take to task.

He had left, too, the feeling of his lips on hers; and Aria found herself touching her mouth with her fingertips as if something had happened which must have left an imprint there.

And then with a little smile and shrug of her shoulders she told herself that she must not take this seriously. Lord Buckleigh meant nothing by his philandering.

It was just a passing flirtation; the sort that her father had indulged in so often and which had meant nothing more momentous than that the woman had attracted his ever-changing fancy and that he had an urge to pay tribute to beauty wherever he found it.

"I had forgotten such a world existed," Aria said aloud, thinking of how at Queen's Folly she would have been, at this moment, preparing the lunch or perhaps sweeping and dusting the picture gallery in readiness for the afternoon visitors.

She tried to concentrate on the letters, but Lord Buckleigh's gay, impudent face kept coming between her and the neatly typed pages. It was with almost a sense of relief that Aria heard the gong booming out from the hall and hurried down the stairs.

Someone was following her and she looked back to see the stiff, rather formal countenance of an Ambassador's wife who had arrived late the night before.

"What a nice day, Miss Milbank," she said politely.

"Yes, isn't it, Your Excellency," Aria answered.

She waited for the Ambassadress to catch her up and then, as they descended the stairs together, the older woman said in a low voice:

"I have just had some newspapers from America in my mail. They seem to think that our host will be announcing his engagement at any moment."

"To Miss Carlo?" Aria asked.

"That's right!" the Ambassadress said, then added: "Mr. Huron's a charming man. As I said to my husband last night, it's a pity if we lose him to the Hollywood set."

"I don't think you will do that," Aria said reassuringly.

"Oh, I hope you are right," the Ambassadress replied. "But somehow the fact of her being here makes me think all this rumour and gossip must have some foundation in it."

"They have to talk about something," Aria suggested consolingly.

As she spoke they entered the drawing-room. At the far end of it Dart Huron and Lulu Carlo were standing together. Her hand was on his arm, her lovely face was turned up to his, her head thrown back to show the arch of her white throat and the exquisite curves of her small breasts.

He was looking down at her and they were not speaking, they were just standing staring into each other's eyes. Aria thought that, after all, Lord Buckleigh had been wrong; Dart Huron intended to marry Lulu.

There was no disguising the look of triumph on her

face as they moved apart and Dart Huron came forward to greet the Ambassadress. Other people came into the drawing room from the terrace and soon the party of twelve was collected and they moved towards the dining-room.

It was then, under cover of the noise and the chatter, that Lulu Carlo caught hold of Aria's arm and drew her a little away.

"Listen! she said in a low voice. "I want you to do something for me. I want the name and telephone number of all the main newspapers. Don't say anything about it to anyone, but bring me the list to my bedroom after lunch. Do you understand?"

"Yes, I understand," Aria said.

"And keep quiet about it!"

Lulu slipped into the throng towards the dining-room and a moment later her voice, loud and gay, was answering some quip of Lord Buckleigh's. But Aria, coming along behind, silent and preoccupied with her thoughts, was wondering what this meant.

Why did Lulu want the names of the newspapers? For what purpose?

6

There was a Royal Princess at luncheon and half-a-dozen extra visitors, all distinguished either for their social attributes or because they were gay and witty enough to adorn any gathering.

Aria found, with a sense of relief, that she was not expected to contribute much to the conversation. The two young men on either side of her vied with each other in capping each other's epigrams and inciting argument by making the most exaggerated and sometimes outrageous statements about their friends.

The tempo rose after the first course until by the time they reached the cheese and coffee everyone was talking vivaciously and Aria had little to do except listen.

She had had an exhausting morning. There not only had been an unusual amount of mail from overseas, but the Head Housemaid had had a row with one of her underlings and both had come to Aria to give their notice, and it had taken all her tact and charm to smooth them down and to persuade them to be friends again.

She had no sooner finished this than McDougall had come up with a face of gloom to say he could not carry on without an extra footman.

Aria had rung up Mrs. Benstead only to find that she had no-one on her books, but after a weary search round all the other agencies she had procured a man who was well over seventy and who had promised to give a hand so long as his arthritis didn't trouble him too much.

The gong for luncheon booming through the house had taken her by surprise, and she had only had time to take a hasty glance at herself in the mirror, to wash her hands, powder her nose, and run downstairs before the party was on its way to the dining-room.

Dart Huron gave her a dark look by which she guessed she had offended in some way, but it was Lord Buckleigh who enlightened her.

"You should have been here before the Princess arrived," he said.

"I had forgotten she was coming," Aria confessed.

He grinned at her as he took his place at the table, with on one side of him a pretty socialite who was always hitting the headlines and on the other a lady-in-waiting to the Princess.

Lulu Carlo, Aria noted, was entirely at her ease. She appeared to know all these distinguished people well and they made a fuss of her first like millions of the ordinary people because the aristocrats of the celluloid film had the *entrée* into every heart and home.

Lulu was looking entrancingly lovely in a simple dress of white sharkskin, which had cost a fortune, with huge aquamarines blazing in her ears and round her wrists. She was being charming, too, in a way which made Aria understand how any man, even someone like Dart Huron, could not help being in love with her.

They were nearing the end of the luncheon when McDougall aproached Lulu Carlo's side and Aria heard him say:

"There is someone to speak to you on the telephone, Miss."

"Who is it?" Lulu demanded.

"A woman, Miss. She would not give her name, but said she wished to speak to you about your grandmother, Mrs. Hawkins."

There was a little lull in the conversation and McDougall's voice carried quite clearly to those seated round the room. Aria saw Lulu's face tense. In her eyes there was a sudden look which could only be described as wary.

"I can't speak now," she said to McDougall. She seemed about to say something else when she caught sight of Aria watching her. "Attend to it, please, Miss Milbank," she said with authority.

It was an order given in a peremptory manner which Aria instinctively resented, and yet there was nothing she could do but say quietly:

"Of course, Miss Carlo. I will take a message or ask them to ring back later."

She rose from her seat and went from the room, going into the morning-room to speak as it was the nearest place to the dining-room. She picked up the receiver—a white one which toned elegantly with the white-panelled walls and the curtains of white and blue hand-painted linen.

"Hello!"

"Is that Miss Carlo?"

"No, I'm afraid Miss Carlo cannot speak at the moment. I am Mr. Huron's secretary. Can I take a message?"

95

"I'm speaking for 'er grandma, Mrs. Hawkins," an uneducated voice said. "She read in the paper as 'ow Miss Carlo was staying at that address, and nothing will satisfy 'er but that I should telephone."

"Is Mrs. Hawkins ill?" Aria enquired.

"She's not any worse than she usually is," came the answer. "She's getting on for eighty-two, you know, and 'er rheumatism's bad at times. But what she minds worst is the loneliness. She ain't got many friends; not where she is now."

"And where is she?" Aria asked.

"Ninety-two King George Road," was the answer. "It's on the outskirts of Putney. One-'undred-and-seventy-one drops you at the door."

"I understand. I will tell Miss Carlo and see if it would be possible for her to visit her grandmother," Aria said.

"The old lady'd like that. She's ever so proud of Miss Carlo. Cuts all the bits about 'er out of the papers. It'd be a real treat for 'er to see 'er grandchild, that it would."

"Well, I will tell her, and thank you for telephoning," Aria said.

"That's all right. I goes in to 'elp Mrs. Johnson twice a week. I've got fond of the old dear—you can't 'elp it some'ow."

"Thank you!" Aria said again, and then replaced the receiver.

She did not go back to the luncheon party. She thought it was quite unnecessary for her to join them while they were finishing their coffee and the men were drinking a glass of port. Instead she went back to her typewriter, trying to cope with the arrears of correspondence.

She had been there for perhaps an hour when Lulu Carlo's Italian maid knocked at the door.

With a regretful look at the letter that she was half-way through, Aria followed the maid down the passage to Lulu Carlo's bedroom.

The film star was sitting in front of the mirror

96

powdering her nose and scrutinising minutely a tiny flaw at the corner of her red mouth.

"Oh, there you are, Miss Milbank," she said ungraciously as Aria entered. "What was the telephone call about that came at lunch?"

"It was a woman speaking for your grandmother, Miss Carlo," Aria said. "She is very anxious to see you."

"As if I have got the time!" Lulu said angrily. "I hope you said it was quite impossible."

"I didn't know what to reply," Aria said. "I waited to hear your wishes on the subject."

"How did she know I was here?"

"She saw it in the papers," Aria replied. "Apparently your grandmother is very proud of your success and cuts out all the references to you."

Lulu Carlo put down the hand mirror with a decided slap on the dressing-table.

"It's ridiculous and extremely annoying," she said. "I do the very best I can for her. She should have more sense than to get people to telephone me at inconvenient moments."

"That the moment was inconvenient was perhaps not her fault," Aria said. "The woman speaking was, I gathered, a cleaner in the house where your grandmother is living."

"Well, you tell McDougall," Lulu went on, apparently not listening to Aria's explanation, "that in future he should not mention names at the table. Saying 'your grandmother—Mrs. Hawkins,' in front of all those people."

"You asked him who was on the telephone," Aria protested. "He had to give you the correct answer."

"Well, how was I to know who it was likely to be?" Lulu asked irritably. She looked at Aria as she spoke and then added even more irritably: "You wouldn't understand, of course, but everybody has always believed that I'm an American. There's no prestige in being English. Besides, the studio put out the story of

97

my origin and where I came from. They won't care for this sort of thing."

"I don't see why anyone should know about it," Aria said soothingly.

"Know about it!" Lulu said with something like a scream. "Didn't you see their faces at lunch when McDougall said "your grandmother, Mrs. Hawkins"? Hawkins sounds like an American name, doesn't it? Or even Scandinavian, which is supposed to account for my fair hair? Do you suppose they weren't all agog and at this very moment aren't whispering among themselves? Oh, I know how people talk, I tell you—especially about someone like me."

She was so upset that Aria could not but feel sorry for her. She could, in a way, sympathize with Lulu for having her schemes upset by a chance word, a telephone call which had come at the wrong moment.

"I am sorry," she murmured ineffectually.

"I could say that she married again, couldn't I?" Lulu said. "I never thought of that until this moment. She can be my mother's mother, the Scandinavian one. I don't know what they said about my old home in Sweden. I shall have to check up. But as far as this lot are concerned my grandmother has re-married."

She smiled suddenly, the lovely, flashing smile which had captured the hearts of the so-called civilized world.

"That's all right then, Miss Milbank."

"But what about your grandmother?" Aria asked. "I think that, as she knows you are here, she will be hoping to see you."

"Well, then she'll have to be disappointed," Lulu Carlo said, and the hard note had returned again to her voice. "I pay for her rooms, that ought to satisfy her. Six pounds a week it costs me. But then, some people are never satisfied. Order her a bunch of flowers or something and have them sent there. Or, better still, take them from the garden.

There will very likely be some fruit to spare as well. Mr. Huron won't mind. Of course he knows the truth about all my family, you realise that. I have no secrets from him, because we are going to be married."

"So you told me," Aria said.

"Not that there's any reason to discuss it with him," Lulu went on. "Men are bored with their wives' relations—we all know that. But you send the old girl some fruit and flowers."

"She's eighty-two," Aria said hesitantly. "You don't think you could find the time to see her if only for a moment?"

"No, I don't!" Lulu Carlo said abruptly. "And that's definite, Miss Milbank. And, incidentally, it's my business what I do about my grandmother. You send her the flowers and the fruit, as I have told you, and that's the end of it."

There was nothing Aria could say and she went from the bedroom back to her own room. There she found Lord Buckleigh lounging in an armchair.

"I wondered where you had disappeared to," he said. "The others are changing for tennis. Are you coming to play?"

"No of course not," Aria answered. "I am far too busy."

"Why didn't you come back to the luncheon table?" he enquired.

"There didn't seem much point. I had finished and I thought everyone could get on very well without me."

"I missed you," he said, his eyes on her face.

"Thank you for the compliment," she smiled. "But I am not so stupid as to believe it."

"You don't take me seriously, that's what's the matter," Lord Buckleigh said. "I'm falling more in love with you every moment, and you either laugh at me or avoid me. What am I to do about it?"

"At this moment I suggest you go and play tennis."

"What did Mrs. Hawkins have to say?" he asked disconcertingly.

"It wasn't Mrs. Hawkins speaking," Aria said evasively.

"You're trying to put me off," he said accusingly. "I

had no idea that the fair Lulu had relations in England. Was her name originally Hawkins, do you think?"

"I understand from Miss Carlo that her grandmother married again," Aria said primly.

She didn't like Lulu Carlo, but she was determined to be fair to her. Lord Buckleigh threw back his head and laughed.

"So that's her story, is it?" he enquired. "Well, I would rather like to see this grandmother of hers. I bet, if the truth be known, she's a skeleton in our little Lulu's cupboard."

"Don't be so horrid," Aria said. "You may not like Miss Carlo, but at the same time she has made a big name for herself. She has a right to some privacy in her personal life."

Lord Buckleigh rose to his feet and walked across to the desk where Aria was already seated at the typewriter.

"You're a loyal little thing," he said in a gentle voice. "The sort of wife that any man could rely on. It's a pity I have got no money and can't ask you to marry me."

Aria was so surprised that she could not help turning her head to look up into his face.

"Yes," he said, seeing the expression of interrogation in her eyes. "Yes, that's how I feel about you. Stupid, isn't it? I have met so many different girls who have meant nothing to me; but you're different."

"But you haven't known me long enough to be sure of anything, let alone your own feelings," Aria said.

"Who's been telling you that sort of nonsense about love?" he asked. "Love is either there or it isn't. From the first moment I saw you I knew I was in love. It's hopeless, it's insane, but there it is. I love you!"

He picked up her hand as he spoke and turning it over kissed her palm. Then before she could recover from her surprise at his sudden seriousness, Lord Buckleigh had gone from the room and she heard him singing as he went down the passage.

Her smile was tender as she fitted a fresh piece of paper into her typewriter. Even if he could afford to keep her, she decided, she would not want to marry him. At the same time, she liked him—liked the gay irresponsibility about him, his boyish frankness, the aura of almost perennial good humour which seemed to exude from first thing in the morning to last thing at night.

She finished the letter, did two or three of the more urgent ones, and then sat for a moment deciding what to do next. The thought of Lulu Carlo's old grandmother was so vividly in her mind that she knew her conscience would not rest until she had gone to see the old lady.

There was something pathetic in the story of her cutting her grandchild's Press notices out of the paper, yearning to see her, hoping against hope that she would pay her a visit. And she never would, Aria thought. Lulu Carlo was a snob as well as an adventuress.

It was quite obvious that she would never risk visiting her grandmother in case the Press should get hold of it.

On impulse Aria picked up the house telephone and rang through, first to the gardens and then to the garage. Twenty minutes later she slipped downstairs to find a car waiting for her at the front door. The back seat was filled with flowers and beside them was a big basket of early strawberries from the hot houses.

Aria sat in front with the chauffeur, a young man who had not long left the army and who regaled her with tales of his experiences overseas until they reached the outskirts of London.

There was a map in the car and they asked the way of a large number of policemen, but even so they got helplessly lost, until finally they found King George Road— a dingy back street sloping down to the river. Number ninety-two was a high house badly in need of repair.

The paint was peeling off the window frames and there was a smell of bad cooking and accumulated dirt, which was obvious from the very moment one stepped under the crumbling portico.

101

Aria rang the bell, but there was no answer. She rang again with the same result; and then a young woman in slacks, with a handkerchief over her head and a cigarette hanging out of her mouth, came out of the door carrying a shopping basket.

"Can I see Mrs. Hawkins?" Aria asked. "I have been ringing for some time. I think the bell must be broken."

The woman stared at her in surprise.

"Hasn't been working for years," she said. "You 'ave to shout. I'll tell Mrs. Johnson that you're here. She'll show you which room it is."

She walked across the narrow hall and putting her head round the glass partition shouted down the stairs to the basement.

"Hi, Ma! Are you there?" She waited and shouted again. "Ma! Someone wants you."

Again there was no answer. She came back and said to Aria:.

"Mrs. Johnson must be out or upstairs. You'll find Mrs. Hawkins in the third back. Go straight up."

"Thank you!" Aria said.

She took the flowers from the chauffeur and the basket of strawberries and started up the narrow stairs. Many of the banisters were missing and the linoleum on the staircase was so worn that Aria felt its condition must be dangerous for anyone as old as Mrs. Hawkins when she came downstairs.

Up she climbed. There was the sound of voices and radios coming from the rooms she passed. She gathered that this was a boarding-house—evidently a successful one for it was obvious that every room was occupied.

There were two doors on the third floor, one had a piece of paper pinned to it and Aria paused to read it. *"Keep out,"* she read. *"This room is private and I don't want any nosey parkers prying about in it."*

She looked at the message in astonishment when she heard the voice coming from the room next door. It was a raucous, ugly voice, high in anger.

"And I'll thank you not to encourage them to write me rude messages," it said. "Is this my house or isn't it,

102

I should like to know? Any more from either of you and don't think I'm carrying your meals upstairs in future. You can come down like the rest of them or go without. I've only got one pair of hands, that's all, and I can't do any more than I do, and that's a fact."

Another voice said something gently, but was hardly allowed to speak.

"It's all very well for you sitting up here as if you were a duchess, waited on hand and foot. But I'm not having any more of it, do you understand? You and your aches and pains. I'm sick to death of you! Well, I've made myself clear. No more meals upstairs. I can't help it that you can't walk. You should be in hospital or in the grave at your age!"

The door opened suddenly and a woman came out on to the landing.

She was a short, red-faced woman with eyes that were too close together and hennaed hair frizzed into tight curls on top of her head. She was dressed in tight, lacey jumper and a skirt that was too short and strained across her behind.

Her coarse fat hands were bedecked with cheap rings and flamboyant pearl ear-rings graced her thick ears.

She was still shouting when she saw Aria and her voice died abruptly in her throat.

"What do you want? she asked aggressively. At the same time a hint of respect appeared in her small, shrewd eyes as she took in Aria's general appearance and the flowers and fruit in her arms.

"I have come to see Mrs. Hawkins," Aria replied.

The woman pulled the door behind her close to.

"I'm afraid she isn't well enough to see anyone today," she said quickly. "It's a pity, but it's doctor's orders. Are those flowers for her and the fruit? I'll give them to her when she's a bit better."

She put out her hand for the flowers, but Aria took no notice.

"I have come from her grand-daughter, Miss Carlo,"

103

she said. "And I am afraid I must see her. It's important."

"Well, I tell you that's impossible," the woman said.
"I'm Mrs. Johnson. This is my house, where Mrs.
Hawkins lodges, and I look after her, you see. And
when the doctor was here last week he said, "No
visitors, Mrs. Johnson; not until I say so." And so you
understand, I must carry out his orders."

The woman's voice was more ingratiating now, but
there was no mistaking the determination in her general
attitude.

"You can go and ring up the doctor if you like,"
Aria said. "But I have come here to see Mrs. Hawkins
and I intend to see her. If she is really ill, I expect Miss
Carlo would like a second opinion."

"Well, it's like this," the woman said, taking a step
nearer to Aria and lowering her voice. "She's not herself, as it happens. Senile she is. Eighty-two! You can't
expect much else, can you? I've looked after her as if
I was her daughter.

Nothing's been too much trouble for me, but when
people get old, they get difficult; they get ideas in their
heads and think people are being unkind to them. You
mustn't take any notice of anything she says. It would
be better, really, if you would just leave the flowers
with me. I'll see she has them."

"This is really a waste of time, Mrs. Johnson," Aria
said sharply. "Suppose you open the door behind you
and let me see Mrs. Hawkins for myself."

"Well, see her then," Mrs. Johnson said rudely. "But
don't say I didn't warn you. At that age they aren't
responsible for anything they says."

She flung open the door and Aria moved past her
into the room. It was a small, narrow back bedroom
with a window which admitted very little light.

There was an iron bedstead in one corner of the
room, a chair with the upholstery torn and sagging
springs which nearly touched the floor, and a chest-of-
drawers which had lost most of its handles.

There was a fireplace where a fire had obviously not

been lit for a very long time, and no sign of any other form of heating. An old-fashioned marble washstand was stacked with dirty plates, a cracked basin and several other toilet utensils.

The worn and torn linoleum on the floor had one little mat to cover it, which was so dirty that it was difficult to see what the colours had ever been.

An oleograph of Queen Victoria was the only decoration on the faded wallpaper, which was peeling away in the corners from damp and old age.

In the bed, covered by several very thin and inadequate blankets, lay an old lady. She looked very ill. Her face was the colour of old ivory and her lips were almost bloodless. Nevertheless, as Aria advanced across the room, she managed a little smile.

"I heard you say as how you'd come from my granddaughter, dearie," she said. "She got my message?"

"Yes, she got your message," Aria said gently. "And she sent you these."

She put the flowers down on the bed as she spoke and set the strawberries on a hard chair on which rested a candle in a tin candlestick and a small, worn bible.

"That's real kind of her," the old lady said. "I haven't seen a flower for a long time. They're beautiful, aren't they? And strawberries, too! Makes me think of when I was a girl. I always was a one for strawberries when they came into season."

Aria walked suddenly to the door and opened it. As she expected, Mrs. Johnson was standing just outside and listening.

"That's quite all right, Mrs. Johnson," she said. "Mrs. Hawkins is quite well enough to see me. We shall not require you any more."

Mrs. Johnson shot her a glance of venomous dislike.

"If anything happens after you've gone," she said nastily, "you mustn't blame me. 'No visitors,' is what the doctor said. I was only carrying out his orders."

With a toss of her head she flounced down the stairs.

105

Only when she had gone down to the turn in the staircase did Aria shut the door and go back into the room.

"Tell me, what does the doctor really say about you?" she asked gently of the old lady.

Ill though she looked, Mrs. Hawkins' eyes managed to twinkle.

"I haven't seen a doctor," she said in a whisper. "But don't tell Mrs. Johnson I said so. She's angry with me at the moment. The lady as lodges next door—ever so kind she is to me—caught her reading her letters yesterday. So she's left a message outside her door and locked it. It's upset Mrs. Johnson."

"So I heard," Aria said drily. "But why do you stay in this place?"

"She'd never let me leave," the old lady said. "The money comes regular."

"But your grand-daughter told me she was paying six pounds a week," Aria said. "Is that true?"

Mrs. Hawkins nodded.

"Yes! She's real good to me is Maggie."

"Maggie?" Aria enquired.

The old lady chuckled.

"Lulu Carlo is what they call her on the films, but Maggie Hawkins is her real name. Margaret, she was christened, and an ugly little baby she was, too. I never thought she would turn out as she has. Strange, isn't it, when you come to think of it? You never knows when they're born what they'll grow up to be like."

"Maggie Hawkins! What a name for a glamorous film star, Aria thought. No wonder Lulu Carlo wished to keep her grandmother a secret. At the same time, surely she wouldn't countenance the old lady being treated in such a manner?

"How did you come here in the first place?" Aria asked.

"Oh, it wasn't always like this," Mrs. Hawkins said. "When my daughter was alive, it was very different. She lived next door, you see—at least, about three doors down—and when she was expecting her fifth she says to me: "Gran, we'll have to have your room,

106

we shall really, and there's a place up the street with Mrs. Roberts, where you'll be ever so comfortable."

"Well, I knew Mrs. Roberts; a really decent woman she was, and clean—well, you could have eaten any of your meals off her floor! I came to see her—I could get about in those days—and she let me have the front room on the first floor. A beautiful room it was, and nicely furnished, too. I moved in and I was very happy there. Nothing to complain about, nothing at all.

"And then comes the blitz. My daughter was killed. You knew about that, didn't you?"

"No, I'm afraid I didn't," Aria said.

"A direct hit," the old lady said. "The whole lot of them killed—my daughter, her husband and four of my grandchildren, and a friend as they had staying there. Maggie was the only one that was all right. She was working in an office then and had stayed the night in the air-raid shelter.

"Well, it was shortly after that Mrs. Roberts felt her nerves going. She couldn't stand them doodles coming over night after night, and so she sold the house and the lodgers in it, so to speak. Not that there were many of them then! Most of them had gone away."

"And Mrs. Johnson bought it," Aria said.

"Yes, she bought it. Then about three years ago she said I couldn't have the front room any longer. I tried to argue with her, but she wouldn't listen, and I hadn't got anyone I could ask to help me.

"Maggie was my only relation and she had gone to Hollywood. I couldn't worry her with my troubles and she was sending me money regular. At first it was only two or three pounds a week, and then she put it up to six. A lot of money for a girl to part with when she's earning her own living!

Aria said nothing. She had a sudden vision of the diamond necklace that Lulu had worn at dinner last night, of the aquamarines flashing in her ears at luncheon, of the tales she had read of her fabulous house in Beverly Hills, of the platina mink stole which

107

she had flung carelessly down in the hall yesterday evning when she had come in from a drive.

"Yes, she's a kind girl," she said with an effort.

"That's what I always says," Mrs. Hawkins said. "And look at all those cuttings about her. Open that drawer over there."

Aria did as she was told. The badly fitting drawer was hard to pull out. When she managed it, she found it crammed full with newspaper cuttings:

"Lulu Carlo hits the headlines." "Lulu Carlo walks away with the film." "Lulu is mobbed by her fans." "Lulu. . . ." "Lulu. . . ."

Aria shut the drawer again.

"A wonderful collection," she said.

"They all know in the street what I feel about her," Mrs. Hawkins said. "There's quite a lot of people as cuts bits out of their papers for me and sends them up. But not as many as there used to be," she added with a sigh. "They forget about me now they can't see me."

"Don't you ever get out of here?" Aria asked.

"No dearie! I haven't been out for nearly two years. It's my legs, you see. I can get down the stairs all right, but I can't get up again."

"But how do you manage?" Aria asked.

"Oh, Mrs. Johnson does sometimes bring me up a bit of something to eat, and the lady next door is ever so kind. She carries up my breakfast and usually my supper. I manage all right. I'm a bit hungry at times; but then, when you're old it doesn't do to get fat, does it?"

"Fat!" Aria exclaimed, looking at the blue veins on the thin bony hand resting on the worn blankets.

She remembered that harsh, bullying tone in Mrs. Johnson's voice; she remembered her threat that she would do nothing more; she remembered that shifty manner in which she had tried to prevent her from seeing Mrs. Hawkins.

She looked round at the room and made up her mind.

"Well, you are going to go down these stairs once

108

more," she said. "And you will never have to come up them again. I am taking you away."

"Taking me away!" Mrs. Hawkins exclaimed. "But where to, dearie?"

"I am taking you to see your grand-daughter," Aria said gently.

7

Aria knocked on Lulu Carlo's bedroom door.

It was a timid, rather hesitant knock, for suddenly she felt apprehensive and afraid, unsure of herself and almost regretful of having the courage to act in the way she thought was right.

She entered the room a second later to find, as she had expected, that Lulu was nearly ready for dinner. She was wearing a dress of soft aquamarine blue chiffon, which made her skin look very white and her blonde hair like gleaming gold.

She was in the very act, as Aria entered, of clasping a fabulous necklace of diamonds and aquamarines round her neck, while already similar stones glittered in a wide bracelet on her wrist and in the lobes of her ears.

"What is it, Miss Milbank?" she asked, with a sharp note in her voice.

"I came to tell you about your grandmother, Miss Carlo," Aria replied.

"Oh, yes! I hope she was pleased with the flowers and fruit," Lulu said carelessly.

She clasped the necklace round her neck and then gave an exclamation of annoyance as she noticed that the varnish had chipped from the tip of one of her long, red fingernails.

"Really, it's impossible to get decent varnish in this

109

country," she said. "I brought some from America with me but it's all finished now."

"I think you will be worried to hear about your grandmother," Aria said in a low voice. "The place in which I found her was horrible. She had no comforts of any sort and the landlady, who was perfectly prepared to take her money, was bullying her unmercifully. In fact I actually heard her tell Mrs. Hawkins that she did not intend to carry her food up to her any longer!"

"If she doesn't like it, I suppose she can always move," Lulu replied indifferently.

"Mrs. Hawkins is eighty-two," Aria answered. "She has no-one to speak to her and it is very difficult for an old person to take the initiative or to move anywhere when she is really bed-ridden."

"Well, I can't do anything about it," Lulu said positively. "And I hope you told her so. She used to bombard me with letters about all sorts of things until she realised I hadn't got the time to answer them.

Aria's feeling of nervousness and apprehension had left her. She stood for a moment looking at the pretty, petulant face bent over the chipped finger-nail, and then she said:

"I think something has got to be done about Mrs. Hawkins. I do not know how anyone with any decent feelings could stand by and see an old lady badly treated."

"I don't suppose it's as bad as you are making out," Lulu replied.

"I assure you that I am not exaggerating," Aria answered. "So perhaps you will tell me what action you would like me to take on your behalf."

Lulu Carlo put the brush back into the bottle of nail varnish and then looked at Aria.

"I think you are taking a great deal upon yourself, Miss Milbank. I do not care for the tone of voice in which you are speaking to me. I suggest that you don't interfere in things which do not concern you. Or else, if my grandmother's affairs trouble you so greatly, you had better find some other lodgings for her to go to."

"That is exactly what I have done," Aria said quietly.

"Oh, well, you have been very quick about it," Lulu remarked. "I hope at any rate she will be more satisfied with these lodgings than the last ones."

"I think she will be," Aria answered. "You see, I have brought her here!"

Lulu Carlo stared at her for a moment in silence.

"What—what did you say?" she asked at length.

"I said that I had brought your grandmother, Mrs. Hawkins, here," Aria replied.

"Are you mad?"

Lulu got to her feet as she spoke and walked towards Aria with her face almost contorted with anger.

"You have brought her here?" she questioned. "Here to this house? How dare you do such a thing? You will take her away at once, do you understand? Now, this moment!"

"I shall do nothing of the sort," Aria answered. "I don't think you understand. Your grandmother was being not merely harshly treated, but criminally treated. She is ill—not mentally, old though she is, but physically I couldn't go away and leave her, whatever you might feel or think about it, so I put her in the car and brought her back here."

"I don't know what to say to you," Lulu Carlo cried. "How dare you do such a thing? How dare you interfere? You beastly, sneaking, stuck-up servant; worming your way in here and daring to try to insinuate your ideas and your opinions into my life. But, anyhow, you won't get far over this sort of thing. I give the orders in this house, do you understand? And out my grandmother goes, now and at once!"

She walked towards the bell as she spoke, but Aria's voice arrested her.

"Wait a minute," she said. "I have told you that I have brought Mrs. Hawkins here. Nobody else knows who she is. I have told no-one but you of her arrival. I have put her in the room downstairs which is known as

111

the Garden Room because it is on the ground floor and it opens into the rose garden.

At this moment she is in bed sleeping off the effects of the journey. She is very old and frail. If you move her now, or even if you upset her, she won't stand it. It would, in my opinion, be deliberate murder!"

Lulu's hand fell from the bell.

"You say that nobody knows that she's here?" she asked, the furious expression on her face lightening a little.

"No-one!" Aria repeated.

"Very well then. I will not disturb her tonight," Lulu said. "But she goes tomorrow. You have taken this on yourself, so you can go and find somewhere else for her to go to. I don't care where it is as long as it's out of here, do you understand?"

"I understand," Aria replied. "I won't attempt now to tell you what I think of you, Miss Carlo; but perhaps your own conscience will do that."

She walked out of the bedroom and slammed the door behind her. She knew it showed lack of self-control; but her temper had got the upper hand.

She was angry, as few people had seen her angry in the past, with a slow, smouldering anger which was fanned by her sense of justice and the pity she felt for the poor old woman who had no-one to care for her.

Mrs. Hawkins had been quite happy to let Aria make decisions for her. She had made no protest about being dressed and half-carried down the stairs by Aria and the chauffeur.

Aria had settled her comfortably in the car and then gone upstairs again to collect the poor old lady's pitifully few belongings into a battered suitcase which she had noticed under the bed.

"And the newspaper cuttings about Maggie." Mrs. Hawkins had whispered when Aria told her where she was going. "I can't leave those behind; they are very precious to me."

"You shall have them all," Aria promised, and

112

having nothing to pack them in she was forced to wrap them up in a woollen shawl.

It was only then, when she was taking a last glance round the room, that she remembered the flowers and fruit she had brought for Mrs. Hawkins. She carried them and laid them outside the door of the room next door, and taking a piece of paper, she wrote on it: *To thank you for your kindness to an old lady.*

Then she went downstairs and found Mrs. Johnson waiting for her in the hall.

"Where are you a-takin' 'er?" the latter had asked truculently. "I don't know as 'ow I ought to let you go junketing off with someone who's committed to my charge."

"If you have any complaints to make, I suggest you make them to the police," Aria said. "I shall very likely be seeing them on Miss Carlo's account. I have seen how you treated Mrs. Hawkins and I don't believe that people like you are allowed to cheat and defraud the public indefinitely."

She walked past Mrs. Johnson as she spoke and only as she got into the car did she hear the landlady, having finally recovered her breath, begin to shout at her. But by that time it was too late!

The car drove away leaving Mrs. Johnson staring after it, crimson with rage and frustration; and Aria, with a little sigh of relief, turned to pat Mrs. Hawkins' hand.

"You will never go back there again," she said.

"You're very kind to me, my dear," was the gentle reply. "Are you taking me to see my Maggie?"

"You shall see her," Aria promised.

She wondered now, as she went down to dinner, whether that promise would be fulfilled.

Lulu was in the drawing-room, the centre of a laughing chattering group of people. Her jewels flashing in the light from the chandeliers, her face as smooth and untroubled as that of an angel.

Aria saw that Dart Huron's eyes were on her and though she disliked him she could not help a feeling of

113

pity if he should be fool enough to tie himself up to a woman like this. He had evaded matrimony for so long; was he going to be caught by a hard little schemer who had no love in her heart for anyone or anything except herself?

"What does it matter to me if he is?" Aria asked herself, with a metaphorical shrug of her shoulders.

"You are looking lovely!" a low voice said in her ear.

She looked round with a smile to find Lord Buckleigh beside her.

"You need to see an occulist," she answered. "Haven't you looked at Miss Carlo tonight?"

"She's not my type," he answered. "I have told you, I only love red-haired women."

"All those people make me feel more like Cinderella every moment," Aria answered, intensely conscious, because his words had drawn her attention to it, of the shabbiness of her one and only evening dress.

It was, however, well cut because it had been bought in Paris; and she had tried to make it look different by wearing it sometimes with no ornamentation, sometimes with a bunch of flowers at the waist or on the shoulder, and on other occasions with a chiffon stole of varying colours.

Tonight she had dressed hurriedly and the gown was severely plain, its black tailored shoulder-straps throwing into relief the magnolia whiteness of her skin and enhancing, although she did not realise it, the dancing fire of her hair and the vivid green of her eyes.

"If I were a rich man, I should give you emeralds," Lord Buckleigh said.

"Why?" Aria enquired innocently.

"Don't you ever look in the mirror?" he enquired.

She smiled at that and said:

"You are making me feel better. I was feeling angry and upset when I came downstairs, and so I am grateful to you—though really I ought to be very angry because you talk so much nonsense."

"I love you! You know that," he said. "Why couldn't you be an heiress like that dumpy girl on the right talk-

114

ing to Lady Westwood? Or the divorced wife of an oil king like Mrs. Davenall? The fat one in pink with the outsize pearls."

Aria looked at the two women he mentioned and felt herself beginning to laugh.

"I would rather be me," she said.

"That's just what I was thinking," he smiled. "I don't want to kiss either of them, I would much rather kiss you."

Aria looked hastily over her shoulder to see that no-one was listening.

"You are embarrassing me," she protested. "Go and be nice to the new guests who have just arrived. I am sure Mr. Huron disapproves of his secretary monopolising one of the most eligible young men in his party."

"I am not eligible, that's just the point," Lord Buckleigh retorted. "If I was, we could walk out of here—you and I; drive to London Airport and take a 'plane to some forgotten island in the Pacific where we could be alone, away from all these chattering fools. Would you like that?"

"I am not going to answer that sort of question," Aria said evasively.

At the same time she could not deny that it was fun to be made love to by someone as charming and good-looking as Lord Buckleigh. It was also exciting, in some ways, to be here; to see all these well-known, glamorous people; to know the luxury and the ease which only great wealth can bring. All this and at the same time she was benefiting Queen's Folly.

"I am lucky!"

She said the words aloud, almost involuntarily.

"Can't I be lucky, too?" Lord Buckleigh asked.

She looked up at him and saw the question in his eyes; the question she had half expected and which now he had asked it gave her a little sense of dismay.

"I don't know what you mean," she said quickly.

"I think you do," he answered. "We will talk of it later. Can I come to your room?"

"No! No! Of course not!" Aria said decisively.

115

She walked away from him and going to the cocktail table poured out a cocktail which she took across to the Ambassadress. It was only an excuse, for the Ambassadress indicated that she already had one at her side and Aria was forced to carry the glass back to the table.

At the same time, the action had served her need to free herself from Lord Buckleigh, to let the colour subside from her face.

So that was what his love-making had been leading up to, she thought a little despondently. She might have guessed it. And yet somehow, now he had come into the open, she felt as if he had deliberately despoiled something which was rather lovely and had promise of being lovelier still.

Aria was fortunately nowhere near Lord Buckleigh at dinner and when the meal was over she slipped away and went to the Garden Room to see Mrs. Hawkins.

In the doorway she met one of the young housemaids coming out—a girl whom she had asked to keep looking in at the old lady in case there was anything she wanted. She was Italian and spoke very little English, so Aria knew that any secrets the old lady might reveal were safe as far as the staff were concerned.

"How is the lady?" Aria asked in Italian.

"The *Signora* seems very comfortable," the girl replied. "She has thanked me for her dinner. She had very little, but she said it was enough."

"Thank you, Maria, for looking after her," Aria said. "I will stay with her now."

"It was no trouble, *Signorina,*" the girl said.

Aria went into the room. It was large and exquisitely furnished for it had been used by the last Duke of Melchester whose gout had prevented him, in the last years of his life, from being able to negotiate any stairs.

The bed was set in an alcove draped with curtains of misty blue, and the peach-coloured shaded lights gave a soft glow to Mrs. Hawkins' pale cheeks so that she looked better already.

"How are you?" Aria asked.

116

"I had a little sleep just now, dearie, and I thought I must be dreaming. Am I really here in this lovely place?"

"You are, indeed," Aria answered. "And if you want anything, you have only to ring the bell by your side and someone will come."

"I don't want to be any trouble," Mrs. Hawkins declared.

"You would never be that," Aria answered.

"And I will see Maggie? You promised me I would see Maggie. I have been lying here thinking how wonderful it would be if she walked in. She's all I've got left. There was another very like her, but she was killed, the poor wee soul."

The old eyes misted for a moment and Aria said quickly:

"Don't think about it now. Think about yourself and what a good night's sleep you are going to have."

"But I don't want to think about myself, I want to think about Maggie. You brought those newspaper cuttings, didn't you?"

"Yes, yes," Aria said soothingly. "They're over there. I will put them on the chair so that you can see them. They don't look very pretty wrapped up in a shawl, and tomorrow I'll get a big box so that you can put them on the table and look at them when you want to."

As Aria spoke she had a sudden sinking of her heart. Tomorrow, Lulu Carlo had said, Mrs. Hawkins must go away.

"Yes, I can see them now," the old lady was saying. "Everything that's been wrote about her I've got there. I sit reading them, when my eyes will let me, and somehow it's nearly as good as seeing her. She was always beautiful, was my Maggie. Those photographs don't do her justice."

"No, she's very beautiful," Aria said.

"She's here!" Mrs. Hawkins said. "She's here in this very house!"

It was as if she had suddenly tumbled to the idea that

117

she had been brought to the very place where her grandchild was.

"Yes, she's here," Aria said hesitantly.

"And she's coming to see me. Oh, my goodness! Please bring me a looking glass, dearie, and let me see if my hair's tidy. I must look nice for Maggie. I wouldn't want her to be ashamed of me."

The frail old hands with their startling blue veins were trembling. Aria brought a hand glass from the dressing table, but as she did so, she said gently:

"I don't think your grand-daughter will be coming to-night. She would want you to rest and take things easily."

"No, no! I must see her tonight," Mrs. Hawkins said. "I must see her now. I've waited so long. I've a feeling that I can't wait any longer."

There was no mistaking her agitation; the breathlessness of the frail old voice; the trembling of her hands; the look of almost piteous desperation in her eyes. Aria suddenly felt brave and resolute.

"You look very nice," she said gently. She tidied Mrs. Hawkins' pillows. "I am going to fetch your grand-daughter to see you. And then you will be able to go off to sleep."

"I've prayed that I would see her again before I die," Mrs. Hawkins said in a low voice. "I've prayed day after day that the Lord would remember me—and He has!"

Aria turned away so she should not see the tears in her eyes. Then she walked quickly down the long corridors to the hall. She opened the door of the drawing-room. The ladies were there alone for the men had not yet left the dining-room and their port.

Lulu was standing alone at the radiogram, selecting a record from a large pile of the latest tunes which had arrived that morning from America. Aria went to her side.

"I want to speak to you," she said.

"I have nothing to say to you, Miss Milbank," Lulu Carlo replied rudely. "Not here, at any rate."

"You would be wise to hear me," Aria said.

There was something in her voice which made Lulu Carlo glance at her in surprise. Then she almost threw the record down on the table.

"Very well," she said.

She walked abruptly across the room, her dress swinging from the undulating movement of her hips. Aria followed her and they went out together into the hall.

"What is it?" Lulu Carlo asked. "What devilry are you up to now?"

"I am taking you to see your grandmother," Aria answered.

"You are taking me," Lulu Carlo answered scoffingly. "So you think you are giving the orders, do you, Miss Milbank? I don't want to see my grandmother. She has no right to be here. She goes tomorrow, and if I had my way you would go with her."

"What happens tomorrow remains to be seen," Aria said. "But at this moment you are going to see your grandmother and you are going to be pleasant and nice to her.

"If you don't, I am going into the drawing-room and I am going to invite all the other ladies here, and Mr. Huron when he comes from the dining-room, to come and visit her themselves. They would be very interested, I think, in seeing the grandmother of the famous Lulu Carlo."

"You little vixen!" Lulu Carlo exclaimed.

She made a movement with her hand as she spoke, and Aria knew quite well that for a moment she contemplated slapping her across the face. But her self-control prevailed and she merely stood there, staring with smouldering eyes into Aria's face.

Then she acknowledged defeat.

"Very well," she said. "Let's be quick about it."

In absolute silence Aria led the way down the corridor to Mrs. Hawkins' room. Only when they reached it and her hand was on the door did she say quietly to Lulu:

"Be nice to her. Don't say anything about her leaving tomorrow. Just tell her how glad you are to see her. If you don't, my threat still holds good."

"I'll make you suffer for this sort of blackmail," Lulu answered.

Without answering, Aria opened the door.

"Here's someone you very much want to see, Mrs. Hawkins," she said, in a very different voice from the one she had used to Lulu.

For one moment the film star stood in the doorway and then Lulu ran forward, her hands outstretched, her expression one of gladness and delight.

"Granny! How wonderful to see you!" she exclaimed, and took the old lady's shaking hand in hers.

It was an excellent performance, Aria thought drily, as she shut the door behind them and stood outside in the passage. Five minutes passed before the door was opened.

"Good night, Gran darling," she heard Lulu say. "Sleep well. You must take care of yourself, you know."

"I shall sleep now I've seen you, my darling child," was the old lady's answer.

Lulu came out into the corridor and as if she could be switched off like a light her smile faded from her lips. She gave Aria a look of inexpressible venom and walked away down the corridor without another word.

Aria went into the old lady's room. She was weeping with happiness.

"Prettier than ever, she is," she said to Aria. "And as sweet as she's pretty. She was glad to see me. It's been worth waiting all these years to see the gladness in her face at the sight of her old granny."

She went on talking as Aria made her comfortable, rearranging her pillow, putting her glass of water beside her bed and setting a clean handkerchief within reach of her hand. She was still talking when, as the old so often do, she fell asleep, her lips still forming a word as her eyes closed.

Aria turned out the lights with the exception of one very discreetly shaded by the bedside. She didn't want

120

the old lady to wake up in the night and be frightened of her new surroundings, not remembering where she was. And then, having opened the window, she slipped away.

She felt somehow she could not face the party in the drawing-room even though she knew Dart Huron would expect her to be there. Instead she went out into the garden feeling that perhaps the soft, scented darkness would ease her feeling of anger against Lulu and her sense of disappointment about Lord Buckleigh.

She walked away from the house down to the rose garden. The moon was rising and it was easy to find the way along the paths, with their neatly kept box hedges. At the end of the rose garden there was an arbour covered with honeysuckle. It had been built in the Georgian days in imitation of a Greek temple, as was the fashion of the time.

Aria sat down on the seat which stood between two pillars. It had been a long day, she thought suddenly. She was tired and it was very restful. There was just the rustle of the evening breeze in the trees, the sudden scuffle amongst the leaves as if some small animal moved across them.

Otherwise silence! The silence of the night which seemed made for contemplation and reflection.

How long she sat there she had no idea; and then suddenly she realised that footsteps were approaching. Someone was coming slowly down the path; someone who was smoking a cigar because she could see the glow of it very distinct against the darkness.

She sat very still hoping whoever it was would either pass by or return before reaching the temple. But after a moment she realised that she, herself, was clearly discernible because the moonlight fell full upon the seat on which she was sitting.

The man reached her side before she was sure of his identity. And yet, she asked herself as she recognised him, why had she not been sure from the very first moment of his appearance?

No-one else moved in quite the same way with that

curious feline grace that must have been inherited from his Indian ancestor.

"You felt in need of solitude, I gather, Miss Milbank."

It was a statement rather than a question, but Aria felt that it was an accusation.

"I thought perhaps you would not need me any longer, Mr. Huron," she said.

She would have risen, but he put out a hand as if to restrain her and then seated himself by her side.

"I always need a hostess at my parties, Miss Milbank. I thought I made that quite clear."

"I am sorry," Aria said.

Then somehow because in the dark he did not seem so awe inspiring and so frightening as he did in the daylight, she spoke honestly and said what she felt.

"I feel so inadequate to play hostess in a house like yours. I do not know the people and it is difficult to know what to talk to them about. I feel I am letting you down most of the time."

It was only as she finished speaking that she realised how childish and inconsequential she must sound.

"I have no fault to find with you so far, Miss Milbank. You have been, shall we say, entirely satisfactory."

"Thank you! That is kind of you to say so," Aria replied.

"I gather you have not had much experience of this sort of life before," Dart Huron went on.

"No."

"Do you like it?"

The question was surprising in itself, and she turned to look at him. His face was enigmatic in the pale light of the moon, his eyes were pools of darkness, and she could not know what he was thinking.

"Shall I be truthful?" she enquired.

"But of course! Why should you be anything else?"

"Because the truth is often impolite," she said. "You have asked me if I like this life. No, I do not! And yet, in a way it fascinates me. But, I do not know why, I

122

feel all the time in my heart that it is wrong. People shouldn't be so rich and so useless."

"Useless?"

He queried the word.

"Most of the people here have worked hard for their success."

"I didn't mean useless in that sort of way," Aria said. "I meant . . ."

She stopped suddenly. She couldn't put into words what she was trying to say. She had been thinking of Lulu Carlo—hard, selfish, seeking only self-gratification, having no affection for anyone, not even her own kith and kin.

And yet she had worked hard and it would be wrong to say she was anything but a worker, in her own way and for her own self.

And then there was Lord Buckleigh with his charm, his way of saying, 'I love you,' which made her heart turn over even though she told herself it was only a nonsensical falsehood on his part.

What had he contributed to life except an easy gaiety, a superficial veneer, good manners and pleasantry? And yet even he, in his own way, worked.

He looked after many of Dart Huron's affairs, chose him his polo ponies, made arrangements with people to whom he and he alone had the *entrée*.

Yes, Aria supposed he worked, in a sort of way, as did all the other gay young men who came to Summerhill either to stay or to enjoy a good meal. She was not certain what she felt about them except, perhaps, that they lacked depth and fundamental understanding.

Or was she judging everyone by Lulu Carlo and Lord Buckleigh?

She felt suddenly young and very helpless. And then, as she sat there, she knew that Dart Huron was waiting for her to go on speaking.

"I am . . . sorry," she stammered. "I shouldn't have . . . said that. I don't think what I'm talking about."

"Don't you think," he said with a sudden gentleness

123

in his voice that she had never heard before, "that you are trying to change, too quickly, people and perhaps things which need a lot of understanding and, in many ways, a lot of sympathy?

"We are all rather inclined to force people into our own mould, or rather to criticise them if they don't live up to our own particular standards. Yet are our standards the right ones?

"We have got to ask ourselves that, and ask ourselves, too, if our standards being right for us, are also applicable to other people who have, perhaps, a very different outlook and a very different background from our own."

Aria turned to look at him in surprise.

"I didn't think that you would say anything like that," she said involuntarily.

He smiled at her naïvete.

"Perhaps you are also judging me rather harshly."

"I am sorry," Aria replied. "That sounded rude. I didn't mean it to be."

"I know you didn't," he said. "You see, I have knocked about the world a great deal. I have met a great many people. May I say something to you which may sound impertinent? I think that you have come up against something in your life which has prejudiced you against people—at any rate the sort of people whom you meet here."

It was so true that Aria did not know what to say.

How could she tell him that everyone she had met at Summerhill had made her think of the woman and the people with whom her father had surrounded himself; who had encouraged him in his spendthrift, extravagant, rakish way and in the selfishness which had resulted in his destroying the ancient wealth of Queen's Folly and in hurting Charles beyond all hope of the hurt ever being erased.

"I think perhaps that is true in a way," Aria said at last.

"I was sure of it," Dart Huron said. "I have watched your face when people are talking carelessly, saying

124

things which perhaps would be best left unsaid. And I have known that it has all meant something to you personally."

He drew on his cigar and the lighted tip flamed red against the darkness of the sky.

"You must think me very stupid," Aria said at length in a low voice.

"On the contrary, I have the greatest admiration for your courage," Dart Huron said.

"My courage?" Aria enquired.

"Yes! In taking on a job of this sort," Dart Huron replied. "It is not easy, I know. In fact I know it is a very difficult one. But you are doing admirably. Incidentally, I shall be going back to America at the end of the month."

"At the end of the month!" Aria repeated stupidly.

"Yes! I was going to stay until the end of the summer, but I have decided to leave sooner than was intended. I shall want you to stay on a week after I have gone to close up the house and see that the staff leave everything tidy before they go. You will do that, won't you?"

"Yes, yes, of course!" Aria said.

"Well, that gives me another fortnight here," Dart Huron said. "England can be very pleasant at this time of the year."

Aria did not know how to answer him. She was faced with the sense of dismay which was out of all proportion to what she might have expected to feel at hearing that the job which she had just said she did not care for was coming to an end.

She did not know why, but she had the strangest desire to protest, to ask him to change his decision. But there was nothing she could say, and so they sat in silence, Aria consumed by an inexplicable sense of impending loss.

8

A clock in the distance struck one o'clock. At almost the same moment there was a faint sound in the passage outside Aria's bedroom door. She switched off the reading lamp which stood by her side, plunging the room into darkness.

She was still dressed in the black evening gown which she had worn for dinner, but she had flung over her shoulders a warm wrap and now, despite the warmth, she found herself shivering as she listened.

It seemed to her that a century of time rather than a few hours had passed since she had come up to her bedroom and deliberately made no effort to go to bed. Instead she had sat pretending to read, holding the book in front of her eyes, but not seeing the printed pages.

Now, what she had anticipated had happened, and another sound told her all too clearly there was someone outside the door. She waited.

The handle of the door turned very slowly, but it would not open, and after a moment there were several faint clicks as if someone pushed hard, with perhaps a muscular shoulder, against the unbending woodwork.

The handle was turned again, this time less silently, and then came a faint knock.

"Aria! Aria!"

The voice was in a whisper, but there was no mistaking who spoke. In the darkness Aria put her hands up to her cheeks as if to feel the warmth of the blood coursing there in a crimson flood.

The knock came again. Then, reluctantly, as if their owner found it hard to admit himself defeated, footsteps moved away from the door and down the passage.

Only when there had been silence for a long time did Aria reach out and switch on the reading-lamp. Then she rose and went to the window to draw back the curtains and let in the night air, drawing deep breaths into her lungs as if she felt suffocated by the need of it.

This was what she might have expected, she told herself. And yet, somehow it was difficult to face the fact now it had happened. She had a sudden vision of the pretty, painted women with whom her father had loved to associate.

She could see all too clearly the expression in their eyes, the invitation on their curved lips, the voluptuousness of their every movement, everything about them invariably a calculated provocation to sex.

How she hated them! Even before she had understood what they meant and all they stood for in her father's life, she had felt disgusted and somehow a little soiled because she, herself, had come into contact with them.

And now a man had thought of her as being in the same category as those poor creatures whom she had eventually come to pity rather than despise.

She wished now she had opened the door and told him what she thought of him. And then she knew it would have done no good. He would not have understood and she would have merely cheapened herself by ranting at him for something that was instinctively beyond his comprehension.

He would merely reiterate that he would marry her if he could, and he would not realise how poor a compliment such a statement was or that in reality she deemed it an insult.

Hard-eyed, her lips a tight line of anger, Aria undressed and got into bed. She expected to stay awake, incensed by her feelings. But the day had been long and in reality she was very tired.

Soon she was sound asleep and, in the contrariness of the subconscious, dreaming happily that she was with someone she loved and who loved her. She could not see his face, but she knew that she loved him.

She felt herself surrounded by the warmth and protection of his love so that when she was awakened by a knocking on her bedroom door she was smiling happily and the expression in her eyes was soft and gentle.

She slipped out of bed, unlocked the door and then yawning was back against the pillow in the passing of a few seconds. But the opening of the door did not prelude, as was usual, the housemaid's coming in quietly to draw the curtains and place a tray of early morning tea beside her bed.

This morning the door thrust open with a bang and the Italian girl burst into the room, tears running down her face.

"*Signorina,* come quickly! Oh, come quickly!" she cried, her hands going out beseechingly towards Aria who, startled from dreams to stark reality, could for a moment hardly comprehend what was happening or what was being said.

In the dim sunlight seeping through the chintz curtains the girl's emotion and appearance had, in themselves, an almost unreal quality.

"What is the matter?" Aria managed to ask at last.

"The old lady, *Signorina.* Please come to her."

Aria wasted no more time in asking questions. She jumped out of bed, slipped her feet into her mules and covered her nightgown with the pretty dressing-gown of flowered cotton which Nanny had made her the previous summer.

She did not stop to glance in the mirror or to tidy her hair, which rioted in tiny curls all over her head. She quickly followed the Italian maid, who started to run down the back stairs and along the corridor which led to the Garden Room.

The curtains were pulled and Aria realised that the maid must have called Mrs. Hawkins at eight o'clock as she had been instructed, and then turned, when she had done so, to look at the bed.

One glance at the ivory features of the old lady, who

128

had fallen sideways a little on her pillows, was enough for Aria to realise the truth. She bent forward to touch the thin, white, veined hand, but the coldness of it only confirmed what she already knew. Mrs. Hawkins had died in her sleep.

"Poor lady! Oh, *Signorina,* I am so sorry for her. She died alone and without making her peace with God."

Aria realised that this was the Catholic point of view and turned to put her hand consolingly on the girl's shoulder.

"It was as she would have wished to die," she said quietly. "We must not grieve for her."

Even as she spoke the words she heard someone enter the room, and turned with a start to see Dart Huron was standing there. He was dressed in riding-clothes and she knew that he rode very early in the morning and had doubtless just returned from his ride.

He walked across to the bedside without speaking to Aria and stood looking down at Mrs. Hawking. Then he turned to Aria and in a voice of steel said:

"McDougall told me that something extraordinary was happening here. Who is this woman?"

"She is Mrs. Hawkins—Miss Carlo's grandmother," Aria answered.

She thought that Dart Huron looked at her almost incredulously, and then before he could say any more the Italian girl burst into such loud sobbing that it was obvious it would be difficult to be heard above it.

"Come to the library when you are dressed, Miss Milbank," Dart Huron said sharply. "In the meantime I will send for the doctor."

He walked from the room and Aria put her arms round the sobbing Italian girl and tried to console her. When she grew calmer, Aria led her outside into the corridor and sent her to lie on her own bed.

Then she went in search of the Head Housemaid.

Burroughs was a sensible woman with an almost jaundiced view towards life which made her welcome death as if it were a friend rather than an unpleasant occurrence.

129

"Leave everything to me, Miss Milbank," she said crisply when Aria told her what had happened. "I have laid out my mother and three of my father's sisters. I know what to do, and Mrs. Felton, the gardener's wife, will give me a hand. She was a midwife before she married and is used to such things.

If you had told me the old lady was likely to pass away, I should have advised you not to let Maria look after her. If anything happens foreigners always work themselves into a state. It's always the same with them. They love a chance to be emotional."

"I am afraid it was rather a shock for poor Maria," Aria said.

"It would be a shock for anyone," Burroughs answered. "But there's no need for her to carry on as if the lady were a long lost relation, or anything like that. Restraint is what is needed, Miss Milbank, under such circumstances."

Aria could not help agreeing with her, even if she thought it was easier said than done. She was, however, thankful to leave everything in Burroughs' capable hands and go upstairs to dress preparatory to seeing Dart Huron in the library.

She could not prevent her heart sinking at the thought, and a glance at herself in the mirror did not dispel her feeling of disquiet. She must have looked very inefficient and inadequate to cope with such a situation, she thought, staring at her reflection. Her unbrushed hair gave her rather the look of a surprised choir boy, and her face, without powder, and her untouched lips made her appear curiously young.

Then she remembered that it did not really matter whether he was displeased with her or not, considering that he was leaving in a short space of time and the house was to be shut up. And yet, she rather wanted to impress him with how well she had managed since she had come to Summerhill.

It had not been easy to get the household working without rows or departures.

It had not been a simple matter not only to answer

130

his personal letters, but also to cope with the immense complexity of orders, bills, wages and all the million-and-one things which went towards keeping up a big house filled not only with servants but with guests.

She had felt in some ways that she had achieved what at least her predecessors had never achieved before, and now she had ruined what she had fondly imagined was quite a good impression.

She had, too, precipitated herself into a very uncomfortable position in which she must explain her action in bringing to a man's private house not only someone who had been uninvited, but who was extremely unwelcome so far as one honoured guest was concerned.

Whether it was her reluctance to face the row or because of the many interruptions which came while she was dressing Aria was not sure, but it was nearly nine-thirty before finally she got downstairs and went into the library.

The room was empty, but as she looked round her, wondering whether to go or to stay, Dart Huron entered by another door which led into the breakfast room. It was only as she saw him shut the door behind him that Aria realised that she, herself, had not only had no breakfast but had left, untouched, the tea which one of the housemaids had brought up to her room while she was dressing.

She had felt the sight of food or drink repelled her, but now the thought of it must account for the curious sinking feeling inside her as Dart Huron walked across the room, his dark eyes, his face, or so it seemed to her, unusually severe.

"The doctor will be here about eleven o'clock," he said. "I understand that in the meantime everything that ought to be done is being done."

"Yes! Burroughs said she would see to everything," Aria murmured unhappily.

"There will, of course, have to be an inquest," Dart Huron said.

Aria looked at him with startled eyes.

"I hadn't realised that."

131

"I think there are several things that you haven't realised," he said. "The first thing is that it is usual to ask the host's permission or at least inform him that guests are arriving in his house."

"I know," Aria murmured. "And, please, I can only apologise and say how sorry I am about it all. But I couldn't leave Mrs. Hawkins where she was; I couldn't! And there was nowhere else to take her."

It seemed to her as if Dart Huron's expression softened a little.

"Perhaps you had better tell me about it," he began.

Before Aria could answer, Lulu Carlo came into the room. She was wearing a sensational *négligé* of white chiffon and white mink. Her face was exquisitely made up, but her hair flowed loose over her shoulders, and her feet, clad in high-heeled diamond-studded mules, clattered on the parquet as she crossed the threshold.

"I was told you were here," she said to Dart Huron dramatically. "You have heard what has happened?"

"I understand that your grandmother died during the night," he said gently.

"That is what I have been told," Lulu said. "That she has died. And whose fault is it, I should like to know?"

She turned accusingly towards Aria.

"It was you! You killed her! Bringing her away from the home where she had lived so long; over-straining her with the journey and the excitement of coming to a place like this. You're responsible and I hope you're ashamed of what you've done."

Aria went very white and for the moment could find nothing to say.

"Wait a minute, Lulu!" Dart Huron said quietly. "I imagine that Miss Milbank acted in good faith. She was just about to tell me why she had brought Mrs. Hawkins here when you came into the room. Perhaps, Miss Milbank, you could care to go on."

"I hope you are not going to listen to her lies," interposed Lulu, before Aria could speak. "She brought my grandmother here without asking and it was, I consider,

132

a gross impertinence on her part. What right had she to interfere? What right had she to decide that the place where I had put her was not good enough?

"I've got hundreds of letters to say the old lady was perfectly happy. She wanted to see me, of course—she adored me—but that was no reason for dragging her about the place, and incidentally killing her in the process!"

"I don't think you should speak like that," Dart Huron said. "Your grandmother was a very old woman. She would have died anyway. Shall we allow Miss Milbank to tell us exactly what happened?"

"I have told you already. There is no point in listening to her," Lulu cried. "She hates me, and if you ask my opinion, she has done this merely to spite me. She wanted you to see what my grandmother was like, to pretend she was neglected, to try and persuade you that I hadn't beggared myself all these years to send her money that I could often ill afford."

There was almost a sob in Lulu's voice now, and she held out her hand towards Dart Huron as if seeking strength as well as sympathy from him. He took her hand almost automatically in his, but he spoke to Aria.

"You were not satisfied, I gather, with the conditions in which you found Mrs. Hawkins," he said.

"They were deplorable," Aria replied quietly. "She had no comforts of any sort; she was on the third floor; and she could not go downstairs because she had grown too old to climb them again. She was dependent entirely on the kindness of other residents in the building, and with my own ears I heard the landlady inform her that she would no longer carry up her food. She was being bullied and shouted at. Old people cannot stand that sort of thing."

"I don't believe one word of it," Lulu exclaimed loudly.

"I see no reason to doubt Miss Milbank," Dart Huron retorted.

Lulu snatched her hand from his.

"That's exactly what I expected," she said. "You

133

prefer to believe her rather than me. She's trying to show me up in a bad light, to come between us. Why should I let her behave like this?"

"I don't think Miss Milbank is doing any of the things you suggest," Dart Huron said patiently. "She thought your grandmother was uncomfortable and unhappy and she took, perhaps we might say, rather a lot upon herself in bringing her here. But in a way it was understandable.

"At least we can be sure that your grandmother died happy, and for the purpose of the inquest, at any rate, I suggest that you forget anything but your feeling of relief that you were able to see her before she died."

"An inquest!" Lulu's voice almost rose to a shriek.

"I am afraid one will be necessary," Dart Huron said. "The doctor will give a death certificate, I imagine, of heart failure. But, nevertheless, your grandmother died alone and without medical attention and an inquest is, I am afraid, inevitable."

"I won't have it!" Lulu Carlo cried. "I won't! Do you understand? Think of my publicity—my career! Everybody believes that my grandmother was Scandinavian."

"I am afraid there is nothing we can do but tell the truth," Dart Huron said.

Lulu looked at him with her eyes ablaze and then turned towards Aria.

"This is your doing, damn you!" she said, and raising her hand slapped Aria hard across her face.

The sound seemed to re-echo round the room like a pistol shot, and immediately after it the three people standing there seemed turned to stone.

Then, very slowly, Aria raised her hand to where the red imprint of Lulu's fingers had began to burn their way across her cheek.

She was about to speak, and Dart Huron had ejaculated one word, "Lulu!" when the suave voice of Mc-Dougall from the doorway announced:

"The gentlemen from the Press to see you, Sir!"

Dart Huron looked up in surprise; Aria, stunned as she was by the blow from Lulu's hand, angry with a

134

kind of almost smouldering fury which seemed to be seeping like a crimson tide through her blood, could not help but notice the strangeness of the expression on Lulu's face.

Six men were ushered into the room. Three of them carried cameras, the others were quite obviously reporters. They came forward until they reached the group of three people standing in front of the fireplace, then the eldest amongst them appeared to take the initiative.

"Good morning, Mr. Huron!"

"I am surprised to see you, gentlemen," Dart Huron replied. "You certainly wasted no time in getting here, although I cannot quite understand how the information could have reached you even before the arrival of the doctor."

"The doctor!"

The Press men looked puzzled and two of them looked at each other obviously in bewilderment. One of the photographers was smiling at Lulu Carlo, his fingers already busy with his camera, whilst, almost instinctively it seemed to Aria, Lulu was standing in an extremely photogenic position.

The Press man's question, however, seemed to check Dart Huron in what he was about to say.

"One moment," he said. "Perhaps we have got this wrong. Would you like to tell me why you have come here? I've met some of you before, of course. You, I think, are from the *Express*," he said, speaking to the elderly man.

"That's right," was the reply. "And my colleagues are from the *Mail* and the *Sketch*. I daresay another bunch will soon be waiting for you outside. We rather hoped we should be first in the field."

"What field and for what reason?" Dart Huron asked.

"Now come, Mr. Huron. You know the answer to that," the man from the *Express* said. "We have been expecting this for some time, of course; but when we were told the announcement was to be made some time this week, we had to come and see you in person."

"I'm glad you did," Dart Huron smiled. "But I shall

135

be interested to know what announcement you're talking about."

He turned his head a little after he had asked the question and glanced down at Lulu. There was something almost too innocent and too blank in the expression of her face; the wide wonderment in her eyes was an expression which her fans knew only too well. It was what her less admiring critics called her "Orphan Annie look."

"A mixture of idiocy and dumb-wittedness which sometimes passes for innocence," someone had once said scathingly.

Dart Huron's lips tightened, even as the reporter from the *Daily Mail* answered the question.

"The announcement of your engagement, Mr. Huron."

Lulu gave a little cry.

"Oh, Dart! They know about it and we did so hope to keep it a secret."

She laid her hand, as she spoke, on his arm, and at that moment there was a blinding flash of the cameraman's bulb.

"Hold it, Miss Carlo!" called out one of the other photographers who had not been quite so quick off the mark, but Dart Huron had moved abruptly, spoiling the picture.

"I am afraid you are under a misapprehension if you think that an announcement of my engagement is to be made this week."

"Oh, but, Dart," Lulu interposed. "Surely you're making a mistake? It's really no use pretending any longer."

Her voice was hardly a whisper, but it was, as she well knew, perfectly audible to everyone in the room.

It was then that Aria realised who was the instigator of all this. She knew now why Lulu wanted that list of newspapers with their telephone numbers which she had left in her bedroom yesterday morning.

It was Lulu who had engineered that the Press should come here and take Dart Huron by surprise, and who

136

was forcing him into accepting publicly what all the world supposed privately, that eventually he intended to marry her.

"Miss Carlo is right, Mr. Huron," the man from the *Sketch* said. "We'll get the truth sooner or later, so you might as well tell it us now and give us a break. Secret marriages are not only out-of-date, they are out of the question—at least as far as you're concerned."

He laughed at his own *bon mot* and the other Press men smiled good-humouredly.

"Very well," Dart Huron said. "You shall have the truth, gentlemen, since you have asked for it. I am to be married, though I have no idea when the ceremony will take place. But I am going to marry, not, as you seem to imagine, Miss Lulu Carlo, who is only a very old and valued friend, but Miss Aria Milbank, whom I do not think you gentlemen have met and to whom I shall now have the pleasure of introducing you."

There was a startled gasp from Lulu which sounded rather like the hissing of a snake. There was an even more audible gasp from the reporters who all turned quickly towards Aria as if at the command of a sergeant-major.

For the moment she thought she must be dreaming, that she could not have heard Dart Huron's words right. And then, as she saw the rage in his face and realised what he had done, the fury that had been smouldering within herself burst into flame.

"It is not . . ." she began to say, only to find herself, suddenly and to her utter astonishment, caught up in Dart Huron's arms.

"I'm sorry, gentlemen," he said over her head, "but Miss Milbank is feeling faint. You must forgive me if I take her into another room for a breath of fresh air."

Before Aria could say what trembled on her lips, before she could recover from her utter surprise at being lifted into his arms, he had walked away, kicked open the door of the breakfast room and left an astounded and, for the moment, speechless company behind him.

137

He pushed the door to with his back, then put Aria down on her feet.

"What do you think you are doing?" she began, only to find herself dragged by the arm across the room, through another door which led to a small, panelled *boudoir* which was seldom, if ever, used. Dart Huron shut the door behind him.

"Now you can talk," he said. "We don't want to be overheard."

"Overheard!" Aria ejaculated. "I am going straight back to tell those reporters it is not true. How dare you say you are engaged to me? If you imagine I'm going to stand by and let you tell them lies of that sort and say nothing in my own defence, you're much mistaken."

She was so angry it was difficult to articulate her words. Her eyes were flashing and her face was very pale with the exception of the burning mark where Lulu had struck her. Dart Huron stood leaning against the mantelpiece watching her in what seemed to her an insolent fashion.

"You're intolerable!" Aria stormed. "You think you can do what you like with people—but not with me! I know exactly why you've done this. To get out of an uncomfortable situation in which you find yourself, entirely through your own fault. Well, I'm not acting as your scapegoat. I am going back now and I shall tell the reporters the truth and both you and Miss Carlo can do what you like about it!"

She walked towards the door and had almost reached it before Dart Huron spoke.

"Two thousand pounds!" he said.

It was such an unexpected remark that Aria could not but be arrested by it.

"What does that mean?" she asked.

"That's what I am prepared to give you," he said.

"Do . . . do you think I want money for . . . this sort of . . . thing?" Aria enquired, stammering with rage.

"If you didn't want money you wouldn't be working," he replied. "Presumably, like everyone else, you work

138

because you are in need of money. Two thousand pounds is quite a useful sum to be given free of tax."

"I don't want to be bribed," Aria retorted.

She had turned the handle of the door this time when Dart Huron spoke again.

"Three thousand pounds!" he said. "Even if you don't want it, I imagine you have relatives who would be grateful of a little help."

Almost despite herself Aria paused. Three thousand pounds! What a difference it would make to Charles and Queen's Folly.

The roof could be mended; the beautiful painted ceiling in the Banqueting Hall, which had been damaged by a broken pipe, could be repaired; the window on the north front, which had been boarded up ever since the landmine had fallen in the park, could have the glass put back into it.

And what would three thousand pounds mean to Charles where the farm was concerned. The new Fordson tractor that he had wanted for so long; the bull pen which was so dangerous that more than one herdsman had complained about it; fertiliser for the fields; new stock; the best seed.

She could see the lists now which Charles was drawing up and then throwing into the wastepaper basket because he knew it was quite hopeless even to make a note of what was required.

Three thousand pounds! Almost despite herself she took her hand quietly from the door-handle.

"I thought you would see sense," Dart Huron said. "Shall we talk this out in a reasonable manner?"

"I don't feel reasonable," Aria replied. "I hate you for what you are doing and for what you are making me do. It is typical of you and your sort of people to believe that anyone has their price. But you are right, mine is three thousand pounds!"

She could not help the tears of humiliation coming into her eyes. Then, as she spoke, she felt the room go misty and begin to swim round her, and suddenly Dart

139

Huron's hand was on her arm and she felt him help her to a chair.

"The whole morning so far has been unpleasantly emotional," he said, in a dry tone which made her feel that secretly he was laughing at her. "Sit down and I am going to fetch something to eat from the next room. I don't suppose you have had any breakfast."

"I don't want any," she murmured weakly.

"Oh yes, you do," he contradicted. "Don't forget you have already admitted that I know better than you do what you want."

She felt another surge of anger that he should refer so lightly to what seemed to her something almost too shaming to be spoken of at all.

"I hate you!" she said.

But it sounded weak and ineffectual even to herself.

"You are merely hungry," he smiled, and as he spoke he disappeared into the next room.

9

"I must be mad to do this," Aria told herself a little while later, as Dart Huron, with an easily assumed solitude, led her out onto the terrace where the photographers were waiting to photograph them.

He had been interviewing them alone for some time, and having stuck to his story that she was not feeling well, had insisted, so he had told her, that she should only pose for a photograph, and not be subjected to any questioning.

"I was very firm that we were not ready to answer questions," he said. "I have told them that the engagement will be announced in due course and they will learn all they wish to know."

When she had eaten the breakfast he brought her

from the morning-room and was sitting alone after he had left her to talk to the reporters, Aria wished over and over again that she had the strength of mind to refuse to have anything to do with this ridiculous engagement and all it entailed.

And yet, dazzling her the whole time as if she saw the money actually lying in front of her, was the thought of three thousand pounds.

It was no use, she thought wearily, pretending one was above mercenary thoughts or financial considerations. It was all very well for people to talk of character being more important than cash when they had plenty of money and everything that was absolutely essential to normal living.

It was when one was struggling against debts and mortgages and the wear and tear of everyday economics that money seemed to absorb an almost gigantic proportion of one's thoughts and yearnings.

If Charles failed to farm Queen's Folly competently and had to give up the place, as the solicitors advised him to do, she knew it would not only break his heart but perhaps drive him off his mental balance. After his nervous breakdown the doctors had been very firm in saying that he was not to worry.

How little they understood, Aria thought bitterly. Charles worried incessantly at the thought of losing Queen's Folly. The house and estate might have been a beloved woman to whom he had dedicated not only his heart and soul but his whole life.

Three thousand pounds would enable him to avoid those black patches of depression when everything seemed dark and he was overcome with despair and the hopelessness of ever achieving anything except bankruptcy.

Three thousand pounds would mean, too, that she could go home! That in itself was enough to make her feel that any lie, however much she might deprecate an untruth, was worth while.

She was smiling when Dart Huron came back into the room.

141

"I promised them one photograph," he said. "Nothing more and no questions. Come along."

Aria realised she was to have no choice in the matter, so without comment she rose to her feet and followed him to where the reporters had congregated on the beautiful flagged terrace with its magnificent view overlooking the flat valley beneath the hill on which Summerhill was built.

"Would you like to take Mr. Huron's arm, please, Miss Milbank?" one of the photographers asked. "And smile at each other."

There was the click of half-a-dozen cameras. The number of reporters had grown since Aria last saw them. Then, as those with notebooks surged forward, Dart Huron took her arm and drew her back through the French window.

"That will be all for today, thank you, gentlemen," he said. "I hope you will have a drink before you start your return journey to London."

"We'll drink your health," someone said, as Dart Huron closed the window behind him and turned to look at Aria.

"That wasn't too bad, was it?" he said. "I staved off the worst of the questions, but I'm afraid you will be headlined in the evening papers as a 'mystery bride.' It was only when I started to talk that I realised how little I know about you. I got over that, however, by saying we had not yet informed your family that we were engaged and that I could say nothing until the usual formalities had been effected."

"My family!" Aria stared at him with wide eyes. "You mean they must come into this?"

"But of course," he answered, walking across to a table and taking a cigarette out of an onyx cigarette-box. "And I must ask you not to tell them the truth. If even one person suspects that this engagement of ours is a blind, then rumour, whispering and gossip will start up immediately. Let it run for two weeks until I go back to America and then we can announce that it is broken off by mutual consent."

He lit a cigarette, then, without looking at Aria, went on talking.

"I am afraid there will be a great deal of unwelcome publicity. We can't help that. It is certain to appeal to the type of public who likes the 'She Married her Boss' sort of story. But never mind, our backs are broad enough I hope; and when it is all over, you will he a a good deal richer and have, at the same time, a certain glamour about you which I can't but feel will be help-ful when you are looking for another job."

Aria found it hard to get her breath. She saw now all too clearly that the snare into which she had been precipitated was far deeper and far worse than she had anticipated. She had thought she was mad to agree to his crazy notion of an engagement, but she had not begun to realise what it implied.

She saw now exactly how he looked at it. She was his secretary, a girl who had to earn her own living, of modest, if not humble origin; someone to whom the glaring, spectacular publicity of the national Press would be advantageous rather than the contrary.

She was a girl who was of so little consequence that Dart Huron could, in his own mind, pick her up, use her to his own advantage, then cast her aside without there being any unpleasant consequences, without her personal life being in any way affected.

He spoke of their engagement broken off by mutual consent. Was it likely, under the circumstances, that anyone would imagine for one moment that she had done the breaking?

Everyone would be sure that he had jilted the little secretary who had captivated his attention for a brief moment, or perhaps rushed him into making a declara-tion of marriage when he had intended no such thing.

Because she felt her legs could hardly carry her, Aria sat down in a chair.

"Things aren't as easy as you imagine," she said.

"Why not?" he enquired with a half smile. "You jumped the first fence famously. I must congratulate you."

"I think you are a little premature about that," Aria said. "You see, this has all happened so quickly and in such a rush that I didn't have time to warn you that Milbank is not my real name."

Her words startled even Dart Huron's complacency.

"Good lord!" he said. "Why on earth didn't you tell me? The Press will be rushing round trying to ferret out things about you. They fired innumerable questions at me. As I didn't know the answers, it was easy to say I was not in a position to reply, but that won't stop them investigating."

"Perhaps they won't find out," Aria said. "Perhaps it is best to say nothing."

"Jeez! We can't take a risk like that," Dart Huron exclaimed. "Why on earth didn't you tell me the truth?"

"I had my own reasons," Aria said a little stiffly.

She thought it was too much for him to take up the attitude that she had deceived him by concealing her rightful identity, and he should be apologising to her for landing her in this awkward predicament.

Dart Huron suddenly sat down on the sofa beside Aria.

"Now let's get this straight," he said. "It's best for us both to be frank. You know as well as I do I was run into a corner this morning. I was angry, very angry, and so I did an impulsive and perhaps very stupid thing —wriggling out of an uncomfortable situation without having time to consider or discuss whether my method of escape was a good one or a bad.

"Quite frankly, I acted on the impulse of the moment, and you have been sporting enough to let me go ahead with it. Where do we go from there? It would be impossible for me to retract what I have said now, at this moment."

"Yes, I understand that," Aria said.

"Now you tell me," Dart Huron went on, "that you are not who you pretend to be. Who are you, by the way?"

"I don't suppose you would be very much the wiser if

I were to tell you," Aria replied. "But my name is not Milbank, it is Milborne."

She saw by the expression on Dart Huron's face that the name meant nothing to him.

"Does it matter very much then?" he asked. "I mean, have you got a couple of husbands tucked away somewhere? Or are you wanted for murder or anything like that?"

Despite her feeling of agitation Aria could not help smiling.

"No, nothing like that," she answered. "It is only that there are a certain number of people in England who would know the name."

"You mean you belong to a well-known family?" Dart Huron said, speaking, it seemed to Aria, almost incredulously, so that again her anger and resentment against him rose.

"If you mean are my family ladies and gentlemen," she questioned, "the answer is yes! I am not an obscure little typist from nowhere, if that is what you are thinking. But if you are afraid of repercussions when our engagement is broken off, then you need not be alarmed. There will be no-one to take you to task for having jilted me after a brief fortnight's engagement.

She spoke bitterly and with considerable venom in her voice. Somehow it seemed to leave him unmoved.

"That's all right then," he said. "At the end of a fortnight I shall leave for America and you will have a cheque for three thousand pounds. This is a business arrangement, Miss Milbank—or would you prefer I called you Milborne?"

"I think I had better remain as Milbank and risk the Press discovering who I am."

"It will certainly appear odd that I did not know the right name of the girl to whom I am officially engaged to be married," he said. "But as there will be no official announcement and if later your name is discovered, one can always assume it was my American accent which resulted in their misunderstanding what I said this morning."

"You think you can talk yourself out of any difficulty, don't you?" Aria remarked coldly.

"I can always have a good try," he replied, with a smile on his lips which made her more resentful than ever because she knew she had no power to hurt him.

She glanced at the clock on the mantelpiece.

"It is nearly eleven o'clock. I imagine the doctor will be here soon. There are various things that I must see to."

"Good heavens! I had forgotten the old lady," Dart Huron said. "When you think about it, our engagement, such as it is, will certainly take the edge off any other occurrences in the house. I don't mind betting that nobody will pay much attention to an inquest on an old woman of eighty-two who just happened to die at Summerhill."

"I hope you are right," Aria remarked. "Otherwise Miss Carlo will be very upset."

She rose as she spoke and walked towards the door. As she reached it Dart Huron called her name.

"Miss Milbank!"

She turned back. He was standing in front of the mantelpiece, one hand in the pocket of his riding-breeches, the other arm resting on the mantelpiece. There was something graceful and something very traditional in his attitude.

Posed against the exquisite Chippendale mirror behind him, he might have been part of a conversation piece of the eighteenth century. She took in every detail almost unconsciously as she waited for him to explain why he had called her.

"I only wanted to say thank you!" he said at length.

There was a note of sincerity in his voice and despite herself some of her anger against him evaporated.

"I only hope you will not regret what you have done, Mr. Huron," she said, and went from the room closing the door quietly behind her.

She walked up the front stairs and only as she reached the landing at the top of the first flight did she see that Lulu Carlo's bedroom door was open and

146

realised, with a sinking heart, that the film star was waiting for her.

"Come in here. I want to speak to you," Lulu ordered peremptorily from the doorway.

Aria wanted to refuse, and then she felt it would be cowardly. Slowly and with what she hoped was a show of dignity, she walked through the bedroom door. The sunlight was streaming through the windows and somehow the room seemed exotic.

There was the fragrance of an exotic perfume; there were bowls of orchids, which were Lulu's favourite flower, there was a toilet set of beaten gold decorated with sapphires and an ermine and sable rug flung over the end of the bed.

It was over-luxurious, over-rich, and somehow at variance with the countryside and the soft, warm air of the summer's day.

Lulu had changed from her trailing white *négligé* to a frock of pale nylon which she wore with a dozen ropes of pearls and a huge oriental bracelet of sapphires and rubies. She was looking very beautiful and very angry.

She might, Aria thought, have sat for the model Medusa with snakes upon her head instead of hair.

"Don't think you're going to get away with this," she said in a harsh voice as she stood facing Aria. "I am not a fool and I was not born yesterday. This is a put-up job between you and Dart. I am going to expose it and make you both look idiots."

"I think you had better talk to Mr. Huron about it," Aria replied.

"I'll talk to him when it pleases me," Lulu retorted. "In meantime, you and I are going to come to a reckoning. Ever since you came into this house you have deliberately tried to cross me, and you are going to rue the day you ever did it. I'm not going to take this lying down, and so I'm warning you! You'll find me a very dangerous enemy, Miss Milbank."

"I can quite believe that," Aria answered. "And now,

147

if you have nothing further to say to me, I have work to do."

"Work! When you're engaged to such a wealthy and distinguished young man?" Lulu asked sarcastically. "Oh, well, I suppose you've got your uses. There would have to be something, wouldn't there?"

Aria moved towards the door.

"Just a minute!" Lulu went on. "You've made a great deal of trouble for me, Miss Milbank, but I'm prepared to be generous. Suppose I offer you a thousand pounds to leave Dart Huron alone, to clear out of here and not to come back. What would you say to that?"

"I should say that you were being insulting, Miss Carlo," Aria replied. "And I should also suggest that any money you may have lying about that you don't know what to do with, you might spend either on your relations or on other poor old people like your grandmother, who would really be grateful for it."

Aria meant to be provocative and she succeeded. Lulu gave a scream of rage and picking up the china ornament which stood on the table near her hand, hurled it after Aria just as she slipped through the door. She heard the thud as the ornament hit the woodwork and the clatter of the smashed pieces falling to the floor.

Then, without waiting to hear more, she ran as swiftly as she could down the corridor to her own sitting-room.

There she sat down in an armchair and hid her face in her hands. It was all too much to endure, she thought. And yet, having gone so far, what could she do but go through with it.

However, she had little time for thought. The chef was waiting to see her; Burroughs wished to report on what had been done about the laying out of Mrs. Hawkins; McDougall had sent up a list of fruit which had been ordered from the gardens; and there were innumerable telephone calls to be made, besides the pile of unopened letters which had had arrived by the morning's post.

If the servants had heard of what had been said to the reporters, they showed no sign of it. Aria was still working when, just before lunch time, Lord Buckleigh came striding into the room.

"What's this nonsense I hear?" he asked. "I met Dart in the hall and he told me that he was engaged to you."

"Yes, that's true," Aria answered, trying to prevent the colour from rising in her cheeks as she spoke.

"True!" Lord Buckleigh ejaculated. "It's the most fantastic thing I've ever heard in my life. Of course it isn't true. Why, you've hardly spoken more than a few words to him since you've been here. He has paid no attention to you; he's having this *affaire* with Lulu . . ."

He stopped suddenly.

"What does Lulu say to this?"

"I am afraid Miss Carlo is not very pleased," Aria said demurely.

"I don't believe a word of it," Lord Buckleigh ejaculated. "Come on, tell me the truth. What's it all about?"

"You must ask Mr. Huron," Aria replied.

"You must ask Mr. Huron," he repeated, mimicking her voice. "Listen! I love you! You know that. Tell all this poppycock to the other people if you like, but not to me. What's it all about?"

"I am engaged, unofficially and secretly if you like, to Mr. Huron," Aria smiled.

"Secretly!" Lord Buckleigh snorted. "McDougall told me that half the Press were here this morning. When I saw them coming up the drive, I rode in the other direction. I wondered what they were after. I thought they must have come to see Lulu."

Aria said nothing, and after a moment Lord Buckleigh, watching her face, asked:

"Who invited them?"

"I am not going to answer any of your questions," Aria answered. "It wouldn't be fair to Mr. Huron."

"In other words you're too frightened to say anything in case you give the whole show away," he said accusingly. "Oh well, if it doesn't mean anything, I suppose

149

I oughtn't to mind. I suppose you know what you're in for?"

"What?" Aria asked apprehensively.

"Well, the dickens of an amount of fuss. For one thing, Dart's an international figure. He has managed to combine the best of all worlds—social, financial, transatlantic. You don't suppose that the lines aren't buzzing at this moment.

"You might like it—the pictures, the probing into your private life. Somehow I didn't think you were made like that. You're not the stuff that Lulu's made of."

"Mr. Huron said that it's only an unofficial engagement," Aria said insistently.

"He can say what he damned well pleases," Lord Buckleigh replied. "If there's even a smell of an engagement ring where Dart is concerned, every newspaper reporter in the world will be tumbling about our ears in the space of a few hours."

"What can we do about it?" Aria enquired.

"Nothing," he answered. "You have agreed to marry him. Well, you must take the consequences."

"I have agreed to an unofficial engagement."

Even as Aria made the correction she thought it was indiscreet. But somehow she could not bear to let Lord Buckleigh, or anyone else for that matter, assume what was not true. He gave a low whistle.

"So that's the way the wind blows, is it?" he said. "I thought he would go to some lengths to get free of Lulu, but not to this. Why did you agree to it?"

"I didn't . . . I mean . . . you're not to ask me questions," Aria stammered.

"My dear, you're transparent as crystal," he remarked. "It's quite obvious what has happened. Dart's got into a panic about Lulu or been driven into a corner, and so he's used you as a blind or a bit of camouflage. Well, it won't work, I can tell you that."

"What do you mean?" Aria enquired.

"I mean that Lulu's a sticker. An unofficial engagement is not going to put her off. The day that Dart

150

marries somebody else he will be free of her, but not until then."

"I think you are attributing her with greater powers of resilience than she has," Aria said. "I imagine that she will leave."

"Then you imagine wrong," Lord Buckleigh said. "As I came upstairs to find you, Lulu was going down. She asked me where Dart was and I told her he was in the library. She didn't look at me like a woman who was packing her box."

"Could he ask her to go?" Aria enquired.

"I imagine not. That was why he was leaving himself," Lord Buckleigh said. "Oh, you little fool! Why did you want to get involved in a situation like this?"

Aria gave a little sigh.

"I haven't admitted to getting involved in anything," she said. "Oh, please! It's been such a dreadful morning, don't go on bullying me."

There was a little break in her voice which brought him instantly to her side.

"Darling, you know I don't want to do anything to upset you!"

He took her hands in his and raised them to his lips.

"You're so sweet and so foolish and so hopelessly incompetent to cope with Dart and the complications of his life.

"Look here! I have known him now for nearly ten years. I have been about with him; I have made myself useful; I have lived on him, if you like to hear the truth. And to me he is still in many ways a stranger. He is a funny person. He does the most accountable things in the most unaccountable ways. You are far too young and too innocent for this sort of set up. Skip out of it."

"But I can't," Aria said, trying to take her hands from Lord Buckleigh's; but he held on to them.

"Why can't you?" he asked, a little suspiciously.

"I cannot tell you that either."

"I can guess," he said. "He has made you give your

151

word of honour that you'll stand by him and he has paid you well for doing it."

Aria drew her hands away with a little exclamation of annoyance.

"Why do you suggest such things?" she asked angrily.

"Because they are true," Lord Buckleigh said. "I know the way Dart's mind works. He is ruthless and he's absurdly generous, especially when it's likely to pay a dividend as far as he's concerned. Oh, Aria! Why didn't you ask me first before you got into such a mess?"

"I didn't have the opportunity," Aria answered. "Besides, why should you concern yourself with me?"

"You know the answer to that," Lord Buckleigh said softly.

"Do I?"

She was thinking of the way the handle had turned the night before, of the taps on the door. Lord Buckleigh's protestations of love and affection, she thought, were not, in reality, any more unselfish than Dart Huron's blatant and quite frankly expressed manner of making use of her.

She rose from the chair in which she had been sitting, tidying up her papers.

"It's nearly lunch time," she said.

"Shall I take you away from here?" Lord Buckleigh enquired. "Shall we go away together, just you and I?"

"For how long?" Aria enquired. "You know that sooner or later you would want to come back. You know this sort of life."

His eyes dropped before hers and he shrugged his shoulders.

"I should never have made a success of sitting in an office," he said.

"I'm not blaming you," Aria answered. "You have the right to do what you like with your life. But you must also allow me to do what I wish to do with mine."

"Damn it! That's not the same thing . . ." Lord Buckleigh began hotly, but the sound of the gong booming through the house checked whatever else he had to say.

"We had better go down," Aria remarked.

Lord Buckleigh hesitated as if he contemplated for a moment trying to take her into his arms. And then as she left the room he followed her, and they walked towards the stairs in silence.

Aria had forgotten that by this time the house party would have been informed of the engagement. She was quite unprepared for the congratulations and the effusiveness of the other guests staying in the house.

"Dart has told us the good news," the Ambassadress said.

While several of the girls who had practically ignored her until now, kissed her with an admirable show of affection.

"I thought . . . it was . . . to be a . . . secret," Aria stammered.

"You can't keep a thing like that secret," someone replied. "What are your plans, old boy? When's the happy day to be?

"Aria and I have not decided yet," Dart Huron replied.

He looked at Aria as he spoke and though she had started at his use of her christian name, she managed to smile a little tumultuously at him.

"In fact the whole thing has been rather sprung on us," Dart Huron went on. "Aria has told me that she wants as little fuss made of it as possible—at least until she has had time to inform her family."

"But, of course, we understand," said the Ambassadress.

"Where do your parents live?"

"My father and mother are dead," Aria answered. "But my brother is alive and he lives in Hertfordshire."

"Whereabouts?" asked a pretty girl. "I live in Hertfordshire."

Aria cast a quick glance at Dart Huron and he rose to the occasion.

"You are not to ask her any questions now," he said.

153

"We have had quite enough with the Press bombarding us. Aria will get into terrible trouble with her family. They will be simply furious with her. For goodness" sake let's have something to eat and behave as if it hasn't happened."

"As if we could!" someone remarked, and a gay voice from the doorway said: "Could do what?"

Lulu Carlo was strolling towards them, smiling and poised. She was, Aria thought, giving a very creditable performance.

"Haven't you heard?" someone asked a little breathlessly, and a hush fell on the rest of the party.

It was obvious that the idea of the tenseness of the situation was uppermost in all their minds.

"About Dart? But of course I have!" Lulu replied. "I have given him my congratulations and my blessing, haven't I, darling?"

She linked her arm through Dart's as she reached him and looked up towards his eyes. Her head was thrown back and she looked very appealing and very feminine.

"Everyone has been very kind," Dart said, looking round the assembled throng.

"And what we've got to decide is what I am going to give you as a wedding present," Lulu said.

There was a sort of *double entendre* in her voice which made everyone feel uncomfortable.

"Shall I lead the way into luncheon?" the Ambassadress asked hastily. "I do hate my food to get cold."

"So do I," another lady agreed.

A pretty American girl took Aria by the arm.

I've never had such a surprise in my life as when Dart told us the news," she said. "You've been awfully subtle about not letting anyone suspect that you were keen on each other."

"We wanted to keep it a secret," Aria smiled.

"Secrets are dangerous things, all the same," a voice said behind her, and she knew without turning her head that it was Lulu who spoke.

It was difficult to know what Lulu's intentions were. She was so charming and so sweet at luncheon that it

154

was hard to believe she was the same virago, Aria thought, who had slapped her in the face that morning and had flung an ornament after her as she had left her bedroom but a short time before.

Although she looked at Dart with big, wistful eyes that seemed to have a hint of tears in them, she nevertheless spoke gaily and brightly of his engagement, and even addressed a sentence or two to Aria, both politely and pleasantly.

It was a change of heart that was difficult to understand. But Aria could see that everyone present was very impressed by it and were telling themselves, almost audibly, that Lulu Carlo was a far better sport than they had thought.

The telephone started ringing halfway through luncheon, and after McDougall had come in four times to report that certain newspapers were on the line and had been told each time to say there was no comment, Dart Huron told him to leave the receiver off.

"We shall all be driven mad by the end of the day if this goes on," he said a little irritably.

"You can't expect anything else," Lord Buckleigh answered. "If you really wanted to announce your engagement and have a little peace, you should have asked me how to manage it."

"And how would you manage it, Tom?" someone enquired.

"Well, if I had been Dart and I had wanted a secret marriage, I should have gone away to an island in the Caribbean or somewhere equally remote. And if I had wanted to announce an engagement and then say nothing more about it, I should have told the Press just the very moment that I stepped on an aeroplane for Timbuctoo. My motto has always been to run away from trouble!"

Everyone laughed at that, but Dart looked serious.

"It's not bad advice, Tom," he said. "I wish now I had asked you."

"I think it's a ridiculous idea," Lulu said lightly.

"Running away from the Press only makes them all the keener."

"Have you found that?" Lord Buckleigh enquired, but she was not to be drawn.

"You're only being horrid to me," she pouted, looking exceedingly attractive as she did so. "You know in my profession we always have to be nice to the Press and give them the right hand-outs. We were talking about Dart, not about me. His life will be a misery now until they get all the details they want."

"I should think they've got enough about Dart," someone suggested. "It's Miss Milbank who will come in for the worst of the questioning."

"There are going to be no questions and no interviews," Dart Huron said. "Let us make that clear from the beginning."

"That's what you think," Lulu answered. "Oh, Dart, dear! You are so naïve where the Press is concerned. You'll find a reporter under your bed and behind your bath; they will be listening at the window and up the chimney. And somehow, by hook or by crook, they will find out what they want to know. Does that make you nervous, Aria, dear?"

There was no sting in the sweetness of her voice, but Aria knew what lay behind the question.

"Not in the slightest," she said quietly. "I don't like the Press and I don't know how to deal with them. But . . . Dart has promised he will do all that."

She could not help a little hesitation in her voice before she said his name, and yet it made her seem all the more feminine, all the more appealing.

There was a little murmur of approval around the table especially from the men. Lulu's face darkened.

"The champion of fair women!" she said, and now there was no disguising the underlying sarcasm. Then, before anyone could speak, Lulu laid her hand over Dart Huron's and said softly: "Darling Dart, you're very, very naughty and, at times, very unkind. But I forgive you. I can't help it, although I ought to be angry with you."

156

Aria could feel the almost physical reaction amongst those present to her speech.

"Dear Lulu," they were thinking. "We never imagined she would take it so well. Dart is really a fool not to marry her. She is much more his type than this quiet little girl with red hair."

It seemed for a moment as if Dart Huron also was hypnotised by Lulu. Her fingers had tightened on his and now he raised her hand to his lips with a courteousness which was somehow very un-English in its ease and grace.

"You are a very sweet person, Lulu," he said quietly.

"No, Dart," she said softly, and yet her words were quite audible. "I am only very loving once."

10

Aria, walking upstairs, met Lady Grania Henley, who had arrived the night before for the weekend.

She was a pretty girl, exquisitely dressed, with rather indecisive features which had, however, been transformed by the clever use of make-up into something of an approaching beauty.

She smiled a little shyly at Aria now and said:

"I'm so looking forward to the dance tonight, Miss Milbank, aren't you?"

Aria gave a guilty start. In the excitement of all that had been happening she had completely forgotten that Dart Huron had told her he had invited a large dinner-party with dancing afterwards, to follow the game of polo which was taking place that afternoon.

Fortunately Aria had given instructions to the chef, had ordered the band and had told the staff to prepare for dancing the big, many-windowed room which overlooked the garden. It was ostensibly used almost entirely as a ballroom, but it rejoiced in the lovely Regency name of the Silver Salon.

She hoped that the gardeners had remembered the decorations, that the platform had been erected for the band, the piano was in tune, and the hundred and one little details, which were all her responsibility, had not been omitted.

"Yes . . . of course, I am . . . looking forward to it," she managed to stammer, hoping that Lady Grania had not guessed from her hesitation that the whole matter had slipped her mind.

"Dances here are always such fun," the other girl enthused. "Last time Dart had the most wonderful Spanish cabaret. It was the best I've ever seen."

Aria murmured something to the effect that she didn't think there would be a cabaret tonight, but Lady Grania was not disconcerted by the news.

"I expect it will be fun anyway," she said. "I brought my best dress because Dart's parties are always so smart. What are you going to wear?"

Aria felt almost angry at the question. What was there for her to wear except the same black dress that she had worn every night? The only choice that lay with her was whether she should wear pink roses at the waist or drape the blue scarf round her shoulders.

She had a sudden vision of how dowdy she would look. She could almost hear Dart Huron's friends saying.

"What on earth does he see in that dull, mousy little thing?"

And she was feminine enough to resent the fact.

All the gayest and most beautiful young women in London were coming; all the young men who graced the Society columns as Royal escorts, as taking part in charity performances, as being everywhere and anywhere, and who represented what was left of the aristocracy and nobility of England.

"I can't go," she thought suddenly. "I can't appear looking so insignificant, so poverty stricken, when everybody's attention will be directed on me; everybody will

158

be asking the same question: "What does he see in her?"

Because she was feeling upset, she spoke abruptly and with an almost sharp edge to her voice to Lady Grania.

"I have got nothing to wear but the dress I had on last night," she said. "If people don't like my appearance it just can't be helped."

As she spoke she started to pass Lady Grania and climb the stairs again, but the girl put out her hand and touched her arm.

"Would you think me really awfully rude if I suggested something to you, Miss Milbank?" she said a little timidly.

"What is it?" Aria asked, ashamed at having spoken as she had. At the same time finding herself envying this pretty girl, with her beautifully cut dress of flowered linen with a fringed scarf to match and shoes that were made of the same material.

"It sounds impudent to say it," Lady Grania said, "but may I lend you a dress to wear tonight?"

She saw the refusal in Aria's eyes and went on quickly:

"Please, it isn't mine. It belongs to Paul Peron whose firm I work for. It's a new dress—a very lovely one which I brought down here just in case I could tempt Miss Carlo with it. You needn't buy it.

"Please don't think I'm trying to sell you something. But in the circumstances I know Paul would be delighted for you to wear it tonight. It's one of his latest models. Nobody has seen it yet, and if people talk about it that's all he would want."

"I don't quite understand," Aria said, arrested in spite of herself. "What advantage can your . . . your firm possibly get from my borrowing a dress for the evening?"

Lady Grania smiled at her.

"Don't you see, you will be the most important person at the dance tonight? Everybody will want to meet you: and if you are wearing a lovely dress, somebody is sure to ask you where it came from. Anyway, I shall be there to tell them and then they might go to Paul and order one for themselves."

"Is business really done like that?" Aria enquired.

"It is indeed!" Lady Grania replied. "You don't suppose I could afford to buy the clothes that I am wearing. Paul Peron dresses me as an advertisement. He has just started up in London. He is very clever and very ambitious."

"I think I have read of him somewhere," Aria said.

"Come and see the dress I brought down for Miss Carlo," Lady Grania pleaded.

Aria, by this time, was far too fascinated to refuse; and although she mentally felt she was getting something under false pretences, she could not help an exclamation of delight and admiration when Lady Grania took from the wardrobe in her room one of the most beautiful dresses she had ever seen.

It was of the very palest green tulle with the bodice embroidered all over with diamonds and tiny green seashells, and a skirt which swept out in frill after frill over a stiffened crinoline and glistened with a million crystal dewdrops so that the whole dress sparkled with every movement that she made.

"You are model size, do you know that?" Lady Grania asked as Aria tried the dress on.

"It's so long since I bought a dress of any sort," Aria replied, "that I have no idea what size I am."

"Look at yourself!" Lady Grania exclaimed as she finished hooking Aria into the dress and then stood back to admire her handiwork. "It might have been made for you," she added.

It might indeed, and Aria, looking at her reflection in the mirror, could hardly believe her eyes.

"Can I really borrow it?" she asked a little breathlessly, she knew that now she had seen herself transformed it would be impossible for her to go to the party in her old black dress.

"But of course!" Lady Grania said. "If it makes you

160

any happier, I will ring up Paul and get his permission. But I know he will be delighted."

"But supposing, after he has been kind enough to lend me this, I can't afford ever to buy anything from him?"

Lady Grania gave a gurgle of laughter.

"Not afford!" she exclaimed. "When you are marrying Dart! Why, you can have the most fabulous clothes in the world. Apart from the fact that you can pay anything you like for a dress, half the famous *couturiers* will want to dress you at a special price. Think of the publicity you will have as Dart's wife."

Aria had stiffened and her voice was cold as she said:

"I don't like publicity and I don't think, after all, that I will wear this dress."

"Oh, but you must," Lady Grania said. "Why have you changed your mind? Have I said something to upset you? Please forgive me. I didn't mean to say anything that you wouldn't like."

She was so sincere in her apology that Aria could only soften and find it impossible to continue her attitude of aloof dignity. Besides, what could she say? How could she possibly explain to Lady Grania that in a fortnight's time she would disappear into the obscurity from which she had emerged.

She would go back to Queen's Folly—a little richer, it was true, but certainly not rich enough to buy new clothes or to waste that precious three thousand pounds on anything but what was urgently needed on the farm.

And yet, wrong though she felt it was intrinsically to borrow the dress, she could not face the evening in her old black.

"I should like you to ask Mr. Peron's permission," she said. "And then, if you are quite sure that he will not be annoyed with you or with me if he receives no order in the future, then I will borrow it for this one occasion."

"He will be thrilled, I know he will," Lady Grania said. "And thank you for helping me, too."

161

She bent forward impulsively and kissed Aria on the cheek.

"We have all been thinking that you were lucky," she said. "But I think Dart's lucky too. I always hoped that he would marry somebody really sweet and not that horrible Lulu or Beatrice, the girl he was engaged to in America. I never liked either of them. He's terribly nice underneath all the frou-frou of being so rich, but he has got spoilt. Women make a fool of him, only he doesn't realise it."

"You don't sound as if you are in love with him, at any rate," Aría said.

Lady Grania smiled.

"No," she answered. "I'm in love with a young man who is earning, at the moment, precisely nothing. He is working to become a Chartered Accountant, and when he has passed his exams and if he gets a good job— well, then we might be able to get engaged.

"Even then it will be years before we shall be able to get married. I know most of my friends think I am mad, but I would rather be poor as a church mouse with the man I love than rich with someone I don't."

"You are right! Of course you are right!" Aria said. "Money doesn't bring happiness. I have seen that here. I have seen it in the past. I often think that poor people have a far better chance of finding love and the real things that matter in life than the rich."

"Oh, but you mustn't say that when you are going to be so rich," Lady Grania cried. "But I knew as soon as I saw you that you wouldn't marry Dart unless you really loved him."

Aria turned her face away and busied herself with getting out of the green dress.

"I have a feeling," Lady Grania chattered on, "that Dart has always been looking for something in his life, and I believe it is real love. He is like Don Juan, who went from one woman to another because he could not find what he sought. The women over here make an absolute bee-line for him, and the same thing happens in America.

"It is not because they really love him. If he were just Mr. Huron with no money at all, ninety-nine out of a hundred wouldn't even look at him. It is only because he's so rich and got so much glamour behind him that they ply him with compliments, hang round his neck and generally behave as if he were a god or a superman. Sometimes it makes me rather sick."

"I feel like that, too," Aria said.

She was thinking of Lulu, with her possessive attitude towards Dart and her softened, almost mesmeric voice when she spoke to him, of her caressing hands and the look in her eyes. And Lulu cared for nobody except herself.

"What fools men are!" Aria said suddenly.

"Not always," Lady Grania said. "Dart has been very clever in that he has found you."

"Please, you mustn't say that," Aria said quickly. "It isn't . . . er . . . anyway, I don't want you to say it."

"You are so sweet," Lady Grania said, not understanding. "And I'm so thrilled you will wear the green dress tonight. You will look wonderful. Everybody will be gaping at you."

"If you mean they won't recognize me, that's more than likely," Aria laughed.

She tried to speak sensibly. At the same time she could not help a little thrill of excitement at the thought of appearing on equal terms with the lovely women who would be coming to dinner and to the dance.

It was only going to be a small party, about fifty couples in all, and yet, she thought a little wistfully as she dressed that night, it was the largest and most important ball she had ever been to.

She had danced in the hotels where she had stayed with her father when she was still a schoolgirl. She had danced in the village hall near Queen's Folly when there had been some special evening arranged in aid of the local Boy Scouts or the Village Institute.

But usually the entertainment at such functions was whist or a concert got up by the vicar, and in the last

163

three years the dances she had attended had been so few as to be almost negligible.

She had said nothing to anyone else about her own appearance that evening and she thought it was typical of Dart Huron, who had, when he returned from polo, talked extensively of the arrangements, not to remember the part that she must play in them.

"We are having a lucky draw," he said to Aria. "There's a gold and sapphire clip for the ladies and a cigarette-case for the men. We don't want to say too much about that, it looks so bad if that sort of thing gets into the Press."

"Are the Press coming?" Aria asked a little apprehensively.

"Not if I can help it," he replied. "They have not been invited and I have told McDougall to refuse them admittance. At the same time, one never knows nowadays who's not a gossip hound amongst one's acquaintances. I don't mind betting you that the most intimate details of what goes on tonight will find their way into the *Evening Standard* tomorrow."

Aria said nothing and noting her serious little face he asked:

"Are you nervous?"

"Very," Aria replied. "I am frightened of letting you down."

"I'm not afraid of that," he answered. "You won't forget to see that the band have plenty of champagne, will you?"

He sauntered from the room, leaving Aria with the feeling that he almost resented her nervousness because it showed inefficiency.

He had made it very clear that, although they were engaged as far as the world was concerned, he still intended her to earn her money as his secretary and housekeeper.

Lulu had not been seen all day. Trays of food had been taken up to her room; but as her hairdresser had come down from London, Aria imagined that she intended to make an appearance in the evening.

She wondered how anyone could be so thick-skinned as to remain on at Summerhill after what had happened that morning. But she she was well aware that Lulu knew that Dart Huron's engagement was nothing but a blind and a subterfuge to avoid his name being linked with hers.

She had not by any means given up the fight. She had taken him away from one woman—a clever and attractive one at that. She was not afraid of an obscure little secretary who was obviously being used as a catspaw.

Aria dressed slowly, savouring, with a sense of anticipated delight, the moment when she could put on her green dress. She had a bath, brushed her hair until it was the colour of copper beech leaves and shone with the gleaming brilliance of old brass.

Then she set it in tiny curls in almost a symmetrical pattern so that she looked not unlike a Greek statue with her delicate features and perfectly shaped head.

Usually she used very little make-up, but tonight she was more daring. She darkened her long eye-lashes, putting a touch of blue on the eyelids and reddening her mouth until in contrast it drew attention to the pearly whiteness of her skin.

Lady Grania had given her a pair of green sandals which matched the dress. Fortunately they fitted. They were mere wisps of green satin with long, high heels studded with diamonds and little diamond buckles to hold ankle straps in place. Aria put them on and admired the effect in the glass.

She had always had tiny and very beautiful feet and never since she had grown up, had she been able to afford the right kind of shoes to show them off to the best advantage.

Then at last the moment came when she could slip on the green dress and ring for the housemaid to do it up for her.

Most of the guests were assembled in the drawing-room when she came downstairs. She was feeling a little shy because what she was wearing tonight made her feel a very different person from her usual self.

165

She was halfway down the staircase when below her she saw Dart Huron come out of the dining-room to speak to McDougall in the hall.

"Where is Miss Milbank?" he said sharply. "Send someone up to her room and tell her to come down at once."

"I am coming now," Aria said quickly, before McDougall could answer.

"You are late," Dart Huron said. "I was wondering what on earth had happened . . ."

He stopped. She reached the last two steps of the staircase, and he stood for an appreciable moment without speaking. She came down on to the floor of the hall and walked towards him, her dress shimmering and glistening beneath the chandeliers, the soft frou-frou of its silken petticoats rustling as she moved.

"You look very beautiful!"

"I expected you to be surprised," Aria said with a flash of humour that she could not help and a little curl of her lips which made her seem unusually provocative.

"Everyone is waiting to see you," he said. "I thought perhaps you had backed out on me."

"I couldn't do that, could I?" Aria asked a little sharply. "Not until I had been paid."

She didn't know why she wanted to strike at him in a manner which she knew would make him angry, and yet perhaps it was because, womanlike, she resented his surprise at her changed appearance even while she was flattered by it.

"You are not as sweet as you look," he said as they reached the drawing-room door.

As she had no opportunity of replying to him she felt that he had the last word.

Dinner was the first meal that Aria had ever really enjoyed at Summerhill. She was seated on Dart Huron's left; Lord Buckleigh was on her other side. A new dress and perhaps the flattery and adulation of the other guests went to her head like wine.

She, who had sat silent at so many meals, now

166

sparkled and chattered, laughed and made repartee, and found that it was all very exhilarating and as frivolous and inconsequential as a glass of champagne.

"I have found out the truth about you at last," Lord Buckleigh said in a low voice.

"What is that?" she questioned.

"That you are really a witch in disguise," he said. "You were testing us to see whether we should recognise you and now you appear before us in your true colours. Don't laugh at me, it's driving me mad."

She looked at him from under her eyelashes.

"Why should my laughter do that?" she enquired.

"Because you know what I want," he answered a little roughly. "I want you! I want you to come away with me. Do you think any of these fools here care for you like I do?"

"I don't think you know the meaning of the word," Aria replied. She was flirting for the first time in her life and enjoying every moment of it.

It was only when dinner was halfway through that she realised that Dart Huron was strangely silent. Lord Buckleigh was engaged in conversation by the woman on his left and she had perforce to turn towards Dart Huron.

"What have you done to yourself?" he enquired.

"Am I any different?" she asked with mock innocence.

"You know exactly what I mean," he said. "It isn't your dress, although that's pretty enough. It's you. You are a different person tonight."

"I have a part to play," she said. "Would you have me give an indifferent performance?"

His lips tightened for a moment as if he would have said something scathing, but the Ambassadress on his right bent forward to speak to him and there was no chance of further conversation.

As soon as dinner was over, outside guests began to arrive from neighbouring houses. Aria was kept busy shaking hands and being introduced.

People who yesterday would have ignored her very

existence today were tumbling over themselves to make her acquaintance. But once everyone had arrived she was free, free to dance with whoever claimed her first—and at this Lord Buckleigh was an expert.

"I had no idea you were so tiny," he said, holding her very close to him so that she had to throw back her head to look up into his eyes.

"I am so very sorry you are disappointed."

He drew her even closer and held her hand so tightly that the fingers were bloodless.

"You know what I feel about you," he said. "I love you! You know that."

"Hush!" Aria looked over her shoulder apprehensively. "If you speak so loud, people will hear you."

"Do you think I care what they hear or what they say? I am going to see Dart Huron tomorrow and tell him the truth. That I love you and——"

"That you don't intend to marry me nor I you," Aria finished for him.

"That's not true. I would marry you by special licence if——"

"If! If! If!" Aria said. "There are so many 'If's,' aren't there? If we had any money; if we loved each other—or, rather, if I loved you. No, there's no future for us and well you know it."

"When you look at me with your witch's eyes I can think of nothing except that somehow I will possess you —whatever the cost," he answered.

There was so much passion in his voice that Aria realised that he was really roused for the first time. This was no playboy flirting with love, seeking a brief, inconsequential *affaire*. This was a man who really seemed to be awakening to love.

There was no chance to answer him or to say more for at that moment the music stopped and they found Dart Huron standing beside them.

"May I be permitted to claim a dance?" he asked Aria with a sarcastic note in his voice.

"But, of course," she answered.

"You have been so preoccupied," he said, "that I

haven't liked to interrupt your tête-à-tête with Tom. However, as, doubtless, people are talking, it would be wisest for us to take the floor together."

"It is the first time I've ever known you worry about what people are thinking, Dart," Lord Buckleigh said. But he walked away and Dart Huron put his arm round Aria's waist.

It was a tune she particularly liked. She swung into the rhythm of it, realising almost at once that, as she might have expected, he was a magnificent dancer.

Lord Buckleigh had only really propelled her round the room, but with Dart Huron she was made to dance, following his steps with a sense of almost breathless excitement as the tempo of the music quickened and they found that, in some curious way, they were almost ideally suited to each other.

"Are you enjoying yourself?" he asked after a moment.

"I am," she said. "More, I think, than I have ever enjoyed myself before at a party."

She spoke simply and without the sarcastic note in her voice which she knew could goad him to anger.

"You are looking lovely," he said. "People are astonished and excited about you. They can't think why they have never seen you before."

"Cinderella is ready to disappear at midnight," she said. "Or, shall we say, when the party ends. Tomorrow she will be back in her rags and tatters, sweeping the hearth."

"But tonight she is Princess Starlight," he said. "Wasn't that what she was called in the story?"

"I think it was," Aria said with a little smile.

"And, if you remember, she thought that the Prince was charming," he said.

She glanced up at him from under her eyelashes.

"All the same, he didn't trust her," she said. "He disguised himself as Dandini—more, I have always thought, for the selfish motive of wanting to have a good time without any responsibility than because he wanted to be loved for himself alone."

"Perhaps he wanted both," Dart Huron said. "And because it was a fairy story he got it."

"Something that never happens, of course, in real life," Aria finished.

"I wonder," he said. "Even in real life the unexpected can happen."

Aria smiled as she thought of his surprise as she had come down the stairs. That had been unexpected, and the fact that they were dancing so close and so well together was unexpected, too. Tomorrow seemed far away, when she must go back to being herself.

Tonight she was Princess Starlight, and she felt as if there were stars in her eyes as she said:

"I don't believe that Cinderella worried about anything except that the ball was the most wonderful party she had ever been to and the Prince said all the right things, so it didn't matter who he was so long as he was kind and sweet to her."

"Shall I be kind and sweet to you?"

She hardly heard the question, it was asked in such a low, rather deep voice.

"You might try—just for tonight?" she replied.

The music came to an end and they stood for a moment looking at each other.

She hated him, Aria thought, but it was hard to go on hating anyone when the ballroom was bathed in a soft, seductive light, there was the scent of the great bowls of fragrant roses arranged along every wall, the music was soft and romantic, and through the open windows there was a glimpse of a moonlit garden with the stars hanging pendant in the sable sky.

"It's my dance now, Dart. You can't be so selfish as to keep her any longer."

It was Lord Buckleigh who spoke and he whirled Aria away in his arms before Dart Huron could reply. They danced round the room once, and before she realised what was happening he had taken her by the hand and drawn her through one of the windows into the garden.

They walked down the centre of the lawn to where a

little arbour, covered in honeysuckle, was silver in the moonlight. Chairs covered with soft cushions had been arranged all over the garden, and in the arbour there was a sofa pulled a little back into the shadows, on which a couple could sit in seclusion without being seen.

Aria seated herself and spread out her skirts.

"I mustn't stay long . . ." she began, but stopped abruptly because Lord Buckleigh, having seated himself beside her, had bent forward to kiss her naked shoulder.

"You are entrancing," he said. "We can't go on like this. Aria, I am really serious. Marry me. I love you and I will make you happy."

"Please, you mustn't say things like that to me," Aria said. "I have told you that I don't love you, and you know, too, that I am engaged to Dart Huron. You're employed by him, and so am I. We must be loyal."

"Loyal! What's loyalty? What's honour? What's anything when one is in love?" Lord Buckleigh said through his teeth.

He would have put his arm around her waist, but Aria rose to her feet.

"I must go back to the house," she said a little unsteadily.

"I won't let you go. I won't let you leave me. I know you despise me because I have made love to you without intending to marry you. I thought, fool that I was, that loving you would be sufficient. But I know now it would never satisfy me. Even if you come away with me, even if you would live with me—it still wouldn't be enough.

"I want you as my wife. I want to own you. I want you to bear my name. I love you, Aria! Oh, God, how I love you!"

He put his arms around her and drew her close to him with a frenzy and a passion that was inescapable. Then his lips were on her mouth. He held her there, captive, for a moment, until gently she stirred and moved away from him.

"It's no use, Tom . . ." she began, only to feel a shadow cross the moonlight and to look round with a

171

start to find that Dart Huron was standing only a few yards away from them.

They both stood silent, feeling there was nothing to say and that words had entirely escaped them and flown from their consciousness. Then Dart Huron moved in closer.

"Go back to the house, Tom," he said harshly. "I shall want to speak with you later."

"But, Dart . . ." Lord Buckleigh began.

"I told you—go back to the house!"

The words came like the crack of a whip. As if he could not help but obey, Lord Buckleigh squared his shoulders and walked away. He moved swiftly out of the moonlight into the shadows of the trees and Aria watched him go. He did not look back.

It was only when he was out of sight that she realised that she was trembling a little, her fingers linked together, her whole body tense. She had not looked at Dart Huron since the first moment when she had seen him standing there and when he advanced upon them.

Now, still keeping her head turned away, she said in a very small voice:

"I think I . . . had better be . . . going back, too."

"What are you trying to do?" he asked.

She raised her eyes at the question, but as the moonlight was on her face, while his was in the shadow, she only had an impression that he was very tall and his shoulders very broad, and there was a tenseness about him as if he were poised on the threshold of something.

"I thought you were different," he said suddenly in a low voice. "I thought you were not like other women. I thought you were cold and indifferent to men. I had a very different picture of you, and now, tonight, you have changed it. You are asking for something, inviting something. Is it kisses that you want?"

She knew then that he was angry, with a strange, uncivilised anger that had something almost savage in it. And then, before she could answer or move, before, indeed, she could realise what he was about, he had taken

172

her in his arms and tipped her head back against his shoulder.

"Is that what you are wanting?" he enquired.

There was something raw in his voice and something brutal about his kiss. His lips were hard, compelling and passionate against hers. She tried to struggle, but his arms were like bands of steel about her slight body.

He held her closer and ever closer. She felt him kiss her wildly and passionately, at the same time so roughly that it was an expression of savagery rather than of any softer emotion.

He kissed her mouth, her closed eyes, her white cheeks, and then her neck. His lips lingered there, seeking the little pulse that was beating wildly, and then finding again the softness of her bruised mouth.

"Please . . . please . . . let me go!"

She tried to cry out the words, but they were nothing louder than the breath against his lips.

"Don't! Please don't!"

His passion was frightening her. It was something she had never encountered before—a man possessed, as it were, by a devil; a man whose self-control had snapped; a man driven only by the wild, surging emotions within himself.

"Please . . . oh, please . . ."

She fluttered and panted against him, her hands pushing ineffectually against his chest, twisting her head to escape his mouth, and finding always that it was impossible and that a moment later she was captive and prisoner beneath his lips.

"Is this—what you wanted?"

He asked the question again, and now his voice was hoarse and for a moment she had a flashing glimpse of the fire in his eyes, as burning and passionate as the kisses that he had rained upon her face.

She struggled and then felt suddenly she could fight no more. She was utterly helpless, utterly weak against his strength.

She was frightened too—frightened to the point when her voice seemed to have died away in her throat and

173

she could only quiver and tremble because her opponent was a man stripped of the veneer of civilisation—primitive and savage in his desires.

"Have mercy . . ."

She heard her voice as if it was the voice of a stranger.

And then, suddenly, her lips were free of his and he threw her from him with a violence that was in keeping with the brutality with which he had held her close.

She fell against the corner of the sofa. Her hands went out to steady herself, but her long dress tripped her and she subsided slowly, a froth of billowing tulle, in a crumpled heap on the floor.

But already he had left her, striding away across the lawns without looking back.

She heard herself give a little frightened sob; and then, as she watched him going, growing fainter and fainter until he vanished into the darkness, the tears of terror that she could not explain, even to herself, began to run down her cheeks.

"How . . . could he . . . how could . . . he?" she whispered.

11

Aria slipped up the back stairs and into her bedroom.

There, with the door closed and locked behind her, she stood trembling. Far away in the distance she could hear the soft strains of music, and outside there was the sound of cars driving up to the house or away from it, the chatter of voices and a sudden burst of laughter.

She realised that she was icily cold, her hands so chilled that when she held on to the back of the chair it was almost as if she could not feel the damask beneath her fingers.

After a moment or two she sat down as if her knees could no longer support her. As she did so she had a glimpse of her reflection in the mirror on the dressing-table.

Her cheeks were very white; but her mouth was red, not with lipstick but from the brutality with which her lips had been bruised and kissed.

Her eyes were dark, with something like terror lurking in the depths of them.

She stared at herself for a long moment, and then with a little moan hid her face in her hands. Could this have really happened to her? She, who had all her life been, not only afraid, but disgusted by any display of emotion and untramelled passion.

She felt as if his arms were still round her. It was as if, with an almost tiger-like fierceness, his lips were still showering those burning kisses on her face while her hands strove ineffectually to push him from her.

Why had she not screamed, she wondered. And knew that her voice had been strangled in her throat, which he had covered, too, with those wild, unrestrained kisses.

She felt herself shiver and yet her eyes were dry and she was very far from tears. She was not even angry, only numb with her own kind of astonishment that this could have happened to her.

After a long time, while the soft melody seemed to mingle with her thoughts, haunting her, taunting her with the very sweetness of it, she rose to her feet and began slowly to take off her exquisite dress of green tulle which Lady Grania Henley had lent her.

Some frugal, practical part of her mind told her that the dress must remain unspoiled. She must not damage it because she could not afford to pay for it.

Strangely enough it showed no signs of the roughness to which it had been subjected.

Aria could feel that her legs and thighs were bruised from the manner in which he had flung her against the sofa and on to the floor; but the dress was unharmed

175

and there appeared not even to be a spot of dust on its twinkling, shimmering surface.

She hung it up in the cupboard and slipping into her cotton dressing-gown sat down in the chair, trying to think, trying to bring the chaos of her thoughts into some resemblance of order.

What should she do? Slowly, as if she almost resisted the decision, she came to the conclusion that she must go away. She could not stay here, even for the short time Dart Huron was remaining in England, and feel that that moment of violence lay between them.

She felt she could not face seeing him again, knowing that his lips held her captive, feeling the imprint of them burning on her face and neck. And yet some proud, resolute part of her character resented the implication that she should play the coward.

Must she run away from something she had contracted to do, an arrangement she had made with forethought, from the decision she had taken, knowing that the consequences might not be pleasant? And yet in her wildest dreams she had not anticipated this.

What was wrong with her that he should treat her in such a manner? What had she done to invite such an insult, both to herself and her womanhood?

Much, much later she realised that the band was no longer playing; the music had ceased. There was no longer the sound of cars outside. There was only silence —the quiet softness of the night.

She got to her feet and went to the window. Should she run away? She had an almost irresistable impulse to leave the house now, while everyone was asleep; to leave no address or message—just to vanish.

Yet even as she thought that she might do such a thing, the conviction came to her that wherever she went, however she strove to hide herself, he would, if he wished to do so, find her.

Again she shivered. Why should she attribute to him such omnipotent powers? the sensible part of her brain asked. But her instinct was stronger than reason. If he wanted her, he would find her.

"He is only making use of me," she told the night.

Somehow the words did not ring true even to herself. Then as she stood there, looking out into the moonlight which touched everything with a magic of its own, making the shadows seem deep and sinister and the lawns and gardens a fairyland of aesthetic beauty, she heard someone come out of the door which lay a little to the left of her window.

The moonlight was full on him. He was bareheaded, his hands were deep in his pockets, and he walked slowly across the grass in front of the house.

She realised he was deep in thought. He walked slowly, and yet it seemed to her with some sort of purpose in his movement, across the lawn, still in the moonlight, until he came up against the huge herbaceous border which blocked his path.

He stood for a moment looking down at it—the flowers a pattern of light and shade with their colour divorced from them by the night. And then suddenly he turned and looked directly up at the house and, so it seemed to Aria, at her window.

She drew back quickly, sheltering herself behind the silk curtains; and yet even as she did so she wondered if he had seen her movement, had known that she had been watching him.

She would have liked to have the strength and courage to draw the curtains again and not to watch him; and yet something stronger than her own wishes held her mesmerised so that she could not take her eyes away from him.

He was standing utterly still; he might have been a statue sculptured on that very spot. What was he thinking? His head was thrown back. She was sure now that he was looking at her room. And yet, how could she be sure of any such thing? It was but a fantasy induced by her fear of him.

And then abruptly he moved away, walking not back towards the house but across the garden towards the drive.

He disappeared in the shadow of the trees and in her

177

imagination she followed him, knowing that he was walking out through the iron gates and on to the Surrey hills.

It was easy there to walk for miles without coming into contact with any human being, and she felt that was what he was about to do.

What devil was he exorcising within himself? she wondered. What thoughts accompanied him as he moved along through the moonlit darkness?

She knew it would be impossible to sleep, and when eventually she went to bed she left the window uncurtained, and she watched the moonlight fade gradually until, so imperceptibly that she was not quite certain when it occurred, the dawn came.

It was then she realised that all through the hours before when she should have been sleeping she had been listening—listening for his return from his lonely walk.

She must have fallen asleep for the last two hours before she was called. When the housemaid knocked, she awoke with a start to find the sun was pouring in through the window, the room bathed in a golden haze.

"I let you sleep a little longer this morning, Miss," the girl said as she set down Aria's early morning tea. "I thought you would be tired after last night. It must have been three o'clock before the band packed up."

"Was it as late as that?" Aria asked vaguely.

"It was, indeed, Miss! I expect you enjoyed yourself. Everyone was saying that you were the prettiest person there."

The girl spoke with undisguised admiration and Aria forced a smile to her lips.

"Thank you," she said softly, and the young housemaid smiled back at her.

"You have all our best wishes, Miss," she said; and then as if shy at having made her expression of goodwill, she hurried from the room without waiting for Aria's answer.

She would need their good wishes, Aria thought, as

178

she rose slowly, realising as she got out of bed that she had not yet made a decision whether or not she should leave. She felt her heart begin to beat almost suffocatingly at the thought that she must see Dart Huron this very morning.

It was too late now to run away. If she went, she must go with propriety, telling him the reason and saying good-bye. Quite suddenly she knew she could not do it. It was one thing to contemplate flight without explanations, without argument. It was quite another to go downstairs and to find him; worse still to take him to task for what had occurred last night.

She knew it was impossible for her to speak of it. It was not only the embarrassment which would be so terrible, it was the thought of arousing again within herself the terror to which he had subjected her.

She put on her plain cotton dress and brushed her hair back from the forehead into some semblance of severity. Last night she had looked alluring, today she would have none of such feminine tricks.

She would appear as she had when he had first seen her, masquerading as someone older than herself, an efficient, level-headed secretary, about whom no-one, she had imagined, would entertain such thoughts and feelings as he had shown last night.

When she was ready she stood hesitating in the middle of the room and realised once again that she was trembling. It required all her resolution to hold her chin high, to open her bedroom door and walk into the passage.

The door of her sitting-room was open. She would have passed it but something outside herself drew her attention to a piece of white paper laid on the blotter.

She walked across to it and picked it up with fingers which seemed to move quicker than her brain. The writing was only too familiar.

I have gone riding. I should like to see you at ten o'clock in the library. D.H.

179

She stared at the message for some moments and then realised it was, in some ways, a reprieve. She could feel her tenseness oozing away from her, her hands were no longer trembling as she put the piece of paper back again on the blotter.

She went downstairs to breakfast. The majority of the female guests breakfasted in their bedrooms anyway, and this morning they had not yet even been called. There was no sign of Lord Buckleigh.

When Aria entered the room there were only two rather pale-faced young men yawning over their coffee.

"We're playing golf this morning," one of them announced to Aria.

"Just the two of you, or are you making a foursome?" she enquired.

Even as she spoke she thought how strange it was she could still speak conventionally, still make the bright, inconsequential conversation that was expected of her, while somehow her whole being rose in revolt against it.

"I must get away! I must! I must!" she told herself.

When breakfast was over, she had little time for private thought. There were a great many arrangements to be made, meals to be chosen, two transatlantic telephone calls to take, and a whole host of other small details to be attended to.

The clock on the mantelpiece striking the hour startled her so that she turned to face it almost incredulously. It could not be ten o'clock! It could not be! And yet it was!

She had a moment of panic when she thought it was impossible for her to face him. What would happen if she disobeyed his command? Would he come in search of her?

That, strangely enough, was infinitely worse than going to him, and almost as if she were drawn by a magnet she walked along the passage and down the stairs into the front hall.

There was no-one about. Somehow she hoped there might have been. She had a longing to speak to someone, anyone, so long as they brought her a moment's respite, delayed even for a few seconds the ordeal that lay ahead of her.

And then her hand was on the library door and, drawing a deep breath, she went into the room.

She had expected him to be seated at his desk, but instead he was standing with his back to the empty fireplace smoking a cigarette. She tried to meet his eyes, tried to look at him as she advanced across the room, but somehow it was impossible.

She could feel the blood rising in her cheeks, she could feel herself tremble, and hated her own weakness.

She wanted to be proud, aloof, indifferent; she knew instead that she was a quivering mass of sensibility.

"I want to talk to you."

His voice was very deep and it seemed to her surprisingly hesitant.

"Yes."

It was an effort to force the monosyllable from between her lips but somehow she managed it.

"You know what I want to say."

"No."

"I think you do."

There was a pause, a silence in which neither spoke, and now at last she was brave enough to look at him. Was it her imagination or did his high cheek-bones seem more prominent than ever, his eyes darker and more inscrutable?

There was something about his mouth, too, and yet she could not dwell on that, could not even bear to think of the lips that had touched hers.

"I want to apologise. You realise that."

The question was almost sharp. Because she had nothing to say she could only incline her head, praying that he did not realise how weak and helpless she felt, while the nails of her clenched hands were digging desperately into the softness of her palms.

He looked at her then suddenly he threw his only half-smoked cigarette on to the unlit fire.

"Oh, hell!" he ejaculated. "You're not helping me,

and I might have expected it. I know that you have got a right to be angry, a right to feel insulted. But let's face it, it's your fault."

"My fault!"

The words were very low and yet the surprise was involuntary.

"Yes, your fault. Do you suppose that your disapproval, your smug disdain, has not got under my skin? I have endured it long enough. Day after day I have seen you watching me and my friends with that impervious aloofness as if you were immune from the ordinary frailty of human beings.

"I told myself that you must have red blood in your veins, too, just like other people. And yet you remained disapproving, divorced from all human emotions."

He spoke jerkily and with a quickness which made his words hard to follow.

"But . . . I don't . . . understand," Aria stammered.

"I think you do," he said. "I've never met anyone like you before. It's . . . it's piqued me, if you like. To know that where other people were eager to please, you were just prepared to do your job and to censure, at the same time with every breath you drew, the person who employed you."

"It's not true!" Aria said.

"Of course it's true," he snapped. "And why should you manage to be so different from other women? With red hair you should be emotional, you should have feelings like every other member of your sex. That was what I told myself. And then, last night, I thought I had caught you off your guard."

He walked away from the fireplace and strode to the window, standing with his back to Aria looking out over the garden.

"I admit the way I behaved was indefensible," he said. "But you drove me to it. I suppose, really, civilisation as far as I am concerned is only a veneer. I'm a savage at heart! There was something about you which drove me crazy. That is the only explanation I can make for what happened."

He waited a moment and then turned round.

"Well, why don't you say something? he asked defiantly.

"There is nothing to say, is there?" Aria said quietly.

"That is the sort of remark you would make," he retorted angrily. "Of course there's something to say. I want to know what you are thinking, feeling. Who are you that you should disapprove of me?"

There was something almost childlike in the question, and yet Aria understood the thought that went behind it.

"You mean that I have not the right to criticise?" she said, her pride coming to the rescue of both her embarrassment and her fear.

"I wouldn't exactly put it like that," he said.

"But that is what you meant, isn't it?" she asked. "By what right has a secretary, whom you have engaged from an agency, an employee who is taking your money, to criticise you, the important, influential Mr. Huron?"

There was a bitterness in her voice now, and he walked back again to the hearthrug before he answered her.

"Put like that it sounds absurd," he said. "And yet, in a way, I must be honest and admit there is some truth in it."

"I don't know quite what you expect," Aria said. "I came here to do a job of work. I have done it to the best of my ability."

"I have often watched your face," he said, ignoring her remark. "I have watched you when people were talking at luncheon or dinner, and I have known all the time that you were sitting in judgement upon what was said and what was done. At first I could hardly believe it was true.

"Then, as I grew to know you better, I saw that you were, indeed, contemplating everyone else as if across a great gulf, a barrier which you intended should be entirely insurmountable.

"I tried to be amused, but somehow it wasn't amusing. I even began to be afraid that I should look at my friends through your eyes and that they would no longer be my friends or amusing to me."

He waited for Aria to say something and after a moment she murmured:

"I am sorry that I should have disturbed you."

"You're not in the least sorry," he shouted. "I don't know what it is, but it seems as if you have been determined to rile me ever since you came here. Perhaps Lulu was right when she said you were a trouble-maker —and yet you have not made trouble in the house, except as far as Lulu was concerned."

"That was not my fault," Aria said, starting to defend herself.

"I must admit that to be the truth," he said, almost as if he grudged her a small victory. "But why, why do you feel like this?"

For one moment Aria contemplated telling him about her father, explaining her suspicion and hatred of Society, telling him about Charles and herself and the struggle they had had to keep going.

And then, before she could speak, he suddenly brought his fist with a crash on to the wooden mantelpiece, which made the ornaments jump and jingle.

"Damn it!" he said angrily. "What are you thinking?"

There was so much fury in his voice and so much fire in his eyes that for the moment he seemed almost demented. Strangely enough his anger did not frighten Aria, instead she felt her own temper rising. She would not be shouted at or sworn at.

"If you speak to me like that," she said, "I shall leave this house."

"If you say that, I . . ." Dart Huron began.

But what he was about to say she was never to know, for even as he spoke the door opened and McDougall announced:

"Sir Charles Milborne, Sir!"

Aria swung round, too astonished for the moment to do anything but stare at her brother as he came into the room.

He was wearing his best suit, she noted automat-

184

ically. It was nearly threadbare, but it had been well cut by a good tailor and he looked very presentable and very unlike his usual untidy self when he worked on the farm in his old corduroys and open-necked shirt.

"Oh, there you are, Aria!"

He advanced towards her and had reached her side before she realised she had said nothing in greeting.

"Charles, why have you come here?" she enquired.

He bent to touch her cheek with his lips before he answered.

"I came up to see what you were up to," he said a little grimly.

"Would it be asking too much that you should introduce me?" a suave voice said from behind them.

Aria started a little guiltily. She had a feeling that this was momentous and at the same time disastrous, and yet there was nothing she could do but effect the introduction.

"This is my brother, Charles," she said a little hastily. "Charles, this is Mr. Dart Huron."

The two men shook hands and then Charles drew from his pocket a rather crumpled newspaper.

"I came for an explanation of this," he said.

He put it down on the writing desk and Aria saw on the front page a photograph of herself standing with Dart Huron on the terrace.

Dart Huron, the international polo player and American millionaire, announces that he is engaged to Miss Nobody of Nowhere, was the caption.

Below was a paragraph explaining that it had been impossible to extract information from Mr. Huron about his future wife apart from the fact that her name was Milbank. She had been acting as secretary and hostess at his house at Summerhill, otherwise he was not prepared to tell the newspapers anything until the announcement should be made formally.

"Joe brought this paper to Queen's Folly last night," Charles told Aria.

Dart Huron gave an exclamation.

"Queen's Folly?" he queried.

185

"My home in Hertfordshire," Charles said stiffly.

"Good gracious! I've been there," Dart Huron said. "The week before last. Somebody had told me about it. I wanted to see the pictures. Actually, I didn't think they were as impressive as the house. It is one of the most beautiful period houses I have seen in my life."

Aria expected Charles to soften at the compliments. Instead he seemed stiffer than ever.

"Queen's Folly is my home and Aria's," he said. "Which is all the more reason for me to resent this sort of publicity about one of my family."

"Your sister told me yesterday for the first time that her name was Milborne and not Milbank," Dart Huron said. "But it did not have any special significance for me. I did not connect her, of course, with Queen's Folly, although I had visited the place and knew by what the guide book told me that the Milbornes had lived there for generations."

"You will understand, then," Charles said, "that as Aria's brother and as head of the family I am entitled to demand an explanation."

"Charles, it was like this——" Aria began.

"I would prefer to have the explanation from Mr. Huron," Charles interrupted.

Aria looked at him in surprise. He was somehow very different from the brother she had thought she knew so well. The hesitant nervousness which had been so much a part of his make-up since his breakdown had gone. Here was a man on his dignity, a man fighting for his family pride, a man affronted, as he believed, quite justifiably.

"I think under the circumstances you are quite entitled to an explanation," Dart Huron said. "But you must believe me when I tell you that I had no idea who your sister was."

"And yet you are engaged to be married?" Charles enquired, a note of incredulity in his voice.

Dart Huron looked at Aria and she at him. For the first time they seemed to be joined together against a common enemy. This was going to be difficult to explain.

"I must ask you, Sir Charles," Dart Huron said after a moment, "to try and understand what will seem to you a very extraordinary chain of circumstances. Your sister came here to me as a secretary and housekeeper at a moment's notice, because I unfortunately had to sack her predecessor."

He spoke firmly as he started his explanation, and then, having got so far, he stopped.

"Do forgive me, Sir Charles," he said. "But I have not asked you to sit down or to have a cigarette."

"I prefer standing," Charles answered. "And I am still-waiting for that explanation."

He was going to be difficult, Aria could see that. And quite suddenly she looked at everything which had happened through Charles' eyes rather than her own. It was certainly rather horrifying, and not particularly commendable.

Lulu Carlo; Mrs. Hawkins' death; Lord Buckleigh; and Dart Huron himself. What strange characters they would seem to Charles, concerned only with whether the kale needed hoeing, the wheat was coming on nicely or the rabbits were eating down the spring wheat. How could anyone begin to explain the peculiarities of the household at Summerhill or, indeed, the strange emotional scene in which she, herself, had been a participant last night.

Then, as she wondered what Charles would think, she heard Dart Huron say:

"And so your sister came here to help me. But now I have asked her to marry me."

Was that all he was going to say? Aria wondered. She looked at him and knew by the expression in his eyes and the twist of his lips that that was exactly all he did intend to say.

"This was rather sudden, wasn't it?" Charles asked.

"My dear fellow! In my country we make up our minds very quickly," Dart Huron said.

Charles turned towards Aria.

"Didn't you think," he began a little ponderously, "that it would have been best to come home first to tell me that you intended to announce your engagement?"

"But I didn't intend to announce it," Aria answered. "It was just——"

"It was just the Press," Dart Huron interposed. "They rushed us before we were really ready for them. We are sorry, very sorry, that this occurred. But there was nothing we could do about it at the time."

"Well it seems to me very unfortunate," Charles said.

He was not as annoyed as he had been, that was obvious. At the same time, having worked himself up into a position of having been affronted, of having his pride and dignity hurt, he was not going to give in too easily.

"There will be no formal announcement," he said, "until everything has been discussed with me as head of the family, and this matter of the name been put right."

"No, no, of course not!" Dart Huron said. "We wouldn't have thought of it. And now, Sir Charles, let me offer you a drink—or coffee, if you prefer it. If you have come here from Queen's Folly you must have had a very early breakfast."

"I should like a whisky and soda," Charles said. "If it is no trouble."

"No, of course not," Dart Huron said, ringing the bell.

"In the meantime Aria had better go and pack," Charles said.

"Pack!"

Both Aria and Dart Huron stared at him in astonishment.

"Of course!" he said. "She cannot stay here unchaperoned. How could she?"

For a moment Aria gaped at him. Then suddenly she felt herself beginning to smile. At that moment he was so like her grandfather. She could see the old man now, rebuking one of his staff for some misdemeanour or speaking sharply to Charles and herself because they had been giggling during family prayers.

Until this moment she had only thought of Charles as needing care and tenderness. Someone who had been hurt and injured and with whom she must be very gentle and almost maternal.

This was a new Charles; one who was assuming the responsibilities which were his by right of birth and breeding; a man to whom authority came naturally.

"I will go and pack," she said obediently. "Have you come here by car?"

"Yes," he answered. "I hired one. It seemed to me the only thing to do."

"Yes, of course," Aria agreed. But at the same time she felt a pang at the thought of what it would cost.

"Wait a minute!" Dart Huron said. "You can't really mean, Sir Charles, that you intend to take Aria away from here now, at this moment."

"But, naturally," Charles answered. "We shall be very pleased to see you, Mr. Huron, if you wish to come to any meal at Queen's Folly or indeed to stay. But Aria cannot possibly remain here, you must see that."

"I am afraid the conventions of English social life are rather beyond me," Dart Huron confessed. "But if you say so, it must obviously be right. However, I don't like to see her go.

"I can understand that," Charles said. "And, as I've already said, you are very welcome to come to Queen's Folly."

"I can't quite get into my head that you really own that exquisite house," Dart Huron said ruminatively, and Aria realised he was not trying to flatter Charles, he was speaking with a note of sincerity in his voice that she knew only too well.

"If I had to settle anywhere in England, I should like to live there. And yet how difficult it would be for me. You have your roots, your background, the place belongs to you. That is what I have wanted, I think more than anything else in my life—to belong somewhere, to feel it was really mine because my ancestors fought and died for it."

Aria's eyes were on Dart Huron's face as he spoke.

189

Charles merely looked embarrassed. This was not the sort of way he thought that ordinary people talked.

"I can't wait very long, Aria," he said quickly. "You know as well as I do that I have got to get back to the farm. There is so much to do."

"I will go and get ready, Charles," she said.

She would have turned towards the door but Dart Huron stopped her.

"Listen," he said. "I don't know quite what your brother wants, but you know as well as I do that I don't want you to leave here. Can we persuade him to stay? If that will satisfy the Mrs. Grundys of Great Britain. Or shall I send for some maiden aunt I haven't got, or invite one or two distinguished ladies who are very good friends of mine to come here tomorrow? Would that make it all right?"

Aria shook her head.

"Charles is right," she said. "I think it would be much better if I went home."

She was seeing, as she spoke, how complicated the whole thing had become. If Charles stayed here even a little while longer, members of the house party would get to know who she really was. It was only a question of time, under those circumstances, before the Press would know too.

Once again there floated before her eyes the headlines which had heralded her father's death. She could see it all being resurrected over again. She could see how both Charles and herself would be dragged back into the limelight of public recognition.

"No! No! I must go," she cried.

She went from the room quickly and ran across the hall. It was only as she reached the staircase that she realised that Dart Huron had followed her. He called her name and she turned her head in astonishment to see he was close behind her.

"You can't go away like this," he said in a low voice.

"But I must, don't you understand?" she said. "And the quicker the better. No one must know who I am. You will just have to say to everyone here that I have disappeared, and to the Press that the engagement is off."

"But why should I say that?"

"Because it is true," she said. "This farce has gone on long enough. I ought never to have consented to it in the first place. It was bound to cause trouble, and you can see how Charles feels about it. Besides, there are other things; things that I cannot tell you now but which will come out unless I disappear. It is the only thing to be done—I've got to go."

"And suppose I say I won't let you?"

He spoke very slowly and she looked up into his face to see a strange light in his eyes.

"I don't know what you mean," she said.

"I think you do," he answered. "I want you to stay, and if you persist in going I might tell your brother the truth."

Aria could only stare at him helplessly.

"You mustn't do that," she said at length. in an agitated voice. "Charles wouldn't understand and he would be furious about the money. I hadn't meant to tell him how I had . . . earned it, anyway. He would think it an insult to his family pride. I hadn't really considered it before, but I see now it was something I should never have agreed to, something rather degrading and shaming."

She spoke almost in desperation, and after a moment Dart Huron said quietly:

"Perhaps you are right."

"I must go, you do see that?"

"Yes, I think I do. And yet it is against all my inclinations."

"But, why? Why?" Aria enquired.

She was standing on the step of the stairs so that her eyes were almost level with his. It seemed to her that his glance flickered over her face, that his eyes rested for a moment on her lips—still bruised and a little swollen from the violence of his kisses.

She felt the colour burning its way into her cheeks.

191

Still, for a moment, she could not move, could not escape his scrutiny.

And then suddenly, to her surprise and astonishment, his expression changed. It seemed to her that something within him galvanised him into action.

"Go, and to hell with you!" he said angrily, and walked back across the hall the way he had come.

He re-entered the library and slammed the door behind him.

12

Lulu Carlo walked into her bedroom and pushed the door to behind her. She had been drinking all the evening and now, at once o'clock in the morning, her eyes were slightly glazed, her cheeks flushed and her silver blonde hair a little dishevelled.

But she was still lovely. As she moved across the floor, the soft, shaded lights seemed to accentuate her beauty so that each reflection of her in the many mirrors which decorated the bedroom showed her from a more alluring, more seductive angle.

She sat down at the dressing-table and stared at her face, but for once she was not concentrating on the perfectly chiselled features, at the clearness of her complexion, or on the exquisite curve of her rather full lips.

"Damn him!"

As she spoke she looked at a photograph of Dart which stood on the adjacent table in an ornate frame of gold set with semi-precious stones. It was only a snapshot taken by a Press photographer at a polo match, for Dart would never consent to enter a studio. But it had caught that arresting quality in his face and the inescapable grace of his lithe body.

"Damn him!" Lulu said again.

She got to her feet and began to walk rather unsteadily up and down the room. Her restlessness and indeed her agitation were sincere enough. But she could not help instinctively over-dramatising her part, throwing back her head so that her neck, rounded and lovely, gave her a swan-like grace, clasping her hands together and then closing them over her small, pointed breasts.

Yet, after a few moments, even her own posturings failed to suit her. She sat down again and started to drum with her fingers on the painted wood of the dressing-table.

She had never dreamed, until tonight, that there was any chance that her plans, so well laid, could end in failure. And now, insidiously, like some awful horror that was inescapable, she had begun to lose her self-assurance, the confidence that all must end well.

She had known from the moment she met him that Dart was going to be hard to catch. And yet she had meant to have him from the very first night that they had been introduced at a party in New York. She could hear her hostess's voice now saying:

"Lulu, you've just got to meet the most attractive man in all America. Mr. Dart Huron—Miss Lulu Carlo."

She had turned almost impatiently from the man she was already talking to and then, it seemed to her in retrospect, her heart had stopped beating. She had heard of him before, of course—who hadn't? She had seen his photographs, she had read about him in the gossip column of every paper she opened. But because his life had not crossed hers she had not been particularly interested.

Lulu had a one point concentration where she herself was concerned. She had known that evening that Dart Huron was going to mean something stupendous in her life, and she never for a single instant imagined that anything could really stand in the way of her getting what she desired.

They had met quite frequently after that first party.

193

But when Lulu had gone to California to sign a film contract, he became engaged to Beatrice Watton.

She could hardly believe it was true when she had opened the papers and seen the announcement of their engagement. Her rage had made her agree to terms which for the first time in her film career did not extort from the company which employed her immeasurably more than they contemplated giving. She was in a hurry and her heart was not in the fight.

"Very well, gentlemen," she said. "Draw up the contract and I will sign it. I'm leaving for New York tonight."

The film company had been astonished. They were also relieved. The arguments with Lulu Carlo, when it came to money, had already made film history.

They usually resulted in shattered nerves, frayed tempers and a nervous breakdown for one or two of the executives, while Lulu invariably emerged triumphant with, in hard cash, exactly what she had her mind on.

She had arrived back in New York in the afternoon and had gone straight to Dart Huron's appartment. She walked in to find that he was out with Beatrice Watton but was expected back somewhere around five o'clock.

She waited and Dart, sauntering into his apartment, had found her curled up on the sofa, looking small, vulnerable and very lovely. She had not berated him. She was far too clever for that. She just told him that because she loved him so much she wanted him to be happy.

Underneath a hard exterior, Dart, like all men of his type, was susceptible to tenderness.

He was used to women who made scenes and clung to him passionately, women who denounced anyone else who had taken their place, and who informed him, not once but over and over again, that they had given him the best years of their lives.

Anything that he had given them in return, such as

194

priceless jewellery from Cartier or Tiffany, was apparently of little consequence.

That evening at his apartment Lulu put on the best act of her life. She was gentle, wistful and apparently utterly unselfish in her desire for him to find all the joy that was possible out of life. She was, at the same time, as alluring and seductive as in any of the films which had captivated the attention of the heart-throbs of world-wide audiences.

"I just had to come and see you the minute I got back," she said, her big eyes raised to Dart's.

"But of course! Why not?" he enquired.

"Miss Watton won't like it," she whispered. "Perhaps we shall never meet again after you are married. But I wanted to thank you for all the happiness you have given me up till now. I knew, of course, that I could never mean anything really in your life, but it has been so wonderful for me just knowing you."

Dart had never known afterwards exactly how it happened, but Lulu was crying softly, and not in the least dramatically, in his arms.

He was never quite certain why he began to kiss her, except perhaps as an act of compassion.

Three days later they sailed for England. They went by ship instead of by air. Lulu was wise enough to consolidate her gains and what, indeed, could be more conducive to intimacy than five-and-a-half days at sea?

"Yesterday is behind us, tomorrow is in front, and now, in the present we are alone together!" she had said to Dart.

They had sat together in the big Royal suite of the liner which was filled, on Dart's instructions, with exotic and fragrant flowers until it had become a veritable bower of beauty.

It was, indeed, a fitting background, he had thought, for Lulu's gold and white beauty, for her love had seemed to anaesthetise him with its soft, sensuous seduction until it was hard for him to think of anything else. And yet he had kept his head.

He admitted that his engagement to Beatrice Watton

195

had been a mistake, but he was not prepared to shackle himself again.

"This is just fun, isn't it?" he said to Lulu, not once but a dozen times. "You have got your life and I have got mine. We couldn't make a go of it together—oil and water don't mix, my dear—but we will enjoy ourselves while we can. We will have fun while I am in England, and when I go back to America and you have to stay behind because of your film, you will go on having fun with someone else."

She had been subtle enough to play up to all his moods; to laugh with him and agree that what they were doing was fun and of no ultimate consequence; to talk seriously or, rather, to listen to him when he talked of his plans for developing his property in South America, for extending American good-will over the whole globe.

And she could be passionate with a fire that equalled and at times surpassed his, when he found the loveliness of her body irresistible and the pouting invitation of her lips impossible to refuse.

But good actress though she was, Lulu was an egotist. Sooner or later her part began to wear a little thin and her real self peeped through the rôle of wistful, innocent girlhood.

Lulu had lived a hard life. No one had ever known and no one would ever be told what she had suffered in her scramble to the top of her profession. She had gone to Hollywood because she had won a beauty competition at Blackpool.

It was one of those crooked, publicity-seeking competitions which bring in a great deal of money and acclaim to those who organise them, and exploit the poor little fools who enter for the glittering prizes. Fools because at the end of all their hopes and aspirations there is nothing but heartbreak.

The prize in Lulu's competition had been the fare to Hollywood.

She was never able to forget the excitement, her sense of exhilaration when she won or the awful pathos and

196

disillusionment of finding, when she arrived in Hollywood, that there was no film contract waiting for her. Indeed, there was nothing waiting for her except starvation and the terror of knowing that she hadn't enough money even to go home.

She had haunted the studios until hunger drove her to take the only obvious method of being able to get a square meal.

But the men who fêted her were of little consequence and she drifted from man to man until, finally, by sheer chance, she met one who was actually working as an assistant to the director in one of the big film companies.

At first he was reluctant to push her forward, to even arrange for her to have a test.

"We're happy as we are, aren't we, honey?" he would ask, when he came back to the squalid little apartment he had rented for her.

It had taken all her cleverness to persuade him that she wanted a part only so that they could both have more money to spend together. And so he had taken her to the casting director.

She could remember so well walking into the big man's office and feeling not anxious but somehow supremely sure of herself.

In the eighteen months that she had waited for this she had somehow never lost faith in her own ability to succeed. She knew that however disillusioned she might be, however hard the way up, she would get there in the end.

She was wearing cheap clothes because she had been able to afford nothing else. But she had youth and a beauty that even amongst the thousands of beautiful women in Holywood had still something a little different about it, that indefinable, elusive quality which makes a star.

"So you want a test," the director had said disagreeably.

"Yes, please."

"I suppose you imagine you can act."

"No, but I think I could be taught."

He had glanced up at her through his heavily lidded eyes. She had seen the look in them, known what he was thinking, and had not been afraid. He was only another man, but this time in a position where he could be of more use than paying for a hamburger or slapping down a few dollars for a night's lodging.

They had come to terms. It had not been as difficult as Lulu had anticipated—in fact it had been surprisingly easy. And the test had been supremely successful.

She had, of course, been given only a small part at first, but it had not been cut and in the next film her name had been among those taking part.

It was then she had changed her name. Not at her own suggestion but at his—the man who was now directing not only her appearance on the screen but her private life, her thoughts, her ambitions.

"You want to capitalise that gaiety of yours," he had said. "You want a name that is frivolous, which makes men think of entertainment, laughter—anything, in fact, except their business and their wives. Something like Frou-Frou—no, Lulu is better."

And so the most alluring star of the century had been born; the girl who could make tired businessmen forget; the girl who was to arouse masculine passion from Yokohama to Alaska. And Lulu was happy.

She had everything in the world she wanted, everything—until she met Dart.

She looked at his photograph now and almost hated him because he still eluded her. She remembered the men who had crawled on their knees to beg her for her favours. She thought of those who had sent her wildly extravagant presents, with even wilder, more extravagant notes.

She thought of the director of her first films, who cried when she left him and then consoled his sorrows, not with drink, which would have been understandable, but with morphine, which ended in his being put away in some obscure home somewhere where nobody ever heard of him again.

Men! Men! Men! Her whole life had been a series of men, and yet she could not get the one she wanted.

She would not believe, when she arrived in England, that it was possible for Dart to be so easily absorbed in a life which hardly included her at all. Not that she wasn't welcome amongst the society he frequented.

Anyone with a world-wide reputation such as hers, who was so successful and so decorative, was accepted as a matter of course.

It became quite an ordinary thing for people to ask Dart to bring Lulu. Nobody worried whether they were or were not living together, the point was that they were both stars in the small firmament of upper class English Society.

They went to dinner-parties, balls, night clubs, small private dances and semi-official luncheons together. At the end of it all, Lulu felt she was further away from Dart than ever before.

Occasionally they would go out alone together—usually to look at the ancient houses for which he had an insatiable predilection.

"I hate ruins!" Lulu cried petulantly.

"They are not ruins, honey," he would answer. "They are relics of an age of elegance which is now lost. That is something I should like to create again—a world in which good manners and beauty went hand-in-hand, and where the bustle and rush and bad manners of the atomic age were unknown."

"Why don't you buy yourself a house, if you feel like that about it?" Lulu asked him.

"I wouldn't belong, would I?" he said quietly.

She didn't understand.

"I would rather say you belonged to me," she said, and was angry because he laughed, not with humour but harshly, as if she had said something absurd. . . .

"I've got to have him! I've got to!"

Lulu was walking again now backwards and forwards across her bedroom floor. She had half hoped that Dart would come to her, but she had known by the way he said good night, that he had no intention of seeing her again.

Suddenly she began to pull off the dress of silver lamé which she had worn for dinner. It made her look like a mermaid, somebody had said, and that the emeralds she wore with it had started thoughts of the sea.

Lulu took off her necklace and ear-rings and put them in the velvet padded case which had been made to hold them. And then she took from its hiding-place at the back of the big wardrobe her jewel box. It was her most precious possession.

In it was the record of all her struggles and all her successes. Diamonds, sapphires, rubies, emeralds—they were all there. A diary written in precious gems; a history in stones, and more valuable than any history book was ever likely to be.

Lulu put away the emeralds. To do so she had to raise one of the trays from the jewel box, and beneath it she saw the small, ivory-handled revolver she always carried in case of burglars.

In America she usually slept with it beside her bed. Here in England she felt safer, but only because she had grown into the habit of hiding her jewel box in different places, changing it day after day and night after night.

She trusted no-one, not even her maid who had been with her now nearly five years. She had a feeling that her jewels were her very life-blood and without them she might fade away or die.

Slowly she took the revolver from the box.

She remembered once that Dart had seen it when they were traveling over on the liner.

"What do you want that for?" he had asked.

She had told him how she always protected her own jewels, and then she had added:

"Besides, it might come in useful. I might one day want to do away with myself."

"Don't talk like that!" his voice had been sharp. "Life is a precious thing. I saw it squandered wantonly in the war and I never want to see death treated lightly again. Remember that! Remember it always!"

She had been impressed by the solemnity with which he spoke, the seriousness in his eyes, as if he was looking back into the past and weeping over what he saw there.

She had thought then, at that moment, that perhaps in this way she would have some hold over him. And now she thought the moment had come.

She took off the last pieces of lace and chiffon that she wore as underclothes, and then she put on her nightgown—as fragile as a cobweb, as transparent and as lovely as the morning mist.

She covered it with a *négligé* of peach-coloured crêpe, with pockets edged with white mink and narrow bands of the same fur on the short sleeves.

When she had buttoned it and tied the belt round her waist, she slipped the revolver almost surreptitiously into the pocket. Then she went to the dressing table and sat down to powder her cheeks until they were as pale as the milky whiteness of her neck, and in contrast her eyes looked very blue.

She combed her hair loose over her shoulders and then, with a last look at herself, opened the bedroom door.

There was only one light burning in the hall, but it told Lulu that she was right in what she had suspected. Dart would be downstairs.

He slept very little, seldom more than four or five hours a night; and invariably after his guests at Summerhill had retired, he would sit reading in the library or sometimes he would take a horse from the stables and gallop away into the night.

It was usually three or four in the morning before he came upstairs to bed, and now, at this moment, she would find him alone.

The satin bedroom slippers she wore made no sound as Lulu walked down the stairs and across the hall. Very gently she turned the handle of the library door;

so gently indeed, that Dart, who was sitting in a big armchair, did not hear her.

There was a reading-lamp at his side and the rest of the room was in darkness. She had nearly reached him before he glanced up and saw her, stepping like a ghost out from the shadows, her silvery blonde hair almost luminous.

"Lulu!" he ejaculated. "I didn't hear you."

"I had to come down and talk to you," she said.

"I thought you were tired," he answered.

It seemed to her that she was dragging him almost reluctantly away from his book. She glanced down to see what it was and saw it was entitled *Country Houses of England* and that on the open page there was a picture of Queen's Folly.

Almost despite herself her voice sharpened as she said:

"Are you still thinking of that tiresome girl?"

"Need we talk of her any more?" he enquired.

"No, because it bores me," Lulu said. "At the same time, I still think you owe me an apology for behaving as you did. Don't think I was deceived for one moment into believing there was anything serious between you —you and that stupid little red-haired idiot.

"Can you imagine anything so ridiculous as her changing her name? Either way she is of no consequence. Could it matter to anyone whether it was Milbank or Milborne?"

"I have asked you not to say anything about that for the moment," Dart said irritably. "You wouldn't have known if you hadn't met her brother while she was packing."

"He's a nice specimen, at any rate," Lulu said spitefully. "Stammering and stuttering as he talked to me. How I hate shy men."

"I shouldn't imagine you've met many," Dart said,

Shutting up his book he walked across to the hearth to switch on the standard lamp on the other side of it.

"Let's talk of something else," Lulu said suddenly.

"Dart, are you really going back to America as soon as you said?"

"I think so," he answered. "I had meant to stay until the end of the summer. I have changed my mind."

"Why?"

"Oh, various reasons," he replied elusively. "I seem to have got myself into a bit of a tangle. If I disappear, people may forget."

"There's no need to disappear," Lulu said. "And as for forgetting, people won't forget what you do, Dart, but they'll always forgive you. Get the Press here and say you made a blurb over that Milbank woman. Tell them it was a joke—a practical joke on me if you like. And tell them we are going to be married when I finish my film."

"That will be making things worse instead of better," Dart said. "Because you know quite well, Lulu, that it isn't true."

"Why do you say that?"

"Because you know that we are not going to get married—now or ever. I'm fond of you and I think you're fond of me. But we are not in the least suited to each other. When I marry anyone, it is going to be for keeps."

He smiled at the word, almost as if he dragged it out of his childhood memories. A word that meant something important, an eternity in a boy's measurement of time.

"But, Dart!" Lulu said earnestly. "You haven't really thought of what it would mean if we married each other. We could be happy, very happy. I like what you like and we could have a great deal of fun together I needn't really do more than one film a year now.

"The rest of the time we could go where you wanted to go—Buenos Aires, California, New York, even London and Paris. It wouldn't matter so long as we were together."

Dart Huron walked across to the sofa where Lulu was seated and sat down beside her.

"Listen, Lulu!" he said. "You've got to be sensible

203

about this. You know as well as I do there was never intended to be a serious ending to our love affair. You came into my life when I had just made a fool of myself over Beatrice Watton. I confess to you what I have never confessed to anyone else—that I never asked her to marry me, she asked me.

"And because I was desperately sorry for her at that moment I couldn't refuse outright. I was a coward, if you like. I evaded the issue, thinking that I would write to her after I had come from the house, or somehow make things not sound so brutal.

"Before I knew what happened she had announced to all her friends at that party that we were engaged.

"The Press were there and there was absolutely nothing I could do about it without giving her what was, to all intents and purposes, a slap in the face from which she might never have recovered.

"She is a neurotic creature, as you know; and so I did nothing until you came into my life and showed me what might have been a cad's way out, but which was, in fact, a comparatively easy one."

Dart paused for a moment and looked down at Lulu's fingers which were curled round his.

"One day," he said quietly, "you will meet someone who will make you really happy. I'm not the right person, I know that. You are very sweet and very lovable, Lulu, but I don't love you as I want to love the woman I marry, and I don't believe, in your heart of hearts, that you love me.

"Wait!" he said quickly, as she tried to speak. "You think you do, but that's only because I am perhaps the first thing in your life that you haven't managed to possess, utterly and completely, at the moment that you wanted to possess it. Admit that's the truth."

"It's a lie." Lulu said hotly. "I love you as I've never loved any man before. I love you not because I can't get you, but simply because I know we were made for each other."

"I wish I could think that too," Dart said quietly. "But I can't. You see, Lulu, there are lots of things

204

about you that I don't really like and I don't understand. Your attitude, for instance, towards your grandmother."

Lulu snatched her hand away from his.

"What do you mean, my attitude towards my grandmother?" she enquired.

"What I say," he replied. "I was thinking about that poor old woman. Do you know what the doctor said when he signed the death certificate?"

"What did he say?" Lulu asked almost defiantly.

Dart got to his feet and moved away from the sofa.

"He said," he replied, "that while it was undoubtedly a case of heart failure, which is the reason for most deaths, what she had really died of was malnutrition."

There was a sudden silence in the room.

"Yes, malnutrition," Dart went on after a moment. "Have you ever thought of the meals that we eat here, Lulu? Those luncheons and dinners we shared on the ship coming over? That night in New York when we had a lot of caviare at fifteen dollars a portion because you said you felt wild and Russian?"

"You are talking like a communist," Lulu said. "If we hadn't eaten caviare in New York but had chosen bread and cheese, it wouldn't have given my grandmother in Putney any more food. Besides, she had plenty of money. I saw to that. If she didn't eat, it was because she didn't want to."

"That isn't true," Dart said. "If she didn't eat, it was because she couldn't get the food. The people where she was living wouldn't take it to her. As you well know, she wasn't capable of going and getting it for herself."

"You've only heard that from the Milbank woman, interfering and spying into my business," Lulu said in a fury. "But, of course, you are prepared to believe her instead of me. I'm not to have a word of thanks or gratitude for all I've done for my family. They were quite prepared to take all the money I sent them and then write complaining letters to say that they never saw me. With the best will in the world one can't be

205

in two places at once. Either one's earning the money in order to be able to send it home, or one's at home starving with the rest of the wasters who can't make a penny piece themselves."

She was spitting out the words in a fury, her voice sharpening and having, as always when she was incensed, an almost Cockney twang to it.

It was then she realised that Dart was just watching and listening to her. She knew what he was thinking. She had not become experienced in men all these years without knowing when they were no longer captivated and she no longer held them spellbound.

Her voice died away. Quite suddenly she was frightened. She rose from the sofa and moved across towards him.

"Dart, Dart," she whispered. "Why are we quarrelling like this? I came down to tell you that I loved you. Help me to forget that there has ever been anything except understanding between us. I love you. You know I love you. Kiss me. Hold me close. I want to be in your arms.

She was touching him and her head was thrown back so that she could look up into his eyes. But his arms did not go round her. There was an expression on his face which she knew only too well as he said:

"It's late, Lulu. I think it's time you went to bed."

"Dart, how can you do this to me?" she said passionately. "Don't send me away. Don't be angry with me. I'll do anything you like, say anything you like, admit I was wrong, if you wish. But don't send me away from you—not now, not tonight."

She beat with her hands against his chest. Still he made no movement to hold her to him. Lulu stepped back a step from him.

"What has happened to you?" she asked. "Why are you like this? I meant something to you once. Have you forgotten those nights as we crossed the Atlantic? Have you forgotten what we felt for each other? What has happened? What has changed you?"

She stared at him a little wildly.

"I love you," she said, and her voice broke on the words.

She moved away from him to where a great bowl of flowers reaching high above her head and stretching out at the sides until it practically covered the table on which it stood was picked out by the light from the lamps.

She stood for a moment with her back to him, her hands, with their pointed red nails, going out to touch first one blossom and then another.

"Roses," she said softly at length. "And carnations. They are so English, and perhaps my favourite flowers. Will you put them on my grave, I wonder?"

"What are you talking about?" Dart asked roughly.

In answer Lulu drew the revolver from the deep pocket of her *négligé*.

"I am talking about death, Dart," she said. "You don't imagine that I want to live if you no longer want me?"

She raised the pistol in her hand as she spoke and held it against her temple. She made a very dramatic and very lovely picture as she stood there, her head haloed by the flowers behind her. There was a faint twist to Dart's lips as he said:

"A splendid curtain to the second act, Lulu. But not entirely convincing."

"I mean it," she said resolutely in a low voice.

"No, you don't," he answered. "You know as well as I do that you are far too lovely and far too shrewd, if you will forgive me saying so, to die by your own hand. You have got everything before you, Lulu; you are at the top of your profession; you are a world-famous figure; you are a very rich woman; and you are still young. What more could anybody ask of life?"

"I love you," she said. "If you will not marry me, I shall kill myself here and now."

"That would be very messy, wouldn't it?" Dart said. "And you wouldn't even look pretty lying in a crumpled heap with blood all over your face and a nasty hole where your eyes ought to be. And suppose you merely wounded yourself. What would happen then? Your scarred and damaged face will hardly be a box-office draw, even if you were still called Lulu Carlo."

Lulu lowered the revolver.

"You think you are talking me out of it," she said. "But you are mistaken. As I told you, I intend to kill myself unless you marry me."

"Do you think we should be happy if I did?"

"Yes, we would," Lulu snapped. "You can't get out of it that way. You know we should be happy. We have been happy these last weeks, haven't we? Deliriously happy until . . . Yes, until that woman came— looking down her nose, disapproving of everything here, interfering. A prying bitch if ever there was one."

"Stop! You are not to talk like that. Do you hear me?"

There was anger in Dart's voice now, an anger which seemed to vibrate across the room between them. And when he had spoken where was a sudden silence. Then, wide-eyed and in a voice as loud as his, Lulu said:

"And why shouldn't I? Because you are in love with her! Is that the truth? Is that the meaning behind all this? The reason for your sudden coldness to me? You are in love with her! Yes, that's it. I tell you, you love her! You love her!"

"And if I do?"

Dart's question seemed to come as if startled from his lips, and there was the sound of a scream that was drowned by the noise of an explosion.

The sound of a shot reverberated round the room; it was followed by another . . . and yet another.

13

Aria woke and could not for the moment remember where she was.

Then, in the light seeping through the thin curtains which covered her window, she saw the outline of her bedroom at Queen's Folly.

Even then she could not comprehend that she was at home.

Then gradually her eyes took in the threadbare silk on the walls, the unfaded patch where the picture had once hung, the cheap wooden furniture which replaced the walnut and rosewood with which the room had once been furnished, and the plain, unframed mirror which stood on the dressing-table.

Yes, she was home and sleeping again with only the ghosts of the past glories to remind her how beautiful the house had once been.

"I am at home," she said aloud, as she rubbed the sleep from her tired eyes.

It had been dawn before she slept. The hours had passed slowly as she had tossed and turned in her narrow bed.

Repeating and re-repeating in her mind the conversations that had taken place in the past weeks and remembering all too vividly, as she tried to thrust it from her, that moment of madness when Dart Huron had rained wild, passionate kisses on her lips and neck.

As if she would escape from her own thoughts, she sprang out of bed and drawing back the curtains stood for a moment looking out over the unkept garden. In the distance she heard a tractor starting up and knew that Charles would already be at work.

Then she began to dress herself.

Last night had been easier than she had anticipated because Betty. Tetley had been there and Charles, with his usual instinctive reserve, would not speak of family matters in front of a stranger.

But Aria knew that he was suspicious of what had occurred at Summerhill. He was not so obtuse or taken up with his own concerns as not to realise that someone like Aria did not become engaged to be married under a wrong name or forget to tell the man to whom she was engaged anything about herself.

As they motored back to Queen's Folly he said, "Are you going to tell me about it?"

She had known exactly what he meant, and she answered quietly:

"Not at the moment."

He nodded his head as if he had expected that particular answer from her, and then said:

"Have you ever known me to lie to you?" Aria enquired, a sudden sharpness in her tone.

"No," he replied. "And that is why I don't want you to begin now. But if I can help you, I am here."

The sudden tenderness made the tears start to her eyes. This was a Charles she did not know, a brother who was not evading his responsibilities, but assuming them.

They had said little during that drive home, and only as they turned down the drive at Queen's Folly and saw the house, breathtaking in its warm, red beauty, with its peaking gables and chimney pots silhouetted against the sky, did Aria regret that she had not unburdened her heart.

Then it was too late and she could only put her hand and lay it for a moment on Charles' knee.

"Thank you," she said softly, and she knew by the smile he gave her that he understood.

But however easy it might be to speak calmly to Charles, to tell him that she had no explanation to make, to try and tell herself that everything was over and done with, she could not prevent or control the chaotic tumult of her mind.

210

She was miserable, with a kind of aching, inner misery that she had never known before. She could not quite understand it or explain it to herself. She wanted to be glad that she had come away from Summerhill, glad that she had escaped from the whole unsavoury and unpleasant set-up.

But instead she could not feel anything but an abject depression.

She kept hearing Dart's voice, kept seeing his face as he had looked at her that last moment at the bottom of the stairs. And then, for some unaccountable reason, she wanted to cry.

She dressed quickly, feeling a sudden urge to be outside the house, to busy herself by making acquaintance with all the familiar objects which she had left such a very short time ago, but which seemed, somehow, to have become nearly strangers to her.

Almost automatically she put on her old tweed skirt and a jumper that had faded through age and Nanny's constant washing. She combed her hair and avoided looking in the mirror.

She had a fleeting impression of a very white face, with eyes underlined by purple shadows, of a mouth that drooped wistfully at the corners; and then she had turned away and run down the stairs.

Nanny was in the kitchen; but old though she was, her ears were sharp. She heard Aria come into the sitting-room and called out:

"Your eggs will be ready for you in a moment, dearie. There's a letter on the table. The postman's just been."

"A letter for me?" Aria enquired in surprise.

She wondered who had written, but one glance at the envelope, with its bold, rather characteristic handwriting, sent the blood rushing into her cheeks. She picked it up and knew that her hand was trembling. He had written to her—why?

As she slit open the flap of the envelope, she knew the answer. Inside was one sheet of writing-paper folded over a cheque. For a moment the words written on the paper seemed to swim before Aria's eyes. Then her vision cleared and she read:

"I must thank you for fulfilling your part of the contract. I enclose my side of it as arranged. Dart Huron."

Aria stared at the letter and slowly sat down in the chair, reading the words over and over again. Almost automatically she opened the cheque.

It was, as she had expected, for three thousand pounds, and with a sudden surge of pride and resentment she made a gesture as if to tear it up.

It was at that moment that Nanny came into the room carrying a plate of eggs and bacon.

"A cheque!" she exclaimed, with the familiarity of a trusted friend of the family. "That's good news, and I was expecting it to be another bill. Who's it from, dearie?"

Without saying a word Aria handed her the pink form. Nanny took it from her, stared at it, her eyes widened in astonishment, and though her lips parted, it seemed for a moment as if no sound would come from them.

"Three thousand pounds!" she exclaimed at last in an awed tone. "But what can it be for and why is it made out to you?"

"Tear it up," Aria said wearily. "I cannot accept it."

"It is a present then?" Nanny enquired. "From Mr. Dart Huron? Why should he be giving you a present like that?"

The sudden sharp suspicion in her eyes and in the tone made Aria shake her head and give her lips a faint twist, a mocking reflection of a smile.

"It's not for what you think, Nanny," she said. "He is not interested in me—except so long as I served a useful purpose. He asked me to become engaged merely to save him from having to admit an engagement to another woman. If I did that, he was prepared to pay me three thousand pounds."

212

"So that is the explanation," Nanny said. "As I said to Mr. Charles last night after you had gone up to bed, there was something wrong somewhere—I could see that as plain as in your face. I haven't looked after you all these years, dearie, without I knew when you're happy or unhappy."

"I couldn't talk about it last night," Aria said. "I am sorry, because I knew you were wanting to hear all about it. It's just that I couldn't talk."

"I understand. We all gets like that at times. Three thousand pounds! Think what it would do to this house. Think what it would mean to the farm."

"Yes, I know," Aria said, "and that's why I agreed to his suggestion at the time. But I can't take the money, I can't Nanny."

She felt the tears suddenly welling into her eyes and there was a break in her voice as she spoke the last words. Nanny gave a little sigh.

"I expect you knows best, dearie," she said. "But t'would mean a great deal of difference to you—and Charles."

"Yes, I know," Aria said. "Can't you understand that is just why we can't take it? It would be charity, or worse still, it would be gaining money by what is really false pretences. I have run out on him, or rather Charles made me leave and so I am not entitled to be paid for something which is only half done, half finished"

She walked across to the window as she spoke and stood looking out, hiding from Nanny the fact that the tears were running down her cheeks.

"Well, if that's how you feel," Nanny said, "there is nothing more to be said, is there? Tear it up, dearie. I've always said as how there was no money in the world that could heal a sore heart."

"A sore heart!" Aria said. "Is that what I'm suffering from?"

She felt the depression that had hung over her all night weighing her down. Desperately she tried to

213

thrust it aside, to whip her emotions into anger rather than despondency.

She hated him, she told herself. Hated him for writing as he had, for insulting her with his money. And yet in justice she had to admit that it was, from his point of view, a debt of honour that he must meet.

"Now come and eat your breakfast," Nanny commanded. "I remember my old mother saying that things never seemed so bad after a meal, and that's true enough, so come along before your eggs get cold."

Reluctantly, feeling the last thing she wanted to do was to eat, Aria sat down at the table. For Nanny's sake she made the pretence of eating, sipping at the cup of hot, but weak tea poured out from the brown teapot.

There was a knock at the back door.

"I expect that's the newspapers," Nanny said.

She hurried off and Aria heard her talking to the boy who brought their newspapers every morning on a bicycle. "Sir Charles says how you were two days late last week with the *Farmer and Stockbreeder*. Don't you be forgetting it this week. Thursday's the day we should get it."

"I can't bring it before it comes in, can I?" the boy answered impertinently.

"Well, tell your father what I've said," Nanny commanded, and shut the door with a slam.

She brought the newspapers—the *Telegraph* and the *Daily Express*—and set them down on the table beside Aria.

"That reminds me," she said conversationally as she did so. "My pools haven't come this morning. I was planning to myself half the night how I would fill them in. One day I shall bring off that big dividend, you see if I don't

"I am sure you will, Nanny," Aria said almost automatically.

This conversation was one which repeated itself week after week until she knew every word of it.

She put down her knife and fork and as she did so caught sight of the headlines of the paper laid in front of her. For a second she could only sit very still as if turned to stone.

"WELL KNOWN AMERICAN SHOT BY FAMOUS FILM STAR," she read. She could hardly take the words in, and then her hands went up towards the paper. Tremblingly she held it before her eyes.

There was a picture of Dart Huron in his polo kit. Theer was another of Lulu Carlo, wearing the exotic semi-naked Oriental clothes she had worn in her last film. Aria could only stare at the photographs, and then, after what seemed to her an aeon of time, she started to read the letterpress.

"Mr. Dart Huron, the internationally famous character and crack polo player, was found badly injured last night in the library of Summerhill House in Surrey. He was discovered by Mr. McDougall, the butler, who entered the library after hearing two or three shots fired in quick succession. He found Mr. Huron lying on the floor and Miss Carlo, the famous film star who has been called the most alluring woman in the world, standing by him with a revolver in her hand. A doctor was fetched and the police visited the house later. They both refused to make a statement to the Press."

There followed after this a long description of Dart Huron's wealth and possessions in America, of the various films in which Lulu Carlo had appeared; but Aria did not read any further. She could only sit trembling, the newspaper rustling in her fingers, every vestige of colour drained from her face.

It was then that she knew what she must do. She must go back!

She got to her feet almost instinctively, even as Nanny, coming into the room to collect the dishes, saw the expression on her face and exclaimed:

"What is the matter, dearie?"

"Mr. Huron has been shot," Aria said, and was somehow surprised that her voice sounded so normal, so unhysterical.

"Good gracious and who has shot him?" Nanny asked, drawing her reading glasses in their black case out of the pocket of her apron.

"I must go to him," Aria said; and now her voice sounded strange and far away, the voice of someone she did not know, a voice that seemed to speak without her conscious volition.

Nanny was reading the newspaper and clucking with her tongue as she did so.

"It's a good thing that you're away from there, if you ask me," she said. "Such goings on. Charles was right to fetch you when he did. He said he didn't approve of what was happening. I should think not, indeed!"

"Nanny, I have got to go to him."

Nanny raised her head in surprise.

"Go to Mr. Huron! But how can you, dear? He's bad, if the papers are to be believed."

"You don't understand," Aria said. "I've got to find out what has happened. I've got to run the house, look after the servants. Who else will do it?"

Nanny opened her lips to speak and suddenly was all solicitude.

"Now, you sit down, dear, while I fetch you another cup of tea," she said. "It's been a shock, I can see that. It's a pity we haven't got a spot of brandy in the house. I gave the last to Charles for that calf that was so ill."

"I don't want any brandy. I don't want anything," Aria argued.

"You're as white as a sheet," Nanny contradicted. "A nice hot cup of tea with a lot of sugar in it—that will do you good."

"I am quite all right," Aria said irritable. "Can't you understand that I can't wait about here? I have got to go to Summerhill."

"And what will Charles say to that I should like to know? He was upset enough when Joe brought the paper up to the house two evenings ago.

"That's Aria, Nanny," he said to me.

"So it is!" I exclaimed.

There was no mistaking that is was you, even though

216

the photograph was none too good. He read everything that was written about you without saying a word. Then he gets up to go to bed.

"I'll fetch her home tomorrow morning, Nanny," he says."

Nanny stopped talking suddenly. She realised that Aria was not listening, only staring at the picture of Dart Huron.

"You had better stay away, dearie," Nanny said uncertainly.

"I love him."

The words seemed to burst from Aria's lips.

"I love him, Nanny, and I didn't know it until this moment."

"There now, dearie, you're overwrought," Nanny said.

Aria jumped to her feet.

"I love him!" she repeated, her voice stronger now and seeming to echo round the room. "I thought I hated him, but I was wrong. I love him, and though he doesn't care anything for me I have got to help him now he is ill. What will happen to her?"

Nanny looked down at the seductive picture of Lulu Carlo. "I don't know," she answered, shaking her head.

But the posters on the London hoardings gave Aria the answer.

"*Lulu Carlo arrested,*" she read, as she stepped out of the bus which had taken her as far as Hyde Park Corner. She got into another which took her to Victoria. There she caught a train to Guildford, having first telegraphed to tell McDougall the time of her arrival.

As she expected, a car was waiting for her. The young chauffeur who was driving it was one she hardly knew at all well and so said nothing to him other than "good morning."

Summerhill looked just as she had left it. The garden was ablaze with blossom as they turned in at the drive and McDougall was waiting for her on the front steps.

"Good morning, Miss. I'm glad to see you," he said. "I think I ought to warn you there are a number of the Press waiting in the morning-room."

"How is Mr. Huron?" Aria asked.

The question had been trembling on her lips and she wondered if the words sounded as strange to McDougall as they did to herself.

"He's as well as can be expected," McDougall answered. "There are two nurses with him and the doctor has just left. Would you like to go up?"

"I think I will wait a moment," Aria said.

She walked across the hall and into the dining-room. It didn't seem possible that she had been gone only twenty-four hours. She felt as if a whole lifetime had passed since she had left this house, driving away with Charles after those last bitter words with Dart Huron at the foot of the stairs.

"Can I get you a glass of sherry, Miss?" McDougall asked in the doorway.

"Yes, please," Aria said.

She did not in the least want anything to drink, but she thought it would dispose of him for the moment. She wanted a few seconds in which to collect herself, to steady the flurried beating of her heart.

She had not realised until this moment what an ordeal it was going to be to come back to Summerhill knowing, as she knew now, that she loved the man who was lying ill upstairs. She had left Queen's Folly impulsively, disregarding Nanny's protests, without saying good-bye to Charles—driven by an urgency which would not be denied.

On the way in the train she had thought of only one thing—that she must get to Dart Huron, she must help him, she must be beside him.

Only now that she was here did she realise how difficult it was going to be. He had nurses and doctors to attend to him. He did not really want her. And now she had come, what was her position?

She had known in the train, as the wheels seemed to repeat his name over and over again, that she loved him enough to brave the headlines, the publicity and the searching questionnaire with the Press.

She was well aware that she had only to stay in

Queen's Folly, to keep out of sight, and there was every chance that she would be forgotten in the general turmoil and excitement over Lulu.

All the horror she had experienced over her father's death was revived again now as she saw Dart Huron's face on every newspaper, Lulu's name on the posters, and knew exactly what would be waiting for her at Summerhill.

She could remember that interrogation in the hotel at Monte Carlo all too vividly. She could remember the quick, searching questions, the flashing of the photographers' bulbs, the shrill, insistent cry of the telephone, the curious glances of the other guests, the whispering which took place every time she appeared.

Was she prepared to go through all that again? She asked herself the question as she stood in the beautiful, long drawing-room with its windows opening on to the terrace.

It seemed for the moment to be very quiet; the sun was making a pattern on the carpet; a butterfly tapped against a pane of glass.

And then suddenly she knew that nothing mattered except the man who had been hurt. He did not care for her, but she loved him enough to know that the only happiness she could ever know was to serve him, to do what she could to alleviate his pain, to take any worry from his mind.

McDougall came back into the room with a glass of sherry on a silver salver. She thanked him with a smile.

"It's all right, Miss," he said in conspiratorial voice. "Nobody knows yet that you've arrived. I didn't show the telegram to anyone."

"That was good of you, McDougall," Aria said. "But I'm not afraid. I want to help Mr. Huron."

"I thought you'd feel like that, Miss," McDougall replied. "As soon as I got your telegram I thought, 'She's the one that'll stand by him in this trouble.'"

Aria felt herself almost flush at the compliment. Then she said quietly:

"How bad is he?"

"Better than we expected, Miss. One bullet went through his arm, the other through his shoulder. The third missed altogether."

McDougall shrugged his shoulders.

"But why . . . why did she do it?" Aria enquired.

"I'm afraid that's something we shall never know, Miss. The police arrested her this morning. She kept saying as how it was an accident and she meant to kill herself, but I don't think they believed her."

Aria drew a deep breath.

"She might have killed him," she said.

"That's what we all felt," McDougall answered. "When I found him lying on the floor, I thought at first he was dead."

"Will you find out if I can see him?" Aria asked.

"I'll go upstairs right away," McDougall replied. "If you ask me, Mr. Huron will be glad to hear you are back."

Aria could only pray that this was true. Suppose he was still angry with her? Suppose he commanded her to go away? She felt herself tremble at the thought. And yet her only feelings, as she crossed the threshold to Dart Huron's bedroom, were anxiety for him.

She had forgotten herself completely as she moved across the big room to where he lay in a four-poster bed.

The curtains were drawn, but it was easy to see him lying there, his dark hair silhouetted against the whiteness of the pillow, his arm and shoulder heavy with bandages.

"Here's Miss Milbank to see you," a nurse said gently, gliding out of the shadows towards the bed, her starched apron rustling as she moved.

Aria drew nearer and realised as her eyes grew accustomed to the darkness that he had turned his head to look at her. His eyes seemed very dark; it was difficult to guess what he was thinking.

"Oh, you've come back," he said in a low voice.

"I thought I might be of use," she said humbly.

"I've wanted you."

She suddenly felt a sudden ecstasy of delight that he should admit his need for her. She said quietly:

"I will stay if there is anything I can do to help, you know that."

"I want you here."

It was more of a command than a statement, and for the first time Aria realised that she was welcoming his masterfulness rather than resenting it.

"He mustn't talk too much," the nurse said from the other side of the bed.

"I understand," Aria replied.

She turned again to Dart Huron.

"I will see to everything," she said. "Don't worry."

She turned and went from the room into a world which suddenly seemed golden. He had wanted her! He needed her! That was all she wanted to know.

Downstairs the Press were waiting and she knew that now at least she had the courage to face them. She went into the morning-room and they jumped to their feet.

"Miss Milbank!" someone exclaimed.

"Milborne." Aria corrected. "The reports which appeared in the newspapers the other day were most inaccurate." She smiled at the curious faces around her. "I am not Miss Nobody from Nowhere. I am Aria Milborne, daughter of the late Sir Gladstone Milborne."

"Not *the* Sir Gladstone?" somebody questioned.

"I am sure by the sound of your voice you are referring to my father," Aria said with a smile. "But let us make one thing quite clear. There is no possibility at the moment that Mr. Huron and I will be able to announce our engagement. We are old friends and there is, if you like to put it that way, an understanding. That is all."

She turned as if to go, but the reporters were on her like a swarm of bees.

"Miss Milborne, we must know more . . ."

"Please tell up . . ."

"When you say . . ."

Questions were being fired just as she remembered them. But somehow they had lost the power to hurt her.

221

"Be reasonable," she said. "I have said quite a lot. It isn't fair to ask me any more at this moment. I shan't run away. I shall be here. You know as well as I do that you've got enough copy for today. Your editors can't fail to be delighted with it."

They laughed at her joke and one reporter raised a glass of beer in her direction.

"Your health, Miss Milborne," he said. "You've brought a touch of humor into these proceedings and one which has been much needed for some time."

They all laughed at that and Aria made good her escape.

Upstairs she went back to her desk. There was a pile of cables, and already quite a number of letters had arrived, all of which wanted answering. She was so busy that she did not hear the door open and only looked up to find Lord Buckleigh halfway across the room towards her with his hands outstretched.

"You're back! By all that's wonderful, you're back! Where did you spring from and why wasn't I told?" he asked.

"I thought I might be needed," she answered demurely.

He took both her hands in his and raised them to his lips.

"I should think you are," he said. "There were three calls in Spanish and one in German this morning. I couldn't understand a word of any of them."

Aria could not help laughing. "You see I have my uses."

"You know I didn't mean that," he answered. "But I thought you had gone for good."

"I thought I had, too, until I saw the papers this morning."

Lord Buckleigh's face darkened. "Damn the woman!" he said. "It's fortunate that she hit his left arm, but even so he won't be able to play polo ever again."

"Why did she do it?" Aria asked.

"We none of us know," Lord Buckleigh replied. "She says it was an accident. But no accident that I've ever

222

heard of would fire three bullets from the revolver in quick succession."

"What will they do to her?" Aria asked.

"She'll stand her trial, I suppose. She'll get a year for a certainty."

"A year in prison?" Aria asked in horror.

"That's what the solicitor thinks. I've just left him. She is briefing the very best counsel available, but British judges and juries are very against people carrying revolvers. And needless to say she hadn't a permit for it."

"Where is everyone else?" Aria enquired. "I mean the people who were staying here?"

Lord Buckleigh grinned and there was a twinkle in his eyes as he answered:

"They scuttled like rabbits. The Ambassador went first explaining that, of course, in his position he couldn't be too careful. And for the rest, I never knew they could get up so early. We are the only ones left—you and I."

"Oh, that's a good thing," Aria said. "Because I have got a lot of work to do."

Lord Buckleigh glanced down at the pile of correspondence on the desk. "You've got to look after me as well," he said. "Dart can't have all the attention."

"What's wrong with looking after yourself?" Aria enquired.

"Everything, and I wouldn't know how!"

His voice was light, but a moment later it was serious again. "There's something I want to ask you."

She had the feeling that the question was going to be one she would not want to answer.

"It's just this," Lord Buckleigh said. "Does Dart care for you—seriously, I mean?"

"No, of course not," Aria answered.

Here at least she could answer in all truth.

"No," she repeated. "I can't think why you should imagine such a thing."

"I had the sort of feeling . . ." Lord Buckleigh began. Then added quickly, "But you would know."

223

"Yes, I should know," Aria replied.

And even as she said the words the hopelessness of them struck her and she knew that not only would she give her chance of salvation for the wonder and glory of knowing that Dart Huron loved her; but also she was prepared, whatever his feelings might be, to sacrifice anything and everything to her love for him.

To follow him, if necessary, barefooted to the ends of the world.

14

Aria put down the receiver after a long and rather complicated conversation in German and turned to her typewriter. But somehow she could not concentrate on the letter she was typing.

She got up and walked across the room to look out over the garden at the mist, damp and rather depressing, which hid the beauties of the valley from sight.

She was nervous and it showed itself in the sudden tightening of the muscles at the corners of her mouth, the nervous fluttering of her fingers as they laced and interlaced each other, the way her thoughts would not concentrate on any one thing.

She had never known the hours pass more slowly. It seemed to her that the day had prolonged itself until each minute seemed to linger in its passing as if time stood still.

Only three o'clock. They should have been back by now. She strained her ears to listen for the sound of a car, but she could hear nothing. And with an effort that was almost superhuman she forced herself to sit down again at the desk, to continue to type the letter where she had left it off.

But after a moment she realised that she was making

mistake after mistake and in a sudden frenzy she took the letter from her machine and tore it up.

She had just deposited the pieces in the wastepaper basket when the door opened. She sprang to her feet and before Lord Buckleigh could even cross the threshold she had run towards him.

"What happened?" she asked. "Is it all right?"

"He's tired," he answered quietly. "But he stood it very well, considering."

Aria looked towards the open door and he added quickly:

"They are bringing him upstairs now. The doctor is with him. You can't be of any help."

Aria gave a little sigh as if he had prevented her from doing something she most wanted to do.

"What happened?" she asked after a moment's pause.

"Lulu got a year's imprisonment," he answered.

"Oh, poor thing!" Aria exclaimed. "I thought Sir Frederick would get her off."

"He did his best. A year was the very least the judge could give her, and, of course, she'll get remission for good conduct."

"I can't bear to think of it," Aria said. "She'll never stand it, will she?"

"She was surprisingly calm when it came to the point," Lord Buckleigh said. "Actually, the sentence, when we heard it, was a relief. At one moment it appeared as if she would get very much more. The prosecuting counsel presented his case very ably."

"I suppose Dart's evidence helped her a lot?" Aria asked in a low voice.

Lord Buckleigh looked at her in a curious manner before he answered.

"I think Lulu helped herself more than anything else. She told the truth, and that was far more convincing than any trumped-up story."

Aria looked at him with startled eyes.

"The truth?" she questioned.

He nodded.

"Yes. Under cross examination she explained exactly what had happened and why she shot Dart."

"But . . . but I thought she always said it was an accident," Aria said.

"That has been her story all along," Lord Buckleigh answered. "And I, for one, never believed it—nor did anyone else for that matter."

"I suppose not," Aria said. "Well, what was the truth?"

Lord Buckleigh took a cigarette from his case and seemed intent on lighting it.

"Dart has not mentioned this to you?" he said.

"No, of course not," Aria replied. "You know how little conversation I have had with him since he has been so ill. Besides, since there were complications over his shoulder, the doctor said particularly he was to talk as little as possible."

"Yes, I know," Lord Buckleigh said. "At the same time I just wondered if he might have said something when you were alone with him."

"I'm never alone with him. Nurse Walters is always there. She has carried out the doctor's orders to the letter. She is right, of course, but I find myself thinking of her as a very efficient watchdog."

"She looks rather like one," Lord Buckleigh said with a grin.

"But never mind about that now," Aria said. "Go on telling me about the case. What did Lulu say?"

"She said," Lord Buckleigh uttered slowly, "that she shot Dart because he admitted to being in love with someone else."

There was no mistaking the effect of his words on Aria. She stared at him with startled eyes, an expression of surprise on her face which could not have been more marked if he had thrown a bomb at her feet.

"In love . . . with . . . someone else," she repeated in faltering tones.

"Yes, Lulu alleged that during a conversation she accused Dart of bringing an end to their love affair be-

226

cause he was in love with another woman. He admitted the truth of this and so she shot him."

"But, Dart . . . what did Dart say?" Aria asked, the words coming from her lips so quickly that she almost stammered them.

"He agreed that what Lulu had said was the truth."

"The truth!" Aria seemed to whisper the words and then, looking away from Lord Buckleigh, she said in a very low voice, "Did he say who the woman was?"

"Yes."

There was a silence that was almost intolerable in its intensity before Aria forced the words between her lips.

"Who was it?"

"You."

She swung round with a passionate intensity, the colour flooding back into her cheeks.

"But it isn't true! How could he say such a thing when it isn't true?"

"That was what he said."

"Then I suppose it was an excuse thought up by Lulu's counsel. There could be no other reason for lying in such a manner and dragging me into it."

"Supposing it is the truth?"

"But it isn't. Of course it isn't. You know as well as I do that Dart announced his engagement to me because Lulu had tried to trap him. She invited the Press here and attempted to force his hand into acknowledging that they were engaged. I've told you what happened. I've kept nothing from you.

"He paid me three thousand pounds to pretend for the time being that there was an engagement. He even sent the cheque to me at Queen's Folly after I had gone. But I tore it up."

"And thereby destroying valuable evidence," Lord Buckleigh said with a grin.

"Don't joke about it," Aria cried. "It isn't funny— not to me, at any rate. But it was a businesslike arrangement. Why should I be dragged in now at the eleventh hour when it was all agreed that my name was not to be mentioned?"

"I know that was what we arranged," Lord Buckleigh said. "Goodness knows, you and I sat long enough with that lawyer going over the facts, trying to find excuses for Lulu, and coming back always to the same conclusion, that her only possible excuse was what she had said originally—that it was an accident, the gun went off in her hand."

"We knew it was weak," Aria said. "But there was no alternative suggestion."

"You never thought that Lulu might tell the truth?" Lord Buckleigh said.

"But it isn't the truth," Aria almost shouted at him. "Don't tell me that you believe such nonsense."

"Is it nonsense?" Lord Buckleigh enquired.

"But, of course it is. Dart has never thought of me as anything except a secretary. He has, in fact, disliked me. He more or less said so, because he thought I disapproved of him and his friends."

"And did you?"

"Yes, of course! I've hated Society ever since my father bankrupted himself and met his death through wantonly extravagant living, through entertaining the same type of people who come here to eat and drink everything they can get hold of and go away without saying 'Thank you.' I don't like Society, I never have. I suppose I was not clever enough to hide my feelings."

"Why should you?" Lord Buckleigh asked. "You are entitled to your own opinions."

"I wasn't paid twenty pounds a week to have opinions," Aria said. "I was paid to run this house efficiently, to make myself a charming hostess. Dart was angry with me about that, and he was angry, too, when Charles came and took me away. His last words to me were "go, and to hell with you"! Does that sound like love to you?"

Lord Buckleigh stubbed his half-smoked cigarette out in an ash-tray.

"Dart is a strange fellow," he said. "I never have understood him and I don't suppose I ever shall. If he ever loved a woman really, apart from his flirtations

228

with pretty butterflies like Lulu, then there is no knowing how he would behave, and I, for one, wouldn't pretend to guess."

Aria was silent for a moment and then she asked:

"Do you really think that Lulu believed that he was . . . fond of me?"

"Unless Lulu and Dart are the most consummate actors the world has ever seen, then they were both of them telling the truth in the witness box," Lord Buckleigh said.

"And yet we know it wasn't the truth."

"You must speak for yourself," Lord Buckleigh said. "I personally believed Dart, at any rate."

"But it is impossible," Aria whispered with a little helpless gesture. "It is quite, quite impossible."

Lord Buckleigh bent towards her and took one of her hands in his.

"I love you," he said. "And I know you don't love me. It is not easy to wish you all the luck in the world and all you wish yourself. Because you are you and the very sweetest person I have ever known, I want you to be happy."

Her fingers tightened over his.

"Dear Tom," she said. "It is the sort of thing you would say, and I think it makes me want to cry. I wish I did love you. It would be so much, much easier."

He raised her hand to his lips and kissed it lightly.

"We can only wait and see what happens," he said. "In the meantime, I am going now to see the Governor of the prison and see if there is anything I can do for Lulu."

"I am glad you are going to do that," Aria said.

"Try not to worry about anything until I come back," he said. "And don't read the evening papers."

"You know they don't even come to this house," Aria answered.

"I wouldn't be too sure about that," he replied with a smile. "I bet the servants have not missed one word of all the sensational claptrap the Press have managed to produce this last day or two."

229

"Sometimes I regret my promise not to read any of it," Aria said with a faint smile.

"No, you don't, he said positively. "You would hate it."

He kissed her hand again and went from the room. When he had gone, she sat down on the sofa and covered her face with her hands.

It was true that she had not read the newspapers this past week. Lord Buckleigh had forced her to promise that she would not do so, and had ordered McDougall to bring none through to the front of the house.

He had understood, because of his affection for her, how besmirched and dirty she felt every time her own name was blazoned, with Dart's and Lulu's, across the pages of the more sensational Press.

It was agony to see pictures of Queen's Folly and old photographs of her father jostling photographs of Lulu's swimming bath at Beverly Hills, of exotic parties taken in night clubs and snapshots of her and her friends lounging half naked on the Riviera.

It was hard, too, to read some of the descriptions of Dart's love affairs; of the women with whom his name had been associated; and to realise that she had joined the long list and that in public opinion she was no worse or no better than Lulu Carlo and her like.

"Why torture yourself?" Lord Buckleigh had said savagely when he had found her in tears over a picture which showed Dart Huron looking his most attractive, while around him in a circle were the heads of every woman with whom his name had ever been coupled.

It was because of this ban on newspapers that Aria had not followed the last-minute excitements over Lulu Carlo's trial and had been concerned only with the difficulty of getting Dart well enough to attend it.

He had trouble with his shoulder as the bullet had splintered a bone and inflammation had set in.

For a less healthy man it might have been more serious than it actually was; but because he was so hard and wiry after long hours in the saddle, because, as one doctor said, he had the constitution of an ox, he was, in an incredibly short time, stronger and better than he had ever hoped.

Even so he had gone to Court today with a nurse and a doctor in attendance and buoyed up by injections and drugs to make him capable of standing the strain of giving evidence.

And that evidence had been something that she, Aria, had never expected even in her wildest dreams. Not for one moment did she imagine it was anything but a lie by which Lulu could extract herself in some little way from the full punishment of the law.

But even so it had the power to unnerve her.

Why, she asked herself must he say that of all things? Why was she dragged deeper into the mire than she was already?

What would Charles, who was already furiously angry that she had returned to Summerhill and had written her long and surprisingly eloquent letters asking her to return home and telling her how shocked and disgusted he was, feel about was being said in the Press.

"Poor Charles," Aria whispered with a sigh.

This would be almost the last straw, and she could not blame him for being angry at it.

At last she had enough control of herself to walk along the passage to Dart's bedroom and knock on the adjoining door where the nurse who was in attendance waited when he was asleep. Nurse Walters, an efficient, middle-aged woman, beckoned Aria into the room.

"I am hoping he is asleep," she said in a low voice. "The doctor has just given him a sedative. He stood it well, but the journey home was rather much for him."

"He should have stayed in London," Aria said.

"You know he wouldn't do that," Nurse Walters replied. "He seems to hate the place. Somehow, before I came here, I always thought the only thing he enjoyed was night clubs."

Aria tried to smile.

"I suppose that is the popular idea of him," she said.

Nurse Walters looked at her in what Aria thought was a slightly embarrassed manner.

231

"I suppose you have heard the result of the case?" she asked a little primly.

"Lord Buckleigh told me," Aria replied. "I am very sorry for Miss Carlo."

Nurse Walters gave a little sniff.

"If you will forgive me for saying so, Miss Milborne, I think she got exactly what she deserves. She was lucky, in many ways, to have got off with a year."

"All the same, I am sorry for her," Aria answered. "Think what it will mean to her being in prison, after the luxurious, wonderful life she has led."

"I expect she will turn it to good account when she comes out," Nurse Walters said. "I remember another film star I was with always used to say to me, "Any publicity is good publicity, Nurse." I couldn't help thinking of that when I saw Miss Carlo smiling at the reporters as she left the witness box. It didn't seem to me she was as upset as poor Mr. Huron."

"Perhaps Miss Carlo was better at hiding it," Aria suggested.

She felt somehow that she must stick up for Lulu, even though she had never liked her. There was something terrifying in thinking of her being shut away from the world she loved, from the adulation and adoration of her fans; of having her beautiful clothes taken from her; of having to work so that her hands were coarsened.

It was no use trying to get sympathy from Nurse Walters that was obvious. She wondered how many more people thought, as the nurse did, almost with pleasure over the downfall of a lovely, alluring woman.

It seemed ridiculous to mind so much, but she could not help feeling that if she had been in Lulu's shoes she would rather die than undergo a term of imprisonment.

Nurse Walters looked at her watch.

"It's nearly four o'clock," she said. "I expect Mr. Huron will sleep for two or three hours. Then the doctor has suggested he has a light meal. I will come and tell you if he wants to see you later this evening, which I am sure he will."

"No," Aria said almost involuntarily.

"Oh, I don't think you need worry about it being too much for him," Nurse Walters went on. "He was better this morning than I have seen him for days. The wound is healing nicely. The doctor is delighted with it.

"I expect he will want a little chat before he goes to sleep. I shan't be as strict as I have been in the past, and you mustn't hold it against me that I tried to keep you out of the sick-room. It was doctor's orders, and in my profession we have to do as we're told."

Nurse Walters was being almost coy, and Aria, with a muttered excuse, fled away from her. She knew only too well what the arch look and innuendoes meant. Nurse Walters was another person who believed Lulu and Dart and were convinced that she was at the bottom of the whole trouble.

"Why? Why?" she asked herself. Why had he done this to me?

It wasn't fair. It was something that she couldn't fight, couldn't battle against all by herself.

She went to her room and had a wild impulse to pack her boxes and go away again. Dart was better, the household was running smoothly, the case was over. What was there to stay for? Just to be thanked once more for doing her duty.

Why shouldn't she go back to Charles and make her peace at home? Queen's Folly was waiting for her. There she would find rest and peace, all the things she had never been able to discover at Summerhill.

And then, as she stood irresolute within her bedroom, she knew that she could not go. She loved him; and so, betrayed by her own heart, she must stay until he had no further use of her.

She knew it was quite useless to talk of finding peace at Queen's Folly or anywhere else. She could never know peace again so long as Dart Huron remained in the world and she could not be beside him.

She thought, with a little smile that was infinitely pathetic, that every woman imagined that her love was deeper and greater than any love had ever been before. And yet she could think of nothing else.

She had never realised that love could turn one's whole body into a battlefield of conflicting emotions; that one could know agony and ecstasy at one and the same moment; that joy and utter misery could go hand in hand.

She loved him and so it was both heaven and hell to be near him. She yearned and longed to see him, and yet, when she did so, it was pain almost beyond endurance because she must control her feelings, her words and even the expression in her eyes.

She dressed slowly for dinner and smiled to herself because she was taking infinitely more pains than usual. Was it likely that he even noticed?

She knew only too well what he would say to her—almost the same thing as he had said every day since he had been ill and she had slipped in to see him for a moment or two.

"Are there any cables from South America?"

"Yes, and I have answered them."

"Good girl. And keep the others quiet until I am well enough to cope with them, won't you."

"You know I will."

"Thank you."

That had been almost the sum total of their conversation. Occasionally she would read him a cable or a message that was more difficult to understand than the others and on which she felt she must have some guidance as to how to answer it.

Otherwise, because the doctor had said he was not to be worried, she told him everything was all right and left it at that.

She put on her old black dress, realising as she did so that because she was worried her skin seemed even whiter and more transparent than usual. There were little lines beneath her eyes, but somehow they enhanced rather than detracted from her prettiness.

The curls on her head seemed to leap into life as she combed them; and then, because the severity of her dress seemed to demand it, she took two large white roses from the flowers arranged on her dressing-table, and pinned them between her breasts.

She could smell the sweetness of their perfume as she walked downstairs for dinner.

They had the usual dinner-party for four—Aria and Lord Buckleigh, and the two nurses—and because the events in Court today hung over them all like a cloud, the conversation was unduly stilted and there were little pauses after which someone began to talk hurriedly on some inconsequential subject.

It was after Nurse Walters had withdrawn "to see my patient," as she put it, that the summons came.

"Mr. Huron would like to see you, Miss Milborne."

Aria started quickly to her feet, and then as she went upstairs she knew that her heart was beating almost suffocatingly within her breast. As she reached the door of his bedroom, she felt it was almost impossible for her to go in.

She put out her hand towards the door knob, and realised it was trembling.

For a moment she stood there striving to get control of herself, ashamed that her breath was coming quickly, that every nerve in her body seemed to quiver.

At length, when she felt that waiting made things worse instead of better, she resolutely opened the door and went in.

To her surprise the curtains had not been drawn. Outside the sun was sinking, crimson and gold, suffusing the sky and casting a strange, rather lovely light over the whole room.

Dart was not, as Aria had expected, in bed, but sitting in a chair by the window, a rug over his knees, a pillow behind his head.

She had expected Nurse Walters to be there, but he was alone; and as she walked across the big room towards him, she was conscious that he was watching her. She drew near, her feet growing slower and slower and yet still carrying her further, until eventually she came to his side.

235

He looked up at her eyes and she saw there was a smile on his lips and a twinkle in his eyes.

"Have they told you?" he asked.

"T . . . told me . . . what?"

"That I have publicly announced my feelings for you."

It was the last thing she had thought he would say.

Because she was so utterly nonplussed, she could only stare at him, the last glimmering of the sinking sun shining on her red hair, the light on her face and on the pain in her eyes.

"Did you have to tell such lies?" she asked at last.

He put out his uninjured hand and took her cold, trembling fingers in his.

"What have they been doing to you?" he asked.

There was a tenderness in his voice that she had never heard before. Because she was so frightened, so uncertain and apprehensive, she felt, to her horror, the tears prick at her eyes.

"Darling, I am a brute to tease you," he said. "I couldn't help what happened today. Lulu, to save her own skin, told the truth; and so, to help her, I had to admit that I love you."

"But, you . . . don't . . . you . . . can't," Aria stammered.

His hand was extraordinarily strong for a man who had been so ill. He drew her forward until somehow, unexpectedly, she found herself kneeling beside the chair, her face turned up to his, his arm around her.

"Are you really so dense?" he asked. "Dear, stupid, disapproving little Aria, who won't listen to anything but the dictates of her own proud heart."

"But you can't really . . . love me. I mean, you don't . . ." Aria said.

"I must have been very ill to disguise my feelings so effectively," he smiled. "I didn't want to say anything to you until after this horrible, unpleasant business was all settled. And, anyway, Nurse Walters has been behaving like a dragon, as you well know."

Aria felt herself giggle a little weakly.

236

"That's better," he said gently. "I want to see you smile. You smile far too seldom, do you realise that? And when you do it's the loveliest thing on earth."

"But, I don't . . . understand."

"How foolish you are, my sweet," he said. "Despite the fact that you speak three languages and can run a house far more efficiently than anyone I have ever met before."

"Is that . . . why you think you . . . love me?" Aria stammered.

"No, that isn't the reason," he answered. "I love you because you've got red hair and the sweetest face I have ever seen on any woman. I love you because I think my heart leapt out of its body and went to you the very first moment of our meeting. I love you just because I cannot help myself, because it is something bigger than me and something I have been looking for all my life."

"But . . . are you sure? Really . . . sure?"

In her agitation Aria put her hands against his chest and threw back her head.

"How can I prove it?" he asked. "Unless you will marry me at once, so that we can go away together. I was sure before I kissed you on the night you drove me almost to madness. I was jealous of Tom because he was obviously so infatuated with you.

I was furious with you because you seemed shocked and disdainful of everything I did and said. And then, when I saw you together in the arbour, something seemed to snap in my brain."

His arm tightened round her before he continued:

"I am not going to be an easy husband, Aria. I am not going to pretend for a moment that I shall be. I have got a savage temper when it is roused. I can be brutal and difficult and altogether exasperating.

"But I always knew that when I loved somebody as I love you, she would have the power to throw the devils out of me. Are you willing to try it?"

He looked down into her eyes and after a moment, because of the wild joy that was leaping within her heart, she could bear his scrutiny no more and with an inarticulate murmur hid her face against his shoulder.

"Darling, I want to kiss you," he said softly. "I have wanted it so much these past weeks that I thought sometimes lying here in this room that I should go mad for the need of you. But I had to wait until I was well enough, until I could say,

"Now we will go away together where there are no newspapers and no curious, prying people and nobody cares what happened in the past; there will only be our present to think about."

"I talked to the doctor tonight, my precious. He has told me that in ten days I shall be fit to travel. Will you marry me before we start our journey?"

Still Aria hid her face, and now he put his fingers beneath her chin and turned her face up to his.

"Oh, my darling, I love you so," he said. "I can imagine nothing more wonderful than to be alone with you, alone where we shall not be disturbed."

"Is it true?" Aria asked almost beneath her breath. "Is it true that you are saying this to me?"

"It's quite true," he answered. "And I will tell you something else—just one more thing before I kiss you. And that is that you needn't be afraid that we shall have to come back to England and face scandal and more talk. We are going abroad for a long time and when we do come back we shan't be coming to London or to Summerhill, but to Queen's Folly.

"I had a long talk on the telephone with Charles this morning. I told him that when the case was over this afternoon I intended to ask you to become my wife. I told him, too, the only ambition I had left in England was to see Queen's Folly restored to its former glory.

"I have been reading about it in all the books on great English houses. Charles has agreed, on your behalf, to buy back all the furniture and pictures that he can. He told me that he will never marry and that when he dies he wants to leave Queen's Folly, restored in all its beauty, to your children and mine."

"Oh, how wonderful!"

Aria could hardly believe his words. It seemed to her that her heart was bursting with happiness and this was the one thing to make her joy complete.

"And now that's settled," Dart said with a little smile. "That leaves only us, you and me, Aria. Could we want anything else?"

"No, nothing," she answered.

Her eyes were bright as the stars which were just appearing over the high tree behind the house.

"There is one thing I want," he said softly. "I want to hear you say that you love me. You have said so many other things to me in the past, so many unkind and cruel things, but you have never told me that you love me."

"But you know it," Aria protested.

"Yes, I know it," he said. "I have seen it in your eyes and on your lips. I knew it when you came back here, braving the talk, the reporters and the scandal. That was very courageous of you, Aria, and I shall never forget it. But still I want to hear you say it."

"I . . . I love you!"

The words came trembling from between her lips, but she felt as if she said them with her whole heart.

"And I adore you, my sweet."

His arms drew her still closer. He bent towards her and now her own hands went up towards his neck.

Then his lips were on hers and she knew, as a sudden ecstasy of joy shot through her, that she would never be afraid of him again.

Once she had shrunk from his kisses, but now she yearned for them, they were all that her body ached for and desired.

She felt his mouth possess her and as she surrendered herself to a happiness that was beyond anything that she had ever experienced in her life before, she felt a sudden flame come to life and quicken within herself.

There was the same fire in his eyes that she had seen there once before and she had shrank away from it in terror.

Now she pressed herself even closer to him.

It was the final and utter surrender of herself and she knew that he understood as she saw the light in his eyes and heard the sudden note of triumph in his voice as he said:

"When I take you away alone, my foolish darling, I will teach you not to be afraid of love—or me."